Hidden
Away

A HEARTS OF MONTANA BOOK

JENNIE MARTS

Entangled Publishing, LLC
2614 South Timberline Road
Suite 109
Fort Collins, CO 80525
Visit our website at www.entangledpublishing.com.

Select Contemporary is an imprint of Entangled Publishing, LLC.

Edited by Allison Collins
Cover design by Louisa Maggio
Cover art from iStock

Manufactured in the United States of America

First Edition November 2015

This book is dedicated to my sons, Tyler & Nick
Both born in Montana
You hold my heart and fill my life with joy and laughter
I love you both

Chapter One

The siren wails of the fire engine were a welcome sound as Cherry Hill shot another burst of white foam from the extinguisher. Panic welled in her chest as she watched the flames creep up the diner's wall above the griddle.

Holy shiz-buckets.

What started as a small grease fire was rapidly turning into a desperate situation.

Cherry swore as she battled to save the only thing she had left.

"Make sure everyone's out of the building," she yelled at Stan, the diner's cook. Thankfully the breakfast crowd had thinned, and only a few people had been left in the restaurant when the grease flamed on the griddle and the fire began. "You should get out, too. I got this."

Stan attacked the fire with a dish towel, keeping the flames from spreading across the kitchen counter. "No way, dude! I'm not leaving you."

The door to the kitchen swung open, and three large firemen filled the small room.

Well, two large fireman and one skinny guy, the best you could hope for on a small-town volunteer fire squad. One of the men dragged a fire hose through the door, and Cherry groaned as she heard glassware hitting the floor, unlucky bystanders in the path of the thick hose.

"I thought you weren't supposed to use water on a grease fire," she said, dredging up old advice her granddad had given her when she'd taken over the diner.

One of the fireman stepped toward her. He held a fire extinguisher in his hands. "Don't worry. You can trust a fireman to always have the right equipment."

Recognizing the voice, Cherry's head snapped up, and she looked into the grinning face of Taylor Johnson.

What in the hamhock is he doing here?

Still not used to having him back in town, Cherry's heart did a flip each time she saw him. She gulped. He had the right equipment for just about anything.

But Taylor was the new Sheriff—since when did he fight fires?

Before she had a chance to ask, another flame shot up, this one catching the side of her arm, and she cried out.

The grin disappeared as Taylor stepped forward, now all business, and put his body between hers and the fire. He yelled at the cook and pointed at Cherry. "Get her out of here before one of you gets hurt even worse!"

The whoosh of the water jetting from the hose drowned out his words, but Stan must have got the idea because he wrapped an arm around Cherry's middle and pulled her out the front door and onto the street in front of the restaurant.

Gasping, Cherry took in great gulps of clean air and prayed that the fireman could save the diner.

Even if they saved the kitchen, the diner would be shut down for days, maybe weeks, as she battled the insurance company and made repairs.

Mentally calculating the lost earnings, she wondered, not for the first time, if the inheritance of the diner from her grandparents had been a blessing or a curse.

Within fifteen minutes, the fire was out, leaving only gray wisps of smoke rising into the air above the building. An ambulance arrived shortly after the fire truck, and Stan had guided Cherry toward the vehicle.

An EMT had just finished wrapping a large bandage around Cherry's burned arm. She looked at the white gauze, bright against her smoke-stained skin, and smiled at the woman. "Thanks, Marge."

She'd known Marge for years. Just like she knew almost everyone in the small town of Broken Falls, Montana.

If she hadn't gone to school or church with them, they were her neighbors or her store clerks or bank tellers. Anyone she might not have known growing up in this town, she'd met through the diner over the last ten years that she'd worked there.

She looked toward the café, the curvy pink letters of Cherry's Diner emblazoned on the windows, and saw Taylor emerge from the smoky building.

He peeled off his fireman jacket and tossed it on the truck. He wore his standard brown uniform shirt and jeans, and the sun winked off the gold sheriff star pinned to his chest.

Why had he moved back here?

She'd seen him a few times since he'd been back, in the diner and once when a friend of hers had needed his help.

Each time she saw him, she was taken aback at the change from the skinny light-haired boy who'd taken her to the prom and stolen her virginity.

Okay, so maybe he hadn't exactly *stolen* it. Maybe she'd given it. Freely.

And with abandon.

But she didn't want to think about that.

Taylor's hair had darkened to a dirty blond, and the years in the military and the police academy had hardened his body and strengthened the muscles that so nicely filled out his uniform.

He strode toward her now, a look of concern in his eyes.

Those were just the same. His eyes hadn't changed. They were the same deep blue color.

And they bore the same intensity that she remembered from all those years ago when he had looked into hers and pledged to love her forever.

To always be there for her.

The same blue eyes that haunted her dreams after he left. Leaving her alone with a broken heart and a handful of empty promises.

Well, not quite alone.

"Are you all right? How's your arm?" Taylor asked, drawing her out of the years-old memories. He picked up her arm and looked down at her bandage as if inspecting the quality of the work.

"You don't need to concern yourself with me. I'm fine." She pulled her arm back, wincing at the pain of the burn but not really caring.

An injured arm was the least of her worries right now.

How was she going to pay for the repairs to the diner? Did she have enough insurance to cover the damage?

The upkeep of the restaurant had eaten into her savings for years, and she wondered even now if she had enough to cover the looming electric bill.

At least she didn't have to pay rent. She looked at the blackened windows above the diner where she lived in a small apartment.

Like everything else about the building, the apartment was old and a little run-down.

But it was free, and she didn't have a commute to work.

Taylor followed her gaze. "I imagine you're gonna need to find a place to stay for a few days. The fire burned a hole through the ceiling, and I'm sure your apartment's gonna have some pretty extensive smoke damage."

How did he know that was her apartment?

Oh right, small town.

"You can stay with me," Stan offered. He sat on the curb at her feet. "My place is small, but I've got a comfy couch."

Cherry smiled down at her employee and friend. Stan always found a way to look at the positive side.

He'd left Chicago three years ago, tired of the city and seeking an adventure out west. He'd wandered into the diner one day looking for work and had been with Cherry ever since. Of Chinese descent, his name was actually Qingshan Lee.

After several attempts at trying to teach the townspeople the correct pronunciation, old Doc Beam had thrown up his arms and declared, "Oh forget it, I'm just going to call you Stan."

Liking the nod to the Marvel hero creator, Qingshan accepted the moniker and had been Stan Lee ever since.

Cherry looked down at her soot-covered uniform, the pink color of the dress barely recognizable, and groaned.

A layer of black dust lay across her pale skin, the light freckles camouflaged under gray smudges. Her substantial cleavage threatened to pop free of her uniform, and she adjusted the bodice of her dress.

She looked at Stan's normal attire of skater shorts and a tie-dyed T-shirt. "Forget the sofa, I may have to borrow some clothes."

Taylor brushed a hand over his chin as he contemplated the apartment, and Cherry had a flash of memory of his hand on her face, caressing her chin before he'd leaned in to kiss her. "She may not be joking, Stan. I don't think you're getting into your apartment any time soon. With the hole in the floor, you'll have to wait until the fire inspector clears it to make sure it's safe for you to be walking around in there."

Great. Now she not only didn't have enough money to keep the power on, she was going to have to find a place to stay and buy some new clothes.

She glanced down, thinking tie-dye and skater shorts might look good on her. She could pull it off. Except all those colors might clash with her red hair.

What didn't clash with her red hair?

As if the name Cherry Hill wasn't bad enough, she'd been gifted with a mass of strawberry-colored hair to go with it.

She reached up, trying to collect the loose strands along her neck, gathering them up and stuffing them back into her ponytail. Her hair must look a mess, and she hoped the stretched-out elastic of the band securing her massive shock of long, curly hair would hold out for another few days.

Her phone buzzed in her front pocket. Thank goodness she'd had it in her pocket instead of floating around the kitchen.

She checked the display and sighed at the number she recognized as her Great Aunt Bea.

Bea was the matriarch of the Hill family. Her grandmother's sister and complete opposite. Bea was stingy and rude, a female mixture of Scrooge and the Grinch. But with gray hair, a raspy voice, and a keen intellect whose words could slice through you quicker than a knife.

Gram had been kind and generous and had a heart the size of Montana.

And was the closest thing Cherry had to a mother.

She waved her phone at Stan and Taylor. "I've gotta take this. I'm sure my family has heard about the fire, and my aunt is calling to remind me what a colossal screw-up I am."

She stepped away from the curb and the crowd gathering around the diner, the townsfolk anxious to see what had caused all the fuss and if it was gossip-worthy.

She imagined someone had already started a prayer chain, and the ladies of the church were probably baking casseroles and pies to bring to her aid.

Although where they would bring them, she had no idea.

After pressing the screen to accept the call, she put the phone to her ear. "Hello."

Her heart stopped as she heard her aunt gasping for breath, trying to speak through shuddered cries.

And with a few simple words, Cherry's world fell apart.

Chapter Two

Taylor watched Cherry's face crumble.

The sudden look of pain in her eyes almost broke his heart.

Again.

How could one woman affect him so deeply? And after all these years?

He'd dated a few women over the years. Even had a long-term girlfriend or two. But never anything that he let get too serious.

How could he when his dreams were still haunted by pale skin and handfuls of red hair?

He'd thought he was over her. Thought coming back to his hometown would be no big deal. They'd practically been kids the last time he'd seen her.

He knew her grandparents had given her the diner to run and thought he could nonchalantly drop in for a piece of pie. Prove to himself that his memories were unfounded.

That she wasn't all he'd remembered.

Unfortunately for him, she was more.

The years had been good to her. She looked older, but in a good way. More confident, secure in herself as she raced between tables, shouting orders and casually flirting with the old farmers lined up at the counter.

Her hair was still long, and she'd filled out since her teenage years.

Lord, had she filled out.

"Well, I'll be jiggered! If it isn't Taylor Johnson. Hometown hero come back for a visit," she'd said, right after she caught him checking out her cleavage.

What an idiot.

He could feel the heat rise to his cheeks. "Yep. Back for good, I guess. I took over the Sheriff's position after Bud Flanagan retired."

How could one word from her take away the normal, easygoing charm he usually had with women and turn him into an empty-headed fool?

Because she wasn't just *any* woman.

She was Cherry, his first crush, his first love.

And the last woman he had truly given his heart to.

"I guess I'll be seeing you around then." She'd smiled at him, and his heart shattered into tiny pieces.

Her smile had always been his undoing.

But her smile was gone now, replaced by an expression of grief and pain as she took off at a run, racing for her car, a late-model blue VW bug.

She yanked at the car door, slid into the seat, and gunned the engine. With a spit of gravel, she tore from the parking lot and headed toward the highway, narrowly missing the yellow fire hydrant on the corner.

What the hell? Where was she headed in such a hurry? And why would she leave the diner right now?

It must have been that phone call.

She said it'd been her Aunt Bea. Could something have happened in Cherry's family?

It was none of his business. He'd let that right go years ago when he'd left Broken Falls.

And her.

She was no longer his concern.

All of these thoughts ran through his head as he crossed the street to where his cruiser was parked in front of the Sheriff's office. Opening the door of the car, a blast of hot summer air engulfed him as he slid into the seat.

She would have told him if she needed his help.

Still, she was a citizen of the county. He was only doing his duty to check and make sure she was okay.

It was his job, after all.

T he engine sputtered and died.

Cherry pulled the car to the soft shoulder of the highway.

"No! No! No!" She beat her fists against the steering wheel. "Not now! You stupid car!"

She took a breath, shot up a silent prayer, and turned the key, desperately hoping the engine would spark back to life.

The car had been giving her trouble lately, and the local mechanic had even offered to look at it the last time it had broken down in town.

But she never had the time. Or the money.

"Please start," she whispered.

Nothing. Not even a spark of life.

That was it. All she could take.

She leaned her head against the wheel and let the tears come. Giant sobs of pain tore from her body as she replayed fragments of her aunt's words in her head.

"There's been an accident. Stacy's car went off the side of the road. She and Greg were killed. Only survivor was Sam, who'd been asleep in the backseat. Stacy left a will. She named you the boy's guardian. In the hospital. You need to come."

How could Stacy be gone?

She'd just talked to her on the phone yesterday.

Though they were five years apart in age, the two cousins had been more like sisters. Stacy was the one she could always turn to when she needed advice or someone to complain to.

Or when she was in trouble.

Like the summer she graduated. After Taylor had left.

Her cousin had been there for her. They'd been there for each other.

Stacy was the only one she'd confided in when she realized her period was late. Feeling desperate and alone, Cherry had nowhere else to turn.

They'd gone to their grandmother who had formed a solution that would help them both.

Stacy and her husband Greg had been trying to have a baby for years. Stacy's body had betrayed her again and again as it failed to hold the life she and Greg lovingly created. The last time had been the worst, and they had given up trying and were looking into adoption.

Broken-hearted and distraught, Cherry knew that she had nothing to offer a child. No money, no future, not even a home where she could take care of it.

Wanting desperately to do what was right for the baby, she made the ultimate sacrifice for the wellbeing of the baby and agreed to her grandmother's plan.

Stacy had been great about keeping Cherry in her son's life. She'd been there for every birthday and special occasion, and Sam loved her as if she were a favorite aunt.

But now Stacy was gone.

And Sam was in the hospital, scared and alone.

Red and blue lights flashed in her rearview mirror. Cherry looked up to see a squad car pull in behind her broken-down Bug.

She groaned as she saw the familiar face behind the wheel. *What's he doing here?*

She swiped at her face, trying to brush away the tears. She rummaged under the passenger seat of the car, unearthing a napkin to wipe her running nose.

Taylor cut the lights as he pulled in behind the ancient blue Bug.

I can't believe she still drives that old thing.

Cherry'd had the little VW since they were in high school, and memories flooded his thoughts of dark nights parked by the river.

He could remember the stickiness of the vinyl seats and the feel of his hands on her body as she squirmed under him in the tiny space of the car.

They took that stupid car everywhere. Road trips to the mountains and to Great Falls. To football games and church on Sunday. They'd spent hours in that thing, talking, laughing, and more.

So much more.

He shook his head to clear his mind of thoughts of Cherry's skin and the way her hair always smelled like strawberries and sunshine.

Get a grip, buddy. What the hell does sunshine smell like anyway?

Like her.

He left the car running, not wanting to have to cool the cab again by turning off the a/c, and approached the car. The engine was dead, and Cherry's pony-tailed head was turned away from the open window.

Geez, that hair, it still got to him.

He patted the top of the car, as he leaned in toward the window. "I can't believe you're still driving this old thing."

"Lay off my car," she snapped. "It's all I can afford, and it's not like I have any place to go."

Whoa. What happened to the light-hearted banter they'd shared outside of the diner a few minutes ago?

She turned to him, a look of fury in her red-rimmed eyes. "What do you care anyway?"

He held up his hands in surrender and softened his tone. "Hey, I was just kidding. Are you crying?"

She laughed, a hard, hollow sound. "Wow. Good deduction. I can see why they made you the Sheriff."

Ignoring her sarcasm, he tried again. "What's going on? Are you okay?"

"No, I'm not okay." She leaned her head on the steering

wheel of the car, her shoulders slumped in defeat. "I don't know that I'll ever be okay again."

He watched her fall apart, her body shaking as she cried, and each sob stabbed at his heart. This wasn't like her.

Cherry was the toughest girl he knew.

He'd only seen her cry once before in his life. And that was when he'd left.

Something was wrong.

Very wrong.

He opened the car door and pulled her from the driver's seat, tugging her into his arms. He held her against him and let her cry as she clutched his shirt, gripping it between her hands as if she were drowning and the fabric were a lifeboat.

Stroking her back, he did his best to offer comfort, not knowing quite how to handle this side of Cherry. "What is it? What's happened? Talk to me, Cherry. You're scaring me."

Cherry tilted her head back, looking up at him with tear-filled eyes. "It's Stacy. You remember my cousin? And her husband Greg?"

He nodded.

He'd met Stacy and Greg several times in high school when he and Cherry were dating. They were older, but Stacy had always been Cherry's best friend, and he knew she thought of her cousin as the sister she never had. "What about them?"

"They're dead." Her face crumpled. "Oh God. They had a car accident. They're both dead." She shook her head in disbelief. "How could they be dead? I don't understand."

Her knees buckled against him, and he grabbed her before she could fall. Picking her up, he carried her to his car.

Recognizing the signs of shock setting in, he set her on

the seat and tilted her face toward him, locking his eyes on hers. "I'm so sorry. I know you loved her. But it's gonna be okay. I'm going to take you home. I'll send someone to pick up your car."

A look of panic crossed her face, and she pushed against him, trying to get out of the car. "No. I have to go to Great Falls. Stacy's son was in the car, and he survived. He's in the hospital. Stacy left Sam to me, and I have to get to him. He's going to need me."

"Okay, take it easy," he said, easing her back into the seat. "We'll get you to Sam. I'll take you."

"You will?" She looked at him in disbelief, and another stab of pain shot through his heart.

What kind of guy did she think he was that he would leave her stranded on the side of the road when she needed him?

Had her opinion of him sunk that low?

Making sure she was inside, he slammed the door and raced around the front of the car. Sliding into the driver's seat, he put the car in gear and eased back onto the highway, then hit the gas and the lights, increasing his speed as they flew toward Great Falls.

This was something he could do. Here was an action he could take. He could get her to the hospital, and fast.

Reaching for her hand, he offered his support. She clutched it in a death grip, as she silently stared out the window.

He could do this for her, wouldn't let her down. He wasn't leaving.

Not this time.

Chapter Three

"They won't let me see him yet, but my family is all down in the waiting room." Cherry spoke over her shoulder to Taylor as she turned from the registration desk and hurried down the hallway.

Thank God for Taylor—he'd sped down the highway, and they'd made record time to the hospital.

She'd told him he could drop her off and go, but he'd insisted on coming in. She hated to admit it, but she was glad he was here.

Stopping outside the waiting room, she looked up at Taylor. "I don't know if I can do this."

"I know you can. Stacy picked you to take care of her son for a reason. She believed in you." He squeezed her hand.

She squeezed back then dropped his hand, as if suddenly realizing that she was holding it.

Pushing back her shoulders, she took one deep, steadying breath then pushed open the doors to face her family.

Two women sat in the waiting room. Her Aunt Susan, her dad's sister and Stacy's mom, curled into the corner of one of the sofas, a crumpled tissue clutched in her hand.

Her Great Aunt Beatrice sat in the center, her back erect as she held court over the Hill family.

Cherry was all too used to the look of disappointment that frequented Bea's face when she looked at her great-niece.

And today was no exception.

"Lord have mercy, Cherry. You are a mess," her aunt said, the snideness slithering through her tone like a nasty little snake in the grass.

Ignoring her mean comment, Cherry headed straight for Aunt Susan.

Dropping to her knees in front of her aunt, she reached to embrace her, then awkwardly dropped her arms when the gesture was not returned. "I'm so sorry."

Susan nodded, bringing the tissue back up to her mouth. "I know you are. I just can't believe it."

"How's Sam?"

"Surprisingly good, all things considered. They think he might have broken his arm, and they're checking for a concussion. They're taking x-rays and running some tests to see if he has any internal injuries. We're waiting to hear from the doctor."

She gripped her aunt's hand. "I'll do whatever it takes to take care of him. You can count on me."

The door to the waiting room burst open and Stacy's older brother, Reed, walked in with his wife, Olivia.

Pudgy and spoiled as a kid, Reed had always been a bully, and Cherry had often been victim to his tactics.

He'd been mean and vindictive as a child, always wanting what someone else had. And except for losing the weight, he hadn't changed much as an adult.

He became a lawyer and married a woman who was as cold and snobbish as he was. They looked the part of success in their designer clothes and expensive jewelry. His watch probably cost more than her car.

Actually her own watch might be worth more than her car now.

She adjusted her waitress uniform, suddenly conscious of her tangled hair and smoke-stained clothes.

They each carried two cups of coffee, and Reed handed one to Aunt Bea before looking down his nose at Cherry, which wasn't hard since she still sat on the floor in front of his mother. "What are you doing here? We didn't need you to come. Besides, we already heard that you burned the diner down, so we figured you'd be busy with that."

Olivia's head swiveled from Cherry to Taylor, and she shot a questioning glance at Bea. "Why did she bring a cop? Did you already tell her she's not taking Sam?"

Cherry's heart stopped.

She never considered the implications of Taylor's sheriff's uniform when they walked in. She glanced at Taylor, who crossed the room and helped her to her feet.

A small gesture, but at least she wasn't sitting on the floor when she addressed her cousin's wife. "I didn't *bring* a cop. He gave me a ride. And what do you mean I'm not taking Sam?"

Olivia made a face as if she smelled something bad, and a tiny spark of anger lit inside Cherry's belly.

She was usually pretty good at putting on a show and

ignoring her family's comments, but Olivia had never even pretended to like her, slinging insults at her every chance she got.

"Seriously, Cherry. Look at yourself. You look like a homeless person. You can't seem to take care of yourself, let alone a child."

Cherry ignored the kernel of truth to that statement.

Instead, she gathered strength from her anger, feeling it growing inside of her, swirling into a ball of rage. "I look like this because I was putting out a fire." She turned to Reed. "And it was a grease fire. I did NOT burn the diner down."

Reed shrugged, his smugness only adding fuel to the fire swelling inside of her. Bubbling like an active volcano, she took a breath, ready to spew lava at these horrible people.

Before she could speak, Taylor took her hand and gave it a warning squeeze.

He stepped to her side and addressed her relatives. "Why don't we all just take a step back here and remember that everybody wants what's best for the boy."

Cherry looked up at his face, recognizing the charming smile that he wore and the easy tone of cop-speak.

She knew he was on her side, but it curdled her gut to have him be nice to them. To show them an ounce of respect when they deserved none.

Reed laughed in disdain, his demeanor even worse than his hideous wife's. "Who do you think you are? Mr. Small-Town Policeman coming in here telling us what we need to do with our family."

Taylor stood his ground, his charming smile slipping only a little. "First of all, I'm not a police officer, I'm the Sheriff. And I think out of respect for your sister, we need to honor her wishes."

Reed took a threatening step toward Taylor. "Listen here. Stacy was *our* sister. You have no idea what her *wishes* were. And I don't care how many piss-ant 'deputies' you bring in here, there is no way in hell that my nephew is going anywhere with that two-bit tramp." He waved a hand in Cherry's direction. "She already swindled the diner away from our grandparents."

Tramp? Who the hell is he calling a tramp?

She hadn't even been with a man in over a year. Who had time?

That diner that she supposedly swindled away from her grandparents took all of her time, energy, and money.

She didn't have time for such frivolous things like a sex life.

A loud banging noise startled her as she turned to see her Great Aunt Bea whacking her cane against the side of the coffee table.

"Everybody needs to shut up," her aunt scolded.

A hush fell over the room as they all deferred to Aunt Bea.

Cherry stepped back against Taylor, surprised at the feeling of comfort and support she got just from leaning against his solid frame.

Bea waved a hand in her direction. "For some reason, unbeknownst to the rest of us, my sister saw something in you. But she was always too kind-hearted. She gave you a chance to run our family's legacy, and you seem to be running it into the ground. Or burning it to the ground, if your clothes and the phone calls I've received this morning are any indication of what happened today."

Running it into the ground? Who did she think she was?

Cherry was the only thing keeping that diner alive. She spent all of her time there working to make the diner a success.

"When the rest of your cousins were seeking higher education and trying to better themselves, you were still goofing off in Broken Falls."

"Goofing off? If by goofing off, you mean spending every waking minute on my feet helping with the diner, then maybe." She'd foregone college, but only until she could raise the money to go. After high school, her grandparents had needed her, with the restaurant and to help them as their health failed.

Her mom had run off when she was a child, and her dad was of no use to her. He loved the bottle more than his daughter and couldn't care less about his parents or their restaurant. But they were all Cherry had, and she would have done anything for them.

"I'm the only one who stayed. The one who took Gram to her doctor appointments and watched as Grandpa's Alzheimer's took over his mind and body. They were always there for me, and I wasn't about to go off to college and leave them with no one to help take care of them." Her voice broke, and she swallowed against the emotion. "I owed them more than that. And I was there for them until the very end."

Her aunt wrinkled her nose in contempt and waved away her comments. "Yes, yes, we've all heard the supposed sacrifices you made for my sister. I'm sure you'll be awarded your sainthood soon."

Cherry gazed at her grandmother's sister and wondered who in this room would be willing to care for her to the end. To feed her and wipe her chin. To bathe her and sit by her bed for hours.

Her Aunt Bea was a bitter woman, and her cousins were snobs. The thought of Sam growing up in this environment of meanness and self-importance curdled her stomach.

How did Stacy stand it? The sooner she could get Sam away from the influence of these cruel people, the better.

Her grandmother had been nothing like her sister. When she and Stacy had come to her with the news of her unplanned pregnancy, she'd had no judgement—hadn't made her feel worse about herself. Instead, she'd cried, hugged them both, then used her connections to quietly get things done.

She'd taught Cherry how to wear her clothes to disguise the rapidly growing bump. When she was too far along for a sweatshirt to hide the proof, she arranged for the girls to take a trip together. A late graduation gift for Cherry and a nice get-away for Stacy.

When they got back, word had come through that a baby was available for adoption.

Through her grandmother's connections, a quiet adoption took place, and Stacy and Greg became new parents. Cherry went back to her life, working at the diner.

Now her great aunt fixed her with a pointed stare, and she felt like she was six years old again and getting in trouble for running through the house. "Right now we need to focus on this situation. We are all aware that you were close to Stacy, and it is unfortunate that she has passed on at such a young age. I can't begin to imagine what she was thinking when she appointed *you* the guardian of Samuel, but it is clear to everyone in this room that you are in no way prepared to take care of a child."

Unfortunate? That's what she was calling Stacy's death?

Cherry opened her mouth to speak, but she had no words. The emotionless words of her aunt left her speechless.

Bea sighed. "You must see that what I'm saying is true. Look at yourself, girl. You have no money, no way to provide for the child. Your sole income comes from a place that requires you to work long hours and won't allow you to spend time with Samuel anyway. You had to hitch a ride here so I assume you now have no mode of transportation. You show up here in dirty clothes with your hair a rat's nest claiming that you are planning to take Samuel with you. Where are you going to take him? From what I've heard about the fire this morning, your apartment is unlivable. So you have no home, no money, not even a car. You have no education, no means of support, and you can't even seem to find a man. Have you considered that you must not be much of a catch if you can't even garner the interest of one of the local yokels in Broken Falls?"

Every word was like a knife delicately and succinctly slicing off a piece of her heart.

Each failing in Cherry's life was being revealed and laid out on the table for everyone in the room to gawk at and inspect.

Her aunt's word were cruel, but they held a ring of truth.

She had no money, no place to live, and a broken down heap of a car. What was she thinking?

Maybe her aunt was right, and Sam would be better off with her cousin.

"I can see by your face that you know what I'm saying is true. You have nothing to offer this boy. No home and no family. No father figure to teach him. Just a broken-down life in a broken-down town. We will be filing the paperwork to get your guardianship revoked, and Samuel will be going home with Reed and Olivia."

"No, he won't. He will be going home with Cherry," Taylor said, his voice hard as steel. "She's a good person and has a big heart. She can provide him a home filled with love."

What was he doing? Why was he sticking up for her?

Aunt Bea looked up at him in surprise, and her eyes narrowed. "And just where is this loving home, Sheriff? Do you propose that a big heart pays the light bill or buys the boy new shoes? How does a big heart take care of him when Cherry is constantly working at the diner?"

Taylor looked down at Cherry, and she glimpsed a keen look in his eye.

What is he up to?

He slipped an arm around her waist and pulled her close.

"Cherry *can* get a man, and she does have a home to provide 'the boy.' It's with me. You can file all the paperwork you want, but she *will* be bringing Sam home to Broken Falls as soon as he can leave the hospital. He'll be coming home with her. With us."

"You can't be serious," Aunt Bea sputtered, obviously not used to having her decisions questioned. "You've only just come back to town. How do we know this isn't some kind of ruse?"

"She's the reason I came back to town. We've been seeing each other for months. We just haven't announced it yet, because you know how small towns can be. So *gossipy*."

He narrowed his eyes at Bea. "But this is no ruse. Sam *will* have a home. With us. Cherry and I are getting married."

Chapter Four

What the hell did I just do?

Did he just tell the matriarch of the Hill family that he and Cherry were getting married?

He'd stood there, watching that old biddy tear Cherry apart. Watched her shoulders slump in defeat. Saw her body cave in as she seemed to shrink with each crushing blow to her self-esteem.

He had known Cherry since they were kids. He knew her heart and knew she would do whatever it took to provide for Sam.

He'd been in town for over a month and had heard only glowing reports from the townsfolk of what Cherry had done with the diner since her grandparent's passing.

Who was this old woman to come in and tear her apart and make her feel like she was less than a human being? Like she had no value as a person? Because her apartment needed a little work, and she had no place to live? Because she didn't have a man?

Well, he was a man, and he had a place to live.

All he could think during Bea's diatribe of cruelty was that if Cherry was married, she wouldn't be saying these things. If Cherry had a husband to defend her.

But that didn't mean it had to be him. He didn't have to be the one to save her. He hadn't spoken to her in nine years.

He barely knew the woman she was now.

And yet he did.

He knew her heart.

He hadn't meant to say they were getting married. He opened his mouth to defend her, and the words just popped out.

What's done is done.

He looked down at Cherry and squeezed her hand. He just needed her to go along with it until they could figure something else out.

Right now, they needed to buy some time for her. And for Sam.

Cherry looked up at him, and he watched her body transform.

She pushed her shoulders back and stood a little taller.

A glint appeared in her eye. The same one he remembered from high school when she'd come up with a plan to steal the rival town's high school mascot right before the Homecoming game.

This was the Cherry he knew. Tough. Determined.

That's my girl.

Wait. Not *his* girl.

Well, sort of his girl. At least his pretend girl.

This was going to get confusing.

What was he doing anyhow? She hadn't asked him to rescue her. Maybe he should back out now. Let Cherry figure this out.

He didn't owe her anything. He didn't even know this kid.

Maybe Sam was a juvenile delinquent or a total brat, and he'd just invited a pack of trouble into his life. Or maybe this kid needed a break.

Reed laughed. A loud bark of a sound that carried disdain and scorn in its one harsh note. "You're going to get married. To her?"

It took all of his restraint to not punch this guy in the throat.

He remembered Stacy as a kind, sweet girl with a big laugh who treated Cherry like a sister.

How could she have come from this family of jackals?

He pulled Cherry closer to his side. "Yes, I am, and I'd appreciate it if you showed my future wife some respect. Regardless of what you think about her, she loved Stacy and she doesn't deserve to be treated like this."

"Whether or not she loved Stacy is irrelevant," Bea said. "That still doesn't make her capable of raising my nephew. Reed is a very accomplished lawyer. We'll go through with filing the paperwork, and they'll see that Cherry walks away without Samuel."

A fierce protectiveness rose in his gut, a determinedness to defend this woman and a boy he had never even met.

His voice took on an edge of steel as he looked Bea directly in the eye. "Let them try."

He took Cherry's hand and turned, slamming the door against the wall as they walked out of the waiting room.

"What the hell was that?" Cherry dropped his hand as they rounded the corner of the hallway, out of earshot of the waiting room.

Taylor ran a hand through his hair and took a deep breath. "I don't know. Your family just made me so mad. I had to get out of there."

"Yeah, welcome to my world. I get that."

She took a step back, one hand going to her hip. "But what's with all this crazy business about us getting married?"

"Oh shit. Sorry. I don't know how that happened." He shrugged. "They were being so mean to you. I couldn't stand it. I kept thinking that they wouldn't treat you like this if you were married. If you had a husband to defend you."

"And that's why you said we were getting married? That's kind of a big leap from 'she needs a husband' to 'it should be me.'"

A sheepish grin crossed his face. "I know. I don't know what came over me. It just felt like you needed a curve ball, something to throw them off center."

"A curve ball? From out of left field? Heck, that pitch wasn't even in the ball park."

She closed her eyes and shook her head. "So what do we do now?"

He shrugged. "I don't know. Go along with it for now. At least until we come up with a better plan. Right now let's worry about Sam and making sure he's okay."

Cherry nodded, tears forming in her eyes. "Some of what they said is true. I don't have a steady income or a car that consistently runs. And thanks to that mother-zinging grease fire, I don't even have a place to live."

"Hey now. Stop that." He pulled her to him, wrapping her in his arms. "Don't you dare buy into their crap. You're not the person they described. You have a lot to offer."

Just not enough to make you stay. Cherry pushed against him, standing up straight and taking a deep breath. "You're right. Screw them. My only focus now is on Sam."

"Thatta girl." He wrinkled his nose. "You do kind of smell like a forest fire." He sniffed at his shirt. "I'm sure I do, too. Why don't I take you somewhere, and we can get cleaned up?"

She shook her head. "I'm not going anywhere. I don't want to miss the doctor."

"You're going back in there?"

"They've been like this my whole life. Ever since I was a kid and my mom left. My dad was Aunt Bea's favorite nephew, and I think she blamed me for my mom leaving and my dad turning into a drunk. Plus, she thought my grandmother spoiled me. My Aunt Bea has always been a crotchety old maid. And Reed's just always been a bully. So, I'm very good at ignoring them. I'm only worried about Sam right now."

"Okay. Why don't I go get us some fresh clothes, at least? The Walmart's only a few blocks down. I'm sure I can find something to hold us over."

Something to hold us over?

That's where she was planning to replenish her entire wardrobe that had been burned in the fire. Great Falls, Montana didn't offer a lot in the way of designer clothes, and her needs were simple.

She looked around for her purse then realized it was still

under the counter in the diner. "I don't have my wallet. I'll have to pay you back."

He waved a hand at her. "Don't worry about it. We'll figure it out later. Give me half an hour, and I'll be back."

Cherry walked back into the waiting room and sat in one of the chairs against the wall, as far away from her family as she could get.

She ignored them, and they ignored her.

The only sound in the room was the low snuffle of her Aunt Susan as she cried softly into a tissue.

The burn on her arm throbbed. She considered finding some ibuprofen but couldn't muster the energy to search for a nurse.

Taylor walked back into the room.

He could have been gone for five minutes or for the last two hours. Time took on a different dimension in this room.

The hard chairs, the fake plants, the cheap painting of a landscape done in muted tones that hung on the wall. The details faded into the distance as she waited.

Waited to hear news about a little boy and how her life was about to change.

A weariness settled over her, and she wanted nothing more than to curl up in a ball and sleep the grief away.

When she argued with her family, she had something to focus on, something to think about. Other than the fact that her cousin had just died and left her the guardian of an eight-year-old boy.

An eight-year-old boy that had her blood running

through his veins.

Taylor crossed the room and sank into the chair next to her.

Will he figure it out?

When Taylor finally met Sam, would he recognize himself in Sam's blue eyes, in his funny grin that tipped up the same way Taylor's had as a boy?

Would everything she and Stacy and Gram had done to help this boy, her son, to have a better life, come crumbling down around them?

She studied Taylor. So handsome.

His eyes were light blue with a deep ring of navy around the iris. She'd always loved his eyes.

She didn't remember him being quite so tall. He must have grown another inch or two after he'd left town. He'd filled out, too, his arms thick with muscle, and his hands seemed strong and capable.

The years had only improved his youthful good looks. His jaw line carried a hint of shadow, and she wanted to reach out and touch his cheek.

Is he real? And really sitting next to me, playing my knight-in-shining armor?

Would he have been so quick to help her if he knew the truth? That she had given away his son, their son, without ever telling him he existed. Without giving him a choice.

She *had* tried. When she found out she was pregnant, she'd texted him a message that they needed to talk. That it was important. She'd texted him twice, and both times he'd responded that he needed time—that they could talk later. Well, later never came. He never texted back again.

So she did what she had to do. Made the choice without

him.

Looking back, she knew she could have tried harder, *should* have tried harder, but she was seventeen—just a kid herself. They were both dumb teenagers, and she'd forgiven their younger selves for the mistakes they'd made. She knew she'd done the best she could. The best she could for Sam.

She'd have to tell Taylor now, though. Just not *right* now.

Right now she could barely form a coherent thought. She couldn't believe Stacy was gone, and she needed to put all of her focus on Sam. She could only handle so much at one time, and she didn't think she could handle telling Taylor, too.

She *would* tell him, though. Later. When the timing was better. When she could think about the words she wanted to say. When she knew Sam was okay.

For now, she needed to focus on Sam. On her little boy.

Taylor offered her an encouraging smile, but before he had time to speak, the waiting room door opened, and a nurse stepped in.

She smiled kindly as the family stood to hear her news. "Hi, I'm Karen. I'm the head nurse on the floor tonight. You must be Sam's family. I don't have a lot of news to tell you. His doctor got called in to do another surgery, but he'll come talk to you as soon as he's finished. I can tell you that Sam was wearing his seat belt, and we think he was probably asleep when it happened, so that helped. We know he's got a hairline fracture in his wrist, so we'll be setting him in a cast this afternoon. Right now we're monitoring his vitals and still running a few tests. And I promise we're taking good care of him. But I wanted to let you know that it's going to be at least an hour before the doctor comes in, so now would be a good time for you all to get something to eat or take a break. Sometimes just getting outside helps a little."

Taylor took Cherry's hand and drew her from the chair. "Come on. There's a little motel across the street. It's not far. I got us a room and some fresh clothes. We can go over and get cleaned up and be back before the doctor comes in."

Too tired to resist, she let herself be pulled from the room, guided down the hall, and out to Taylor's squad car. He drove them across the street to a small mom-and-pop motel.

He unlocked the door and eased her inside.

On the bed were a dozen or so plastic grocery bags. "The couple that run this place were really nice. They said they get a lot of people from the hospital who just need a place to go but don't want to leave the hospital."

"That's nice," she murmured, looking at the bed. She contemplated climbing in, pulling the covers over her head, and staying there for a week.

But that wasn't an option.

Sam needed her. And she wouldn't let him down. Again.

She gestured at the set of bags on the bed. "Geez-Louise, did you buy out the whole shiz-bang store?"

She was afraid to look at what Taylor purchased for her to wear.

Opening the bag closest to her, she was surprised to see a pair of khaki capris and two V-neck T-shirts, one pink and the other white. A pair of pink and white candy-striped flip-flops were also in the bag.

Pulling the pants from the bag, she tried to nonchalantly check out the size, cringing at the thought of Taylor having to return them because she couldn't get them over her ample hips.

Whew. The size was good.

Humiliating fashion-crisis averted.

She tilted her head up at him. "How did you know my size?"

He offered her a sheepish grin. "I found a woman that was about your height and shape and asked for her help. I told her it was for an official case I was working on, and she was glad to offer her assistance."

Yeah, I just bet she was.

She had a feeling the offer to help probably had more to do with the gold strands of his blond hair than the gold in his badge, but she was thankful for his good sense in getting a woman's advice.

"I hope they're all right. She said it was always better to go a little big than to end up with something too small. And I knew you used to like pink. It looks good with your hair."

He remembered that she liked pink. That was sweet.

She didn't have time to think about that right now. "What else did you get?"

He grabbed the bags and dumped them on the bed. "Everything I could think of. I didn't know how long we would need to be here, but I knew both of us would need to shower. I got deodorant, shampoo, toothbrushes, and toothpaste. I figured the motel would have soap."

She looked down at the array of things he'd purchased, and her heart melted a little at his thoughtfulness.

He'd bought a brush, a tube of mascara, a bottle of hairspray, and a package of underwear. He'd even picked out a basic white lace bra. "You bought me a bra?"

His face colored a little. "I put Debbie, that's the woman who helped me, in charge of that stuff. I told her I had five minutes to get everything a woman might need to get by for a few days if her apartment had just caught on fire. She threw stuff in the cart while I went to pick up some extra first aid supplies."

He dumped another bag, this one containing extra bandages, first-aid tape, antibiotic ointment, aloe, and a bottle of ibuprofen.

Relief washed over her as she grabbed the bottle of pain reliever. "Oh, thank the Lord you got ibuprofen. I could just kiss you for this." She froze. "I mean, I could just kiss Debbie, too. This was really nice of her."

She avoided his eyes as she tore into the bottle and dumped two pills into her hand.

He handed her a bottle of water from another one of the bags. "I got some things for me, too. We both stink from the fire. Let's get cleaned up and get back over to the hospital."

She swallowed the pills, the water cool on her parched throat. She could still taste the acrid flavor of the smoke.

She carried the toiletries into the bathroom, set the shampoo and soap on the edge of the tub, then toed off her shoes and peeled off her short socks.

Stepping back into the room, she grabbed an empty plastic bag and tried to wrap it around her bandaged arm.

"Here, let me help you." Taylor double-wrapped the bandage and scanned the room. "I need something to hold it in place with. Maybe I can pull out your shoelace and tie it on."

Cherry reached up and pulled the elastic from her hair. Thick masses of red hair fell around her shoulders. "Here, use this."

"Good idea." He sealed the bag around her arm with the elastic. "Do you need me to help you with your dress?"

She narrowed her eyes at him. "No, I can manage." Reaching for the zipper of her uniform, she winced in pain as she moved her bandaged arm.

"This is ridiculous." He herded her into the bathroom. "You can barely move your arm; it will take you forever to get showered. And we don't have forever. We have about half an hour left to get showered, dressed, and back to the hospital. Quit being stubborn, and just let me help you."

He reached for the zipper.

She put her hand on his arm. "Wait, you're going to help me take a shower?"

"It's not like I haven't seen it before." He was already pulling off his boots and dropping his socks on the floor. He unclipped his badge and laid it on the sink before unbuttoning and tugging off his uniform shirt.

"You saw it almost ten years ago, when it was all fresh and perky and teenagy."

"Fine. We'll leave our underwear on and pretend like it's our swimsuits."

She sucked her bottom lip under her teeth.

She did *not* want to get into a shower with Taylor Johnson, in her underwear or fully clothed.

But he had a point, her arm was useless, and they didn't have time to waste on her pride. They needed to get back to the hospital. "Fine."

He pulled off his T-shirt, now wearing only a pair of white boxer briefs.

She swallowed.

Oh. My. Gosh.

His body was definitely not that of the teenage boy she'd gone to prom with nine years earlier. That had been the body of a boy.

This was the body of a man.

And holy turnips, what a man.

His chest was ripped with tight hard muscles, and she noticed a faded scar that hadn't been there before. The scar could mean nothing, but it served as another small reminder that he'd had a whole other life the past nine years that she knew nothing about.

His biceps were firm, but his touch was gentle as he helped her into the shower. He turned on the water and reached for the zipper of her uniform dress.

Thank goodness she'd at least worn good underwear today. The black lace bra matched her black thong underwear.

She wasn't a huge fan of thongs, but they saved her from having panty lines with her snug uniforms.

The whisper soft sound of the zipper seemed deafening to her ears as Taylor slid it down and opened her dress.

She heard his quiet intake of breath as he took in her body, clad only in the lacy black bra and panties.

Conscious of her pale skin and too-soft belly, she wanted to grab a towel and cover herself.

But she needed to get back to the hospital.

Back to Sam.

Sliding her good arm out of the sleeve, she turned, and Taylor gently slid the other sleeve over her bandaged arm. He tossed the soot-smudged dress on the floor and, after checking the temperature of the water, stepped into the shower behind her.

Pulling the lever, the warm water sprayed down on her back. She held her bandaged arm out of the shower, knowing water would spray out on to the floor, but it couldn't be helped.

Taylor reached for the shampoo on the ledge of the tub, his arm brushing the bare skin of her hip, and she held back a gasp.

Tilting her head back and under the spray, she focused on getting this shower finished as quickly as possible. She didn't have time to think about his muscled half-naked body standing in front of her or the way his chest occasionally pressed against hers as he lifted sections of her hair into the water. His big hands were gentle as he brushed back her hair and tried to keep the water from running down her face.

He massaged shampoo into her hair, the clean fresh scent of the soap replacing the smoky smell of the gray soot that washed off them and filled the floor of the tub.

His movements were quick and capable in a military-style efficiency as he rinsed her hair and slid the lathery soap along her body. His hands gentled as he soaped her arm near the plastic-covered bandage.

Finished with her, he slid around her body and quickly soaped and shampooed himself. Her heartbeat quickened as his bare skin brushed hers, and she tried to slow her breathing as she stood behind him in the shower.

The view she had did nothing to calm her racing heart as she took in the hard ripples of his muscled back. She blinked at his flawless form. The snug briefs went transparent as the white fabric soaked up the water, revealing his tight, perfect buns.

He turned and caught her looking, and she felt a warm flush creeping up her cheeks.

Damn, redheads could never hide a blush.

He grinned and bent to turn off the tap. Was he purposely

giving her a better view of his tush or really just bending to turn off the water?

All business, he grabbed a towel, wrapped it around her and helped her from the tub. He used another towel to wrap her hair and twisted it turban-style on her head.

He dried himself quickly then helped her as she clumsily tried to dry off.

Stepping into the main room, he picked up the clothes and underwear from the bed and set them on the bathroom counter. "I'll let you get dressed. Let me know if you need help with anything."

"Could you just…" Covering her chest with the towel, she turned her back to him and motioned to the clasp of her bra.

He quickly released the clasp and she looked up, catching his expression in the mirror. She caught a quick look of desire, intense and hungry, as he rested his hands just barely above her skin, as if he wanted to touch her but an invisible force field held him back.

Her breath caught, her own need sharp and unexpected, waiting (hoping?) to see if he would touch her.

Then it was gone, and he walked out, pulling the bathroom door shut behind him.

Letting out her breath, she felt both relieved and disappointed. What was she doing worrying about this right now anyway? *Focus, girl.*

Wriggling out of her wet underthings, she pulled on a fresh pair of underwear and the capris. She pulled the towel from her head and finger combed the wet strands of hair.

Wrestling with the new bra, she got her arms through the straps, but couldn't clasp it.

She held the bra to her chest and poked her head out the door. "Sorry, could you help me again?"

Taylor was already dressed in a new pair of Wranglers and a crisp white T-shirt and had pulled on his boots. He grabbed the hairbrush off the bed and slipped into the bathroom behind her.

Pulling the straps together, he clasped the bra and then helped her to slide the pink T-shirt over her head.

Picking up a section of her hair, he quickly pulled the brush through it and had her hair combed in a few seconds. He scanned the small bathroom. "I don't see a hair dryer."

"That's okay. I'll just pull it up. Thank you." She met his eyes in the mirror above the sink and tried to show her gratitude with a smile.

A real one.

She wasn't sure why he was being so nice to her.

Except that he was Taylor. And they did have a history.

They had loved each other at one time.

No use thinking about that.

She needed to focus on Sam now. "Let's get back to the hospital." She grabbed the flip flops off the bed and slipped them on her feet. "I don't want the first face Sam sees when he wakes up to be my Aunt Bea."

Chapter Five

Taylor followed Cherry down the hall of the hospital. He could tell she was shaky. Mostly because she wasn't talking. Or laughing. Cherry was always talking and laughing.

What the hell was he doing here? How was he smack-dab back in the middle of Cherry's life again? He knew he would have to see her when he moved back to Broken Falls. Maybe even hoped to see her.

Hoped to have a chance to repair the damage he'd done.

Time and age had taught him a lot of things over the years, and he realized that he never should have left the way he did. Never should have let Cherry go.

Now he had a chance to make some of that up to her, and damned if he was gonna leave again.

He'd already called in to the station and Alice, the dispatcher, had informed him that everything was quiet. In fact, she'd told him his deputy may have been taking a nap at his desk.

Broken Falls wasn't really known for its huge crime rate. That was part of the reason he'd joined the Volunteer Fire Department. To have one more thing to do.

And to help win over the hearts of the town, several of whom were not exactly thrilled at this young buck who'd come in to take over after their beloved Sheriff Flanagan had retired.

Thank the Lord he was a local. At least he had that going for him.

He felt a shift in Cherry's demeanor as they approached the waiting room. Her back stiffened, and he swore he could practically hear her heart racing. He watched as she took a deep breath and pushed back her shoulders.

Good girl. Don't let those Hill a-holes get to you.

He reached for her hand, not sure if she'd accept his small offer of support, and glad to feel the tightening of her grip on his.

The faces of the Hill family were grim as they stepped back into the room.

"Any word?" Cherry softly asked her Aunt Susan.

Susan shook her head. No one spoke. The only sound in the room was the muffled snoring of Aunt Bea asleep in her chair, her wrinkled face looking almost serene as she slept.

But they all knew better.

That ole biddy was anything but serene. How could such a small, frail body hold so much meanness?

The air was thick with worry and grief as they crossed the room to the empty chairs against the wall. Cherry sat on the edge of the seat, leaning forward in anticipation of a nurse or doctor entering the room.

She didn't look at him. But she hadn't let go of his hand.

They didn't have to wait long.

Karen, the same nurse as before, stepped into the waiting room to tell them Sam had been moved and that he was awake.

Cherry was on her feet, oblivious to the hostile looks her family members were giving her.

She was single-mindedly focused on one thing. Sam.

"Can I see him now?" she asked the nurse.

Karen nodded and held the door open for her to follow.

"Hold on," Reed said, standing up. "Nobody said you were going in first."

Cherry turned to her cousin, fire blazing in her eyes. "Stacy appointed me the guardian of Sam, and that means I make the decisions about his welfare and that he *will* be coming home with me. You're welcome to file any kind of paperwork you want, but right now, I am his guardian, and I *am* going in to see him. And if you try to stop me, I will literally punch you in the throat."

Thatta girl. You tell him.

Reed's eyes widened, and his chest puffed out in indignation. "You can't talk to me like that. You just verbally threatened me with physical violence. I could have you arrested." He turned to Taylor. "Did you hear that? She threatened me. You're supposed to be an officer of the law. What are you going to do about this?"

Taylor shrugged. "Remember, I'm just a–how did you put it?–a 'small town piss-ant sheriff' I think was how you phrased it. So, I wasn't really paying attention, and I didn't hear what she said. But I do know that she *is* the legal guardian so she has the right to determine what will happen with the boy. And she *is* going in to see him now."

He took a step between Cherry and her cousin.

At six-three, Taylor was a good four inches taller than Reed. Though he didn't often have to use his height and muscular build to threaten people, he felt his muscles tense as he looked down at Reed and knew he cut an imposing figure.

"Fine," Reed mumbled as he sat back down. "But this isn't over."

Taylor put a protective hand on Cherry's back to guide her from the room, but she turned and held her hand out to her Aunt Susan.

"Aunt Susan, do you want to come with us? You're Sam's grandma, and I'm sure he'd like to see you."

Susan shook her head, her body crumbling into broken sobs. "I can't. I can't tell him that his parents are gone. I'm not ready. You go ahead."

Taylor hadn't thought about that. Hadn't realized that no one had told the boy that his parents had died in the accident.

None of them wanted Cherry to have responsibility for the boy, but she was the only one brave enough to tell him the truth about his parents.

Cherry took his hand again as they followed the nurse down the hall toward Sam's hospital room.

"He's going to be okay," the nurse told them. "He hit his head but doesn't seem to have a concussion. He does have a hairline fracture in his wrist, but the cast will only be from his elbow down so it shouldn't bother him too much. I'll warn you he's a little bruised up, but he'll be okay and should be able to go home tonight or tomorrow."

"Thank you," Cherry whispered.

The door of Sam's room made a soft whoosh as Karen opened it, then she stood back for them to enter.

Taylor felt Cherry's grip tighten on his hand and heard her inhale a deep breath before she stepped into the room.

Sam's eyes were closed, and he looked so small in the hospital bed.

Something inside of Taylor's heart twisted at the sight of this boy. Sam's perfect little blond head lying against the pillow brought out a protective impulse.

This feeling was beyond his normal sheriff-mode of wanting to protect people.

This was deeper, almost instinctual, and had Taylor wanting to stand guard. To rip the arms off of any of the Hill family who tried to take this boy from Cherry.

She approached Sam, a look of love clear on her face. She lightly touched his arm, and the boy's eyes fluttered open. "Hey, Sammy."

A bulky cast encased the lower half of his right arm, and one of his eyes was surrounded by deep purple bruising. Two black stitches held a cut above his eye closed. He looked like a little broken rag doll lying in the bed.

He blinked up at her, his face a mixture of hurt and hope. "Hi, Cherry." His voice was soft, and Taylor leaned in closer to hear him.

"Do you know where you are, Sam? Do you remember what happened?" Cherry asked.

He nodded slowly. "A little. I know I'm in the hospital, and I know someone wrecked into Dad's car." He looked to the doorway of the room. "I heard the nurses talking, and they said my mom and dad died in the crash."

Sam's eyes filled with tears. "Is that true? Are my mom

and dad dead?"

Cherry nodded, her voice soft and full of pain. "Yes, honey. I'm so sorry. They loved you so much."

His bottom lip quivered, and he searched the room with his eyes, as if hoping his parents would suddenly appear. But no one was there.

A hard, sharp cry emitted from his throat, and his small body shook with sobs as Sam broke down crying. Cherry pulled him gently into her arms, letting the boy cry himself out.

Taylor's heart broke as he watched the tears fall down her cheeks as she hugged Sam to her chest.

Eventually Sam lay back against his pillow and brushed the tears from cheeks with his good arm. He looked up at Taylor, a frightened look in his eyes. "What's going to happen to me? Is he here to arrest me? Or take me away?"

"No. No, of course not." Cherry picked up Sam's hand and cradled it in her own. "This is my friend, Taylor. He is a sheriff, but he's also my friend."

Taylor smiled down at the boy. "Hi, Sam. I'm Cherry's friend, but I'd like to be your friend, too. If that's okay?"

Sam nodded. "Yeah, that's okay. Do you know what's gonna happen to me now?"

Before Taylor could answer, Cherry spoke up. "Sam, you have always been special to me. You know how much I adore you, right?"

He nodded.

"Well, when you were born, your mom knew how much I loved you, and she asked me if I would take care of you if anything ever happened to her and your dad."

"And did you say yes?" The boy's voice was barely

above a whisper.

Cherry smiled down at him. "Of course I did. I promised her that I would always be here for you, and I always will be. So, that means when you're well enough to leave here, you'll come home with me. Is that okay?"

He shrugged, his small shoulders barely moving. "Yeah. I guess so." He shifted in the bed and winced in pain. He looked up at Taylor. "Do you know what happened to me?"

"I do. The nurse told us that you fractured your arm in the crash. You conked your head a good one and have a cut above your eye. So you might have a booger of a headache for a while. You've got some bruises and a couple of stitches, but those'll heal up fine. And you've got a pretty good shiner on your right eye."

Sam nodded. "My head sure does hurt."

Cherry pushed the button for the nurse. "We'll see if we can get you some aspirin, okay, sugar? You just rest now."

He reached for her hand, a panicked look in his eye. "Are you leaving?"

"No," she assured him. "I'm not going anywhere. I'm going to stay right here, with you. You can sleep. I'll be right here when you wake up. I promise."

Taylor's heart hurt for both Cherry and the boy. It was like a physical ache in his gut, and he wanted to do something. Anything to take away their pain.

But there was nothing he could do.

He hated this feeling of helplessness. He was a man of action, but there was no action he could take. Nothing for him to lift or move or crush. And he really wanted to crush something right now.

All he could do right now was the one thing he didn't

do before.

Stay.

Cherry woke with a start.

She looked around, trying to place her surroundings. It was still dark outside, and a dim light illuminated the room and the small boy sleeping in the hospital bed.

It all came crashing back, and a sob filled her throat. She swallowed it back.

She wouldn't cry.

Crying didn't solve anything. She'd learned that years ago when she'd cried over Taylor leaving and cried over having to make the hardest decision of her life. The decision to give up her baby, her son. To let her cousin raise the most perfect thing she'd ever done in her life.

And now her cousin was gone.

And her perfect thing was sleeping in the bed in front of her. Her heart ached just looking at his precious face. A face now cut and bruised.

Her chest filled with a love so huge that it almost hurt, and she knew she would do anything for him. If Reed and Olivia thought they were taking Sam away from her, they were dead wrong.

She was never letting him go again.

The whoosh of the door sounded, and Taylor walked in.

He held two Styrofoam cups of coffee and smiled down at her. A smile that held a hint of promise. Of caring, at least.

How could Taylor Johnson be standing in this room with her? How could he be back in her life?

Nine years ago, she'd lost the two things she'd loved the most in the world. And now both of them were in the same room with her, back in her life, and she didn't know what she was going to do with either one of them.

But she knew she didn't want to let them go.

"You're awake." Taylor held out one of the cups. "It's not very good coffee, but it's hot."

She took the coffee and held the warm cup in her hands. Speaking of hot. Taylor had been good-looking as a boy, but he was ridiculously hot as a man.

How had he not been snatched up already? She tilted her head up at him. "Why are you here?"

He shrugged. "I knew you wouldn't want to go back to the hotel, and I didn't want to leave you."

But you did leave me.

"Not here, in the hospital," she said. "Here in Montana. Why did you come back?"

A look of pain crossed his face. "I had some unfinished business to take care of. Besides, I'm from here. Dad's not as young as he used to be, and he's been bugging me for years to come back and help with the ranch. When Sheriff Flanagan decided to retire, and the town council offered me the job, it just seemed like the right time to come home." He raised an eyebrow at her. "Are you glad I'm back?"

"I haven't decided yet." She offered him a small smile. "I'm grateful for your help, though. I don't know what's going to happen with my family. How long we're going to have to pretend to be engaged."

The rest of the family had all filed in the night before, hugging Sam and telling him how sorry they were about his parents.

Her Aunt Susan was a sobbing mess, laying her head on Sam's small chest as she wept.

Cherry's heart broke at the simple gesture of comfort Sam offered his grandmother as he stroked her hair and assured her that everything would be all right.

Aunt Bea had strode into the room and eyed Sam as if he were a piece of meat in the grocery store. She pronounced that he looked fine and was sure he would be back on his feet in no time.

Olivia fawned all over Sam, straightening his pillows and filling his glass with water. She probably had the best of intentions, but her very presence irked Cherry. She was glad when Aunt Bea asked Reed and Olivia to take her home.

Sam had fallen asleep shortly after.

Cherry and Taylor had sat quietly in the room, the silence more comforting than uncomfortable.

Taylor smiled down at her. "We'll pretend as long as we have to." He looked over at the little boy. "As long as it takes to help him."

Sam must have heard them talking. His blue eyes fluttered open, and he struggled to sit up.

Cherry leaped to her feet to help him. "Here, let me get that." She raised the bed so the boy was more comfortable. "Is that better?"

He nodded and offered her a weak smile.

The first rays of the morning sun shone across his face as dawn broke, and she swore he looked like an angel. His blond hair was tousled around his head, and she just wanted to pick him up and hold him in her lap.

Did eight-year-old boys still sit in laps? She didn't know.

There was so much she didn't know.

She and Stacy were close and had both made efforts to keep Cherry in Sam's life. She'd never missed a birthday party, and they'd tried to get together every month or so.

So Cherry knew that he liked pizza and macaroni-and-cheese. She knew his favorite super-hero was Batman and that he loved dinosaurs. But the day-in and day-out stuff like what kind of shampoo she should buy and what size his shoes were, she had no clue.

She didn't know how many fruit and vegetable servings he was supposed to have in a day. Four? Or was it five? She didn't know how many books he liked to be read before he went to sleep or if he still even listened to books.

She didn't know what kind of laundry detergent to use to make his clothes smell like home, and she didn't know how she would ever be able to take Stacy's place.

Stacy had it all figured out. Being a mom came so naturally to her. The only thing that came naturally to Cherry was misfortune and bad luck.

Everything else she had to work for. Sometimes she felt like she had to work twice as hard to achieve what came so easily to others.

She looked down at the boy lying in the hospital bed, and she knew it didn't matter how hard she had to work. She'd do whatever it took to make a home for Sam. To make a life for the two of them.

Even if that meant pretending to be engaged to Taylor Johnson.

"My head doesn't hurt as much today," Sam said, drawing her out of her musings.

"That's good. Are you hungry? Or thirsty? Do you want me to get you something to drink?" Cherry fell back on her instinct to feed people.

That was one thing she could do right.

The boy nodded. "Yeah, I'm kinda thirsty."

She poured a cup of water and inserted a straw before passing it to him.

He took a few sips then eyed Taylor. "Do you think I could see your badge?"

"Sure." Taylor grinned and unclipped the badge from his belt. He handed it to Sam, who held it with reverence.

He traced his fingers around the five points of the gold star then offered Taylor a lopsided grin as he handed the badge back. "It's pretty cool."

"Yeah it is." Taylor clipped the badge back in place.

"What's a 'fee-on-say'?" Sam asked, carefully pronouncing the word.

Cherry almost choked on the sip of coffee she had just taken. "Where did you hear that word?"

Sam shrugged. "Last night. When all the family was here. Uncle Reed said he didn't know if he believed that Taylor was a real 'fee-on-say.'"

Oh great.

If Reed and Olivia doubted that Taylor was her real fiancé, then that would give them more ammunition for trying to take Sam away from her.

"Is it like a kind of policeman?" Sam asked. "'Cause that badge looks pretty real to me."

Cherry smiled. "No, it's not like that. It doesn't have to do with him being a sheriff. It just means that Taylor and I — um — it means that Taylor and I are going to get married."

"Oh." Sam looked a little disappointed.

Taylor chuckled. "Not as exciting as you thought, huh?

A fiancé is just the name for the person you're engaged to be married to." He looked down at her, and her chest tightened at the thought of having to keep up this charade.

She was starting to feel comfortable around Taylor, starting to count on him. But she knew from experience that she couldn't count on Taylor Johnson. She'd done that before, and he'd left. But this was different.

This wasn't just about her. This was about Sam, too. Her son.

Her and Taylor's son.

The ball of panic she felt tightening in her chest grew another inch.

What would happen if Taylor found out?

There was no way he could. She and Stacy had taken every precaution to keep the adoption a secret.

She couldn't think about that now. She needed to focus on Sam.

She hated lying to Sam. But it was worth it if it meant she could keep him.

And being engaged didn't mean they actually had to *get* married. Some people stayed engaged for years.

Taylor leaned down and spoke softly to her, his breath tickling the inside of her ear. "He's smart. I'm not used to a little kid sounding so much like an adult."

"Yeah, he is." She smiled down at Sam and tried to keep the pride from her voice. Even though she gave Stacy the credit for his advanced vocabulary, he was still her boy. "It's because he's the only child of educated parents, and all he has to talk to are adults. He's always been one of the brightest kids in his class. But sometimes he still surprises me with how deep his thought process is and the big words he uses."

"Do you think I'll get to go home today?" Sam asked. Thank goodness he'd moved on from the fiancé subject.

She wished she could move on as easily.

"We have to wait for the doctor to clear you," Taylor said, "but they told us last night that if everything looked okay today, you should be able to go home this afternoon."

Sam picked at the hem of the sheet, avoiding Taylor's eyes. "Where am I going to go? Back to my house?"

Oh no. She'd been so focused on Sam being okay that she hadn't really thought about what would happen once they let him out of the hospital.

Because of all the fire damage, she couldn't take him back to her apartment. Taking him back to his own house wouldn't work either. He lived here in Great Falls, and it would be impossible to make the forty-five minute commute without a reliable car. Or depending on what was wrong with it this time, no car at all.

Plus, she couldn't just leave the restaurant. She needed to be in Broken Falls to oversee the repairs and get the diner back up and running.

"You're both coming home with me," Taylor said.

Her eyes snapped to his.

Coming home with him? What was he talking about? "Taylor—"

He ignored her protest, his gaze focused on Sam. "I live on a ranch in Broken Falls. It's called the Lazy J Ranch, for the Johnson family. There's plenty of room and lots of things for an eight-year old boy to do. We have horses and cows and even a few pigs. How does that sound? Would you be okay coming back to the Lazy J with us?"

Sam's small shoulders shrugged. "I guess so." He looked

at her. "Is that okay with you, Cherry?"

She sighed. What choice did she have?

She couldn't afford for them to stay in a hotel, and she sure as hell didn't want to ask anyone in her family for help. If she showed any sign that she couldn't take care of Sam, they'd swoop in and snatch him from her faster than she could blink.

"Yeah, Sam. That's okay with me." It had to be okay.

What other choice did she have?

Chapter Six

Taylor pulled the truck to a stop in front of the house. He'd had one of his deputies bring his truck to Great Falls that morning so he wouldn't have to bring Sam and Cherry back in his cruiser. He didn't want Sam's first ride with him to be in the back of a police car.

After Sam was released from the hospital, they'd gone by Stacy's house and picked up some of his things. They'd filled a couple of duffel bags with clothes, toiletries, books, and some of Sam's favorite toys.

Taylor's heart broke as he'd watched Cherry move slowly around the living room, softly touching knick-knacks and photographs. He could almost see the memories flashing across her face as she smiled or grinned at each picture. She'd chosen a few and tucked them into a bag to bring along.

He'd tried to think like a sheriff and reminded her to grab some of the important paperwork from Greg's den.

They'd found a file containing Sam's social security card and health insurance documents.

It had taken less than an hour to pack the most critical things and head for the ranch in Broken Falls. The drive had been quiet as Taylor watched the familiar scenery go by.

Now he stepped from the truck and walked around to get the door for Cherry.

Sam had fallen asleep on the way home but now sat up in the seat, taking in the farm.

Taylor looked around the ranch, viewing it from the eyes of the eight-year-old boy.

The house itself was a sprawling ranch-style home that looked like a big log cabin. The front porch held two rocking chairs, and a swing swayed lazily in the summer breeze. The barn had been repainted a few years back, so the red color seemed bold against the deep blue of the Montana sky.

A fenced-in corral hooked to one side of the barn, and four horses casually munched at a bale of hay in a trough. Large fields lay on the other side, and several hundred cattle grazed on the green grass of the pasture.

The sun was just setting, and the dim light of dusk gave the ranch an idyllic look, almost as if it were lifted from the pages of a book.

He took Cherry's hand and helped her from the truck, then lifted the boy out and set him on the ground. "Welcome to the Lazy J. What do you think?"

A black-and-white striped cat streaked across the yard and pressed itself against Sam's legs.

The boy looked up at Taylor, a lopsided grin on his face. "I like it. It's cool."

The screen door slammed, and his dad stepped onto the

front porch.

Taylor had called him earlier and told him he was bringing home a couple of friends to stay the night. He'd asked his father to make up the guest room and pull something together for supper and said he'd explain everything when they got there.

Taylor herded the group up the steps and onto the porch.

Cherry offered a small wave as she walked up the steps. "Hi, Russ."

"Hey there, Cherry." Russ wrapped her in a hug. "I heard about the fire at the diner. You doing all right?"

Cherry sunk into his dad's arms, and Taylor had a moment of envy that she couldn't get that comfort from him.

She held up her bandaged arm. "Only a slight casualty. But I'll be okay."

His dad had always adored Cherry, and Taylor knew that he still saw her every week at the diner. Russ had wanted them to stay together.

It seemed odd to Taylor that he had left Cherry behind, yet his dad still had a relationship with her. Still saw her and talked to her.

Small towns.

Russ looked down at Sam, his arm still wrapped around Cherry's shoulder. "And who is this young man?"

"This is Sam. He's my cousin's son. He's—" Her voice choked with emotion, and she swallowed, unable to continue.

"Sam and his parents were in a pretty bad car accident, and he's going to be living with Cherry now," Taylor said, reverting to his official sheriff voice. It was easier to say the words if he voiced them in an official capacity.

"My mom and dad died," Sam said, his voice hoarse.

"Well, I am truly sorry to hear that, son. That's a pretty rough deal for a guy to go through." Russ held out his hand and carefully shook the boy's casted hand. "I'm Russ, Taylor's dad. Looks like you busted up your arm there. That's a pretty cool cast though."

Sam held up the cast, now wrapped in orange and blue gauze.

The technician had let him pick the colors, and he'd blurted out his color choices without a moment's hesitation. "Thanks. It's orange and blue, for the Denver Broncos. That's my dad and I's favorite team." He looked up at Russ, sincerity in his eyes. "Do you think they have football in Heaven?"

Russ smiled down at the boy and gave him a reassuring nod. "I'm counting on it, son."

A ball of emotion clogged Taylor's throat, and his heart ached for this parentless boy. He thought he couldn't love his dad more. He was the kind of man that Taylor aspired to be.

He wanted to say thanks but worried he wouldn't be able to get the words out. Instead he just nodded at his father. Universal man-code for "I love you, Dad."

Russ winked at him and held open the screen door. "So, I've got a big pot of sauce simmering on the stove. Are you a fan of spaghetti, Sam?"

Sam nodded. "Yeah, sure. I love spaghetti."

"Taylor, I made up the guest room. Why don't you bring in their stuff, and I'll get the noodles to boiling. We'll eat in fifteen."

Fifteen minutes later, they were sitting at the table, a huge plate of spaghetti steaming in front of them.

Taylor took Sam's small hand in his and bowed his head as his father said grace.

Russ took the lid from the pot of sauce, and a heavenly scent of tomato and garlic filled the room.

Taylor's stomach growled, and Sam grinned up at him. He shrugged. "Sorry, dude. I'm hungry."

He was rewarded with a wide-toothed grin. "Me, too."

Russ filled a plate for Sam then passed it to him, and Taylor was happy to see the boy dig in.

Now if only his dad could get Cherry to eat something.

He'd brought up a sandwich and chips from the hospital cafeteria at lunch and had convinced her to eat some of it only by telling her he was full and going to throw the rest away. He was glad to see her eat but hated that the only reason she took the sandwich he offered was to save it from being tossed in the trash.

His dad spooned a heaping helping of spaghetti and sauce onto a plate then passed it to her, and Taylor was pleased to see her twist her fork into the noodles and scoop a bite into her mouth.

She closed her eyes in bliss as she chewed, and the temperature of the room suddenly went up a notch as he imagined other ways to create the same look of bliss on her face.

Get a grip, man.

They were eating supper. Now was not the time to be fantasizing about the woman sitting across from him. The woman whose red hair spilled from a loose top knot on her head, the strawberry strands resting softly against the cream-colored skin of her neck.

Memories of kissing that neck filled his mind, and he flashed on the last night they'd been together. He'd taken her out to the lake, and he remembered the way the moon and the stars had reflected off the glassy water.

He'd had that old blue pickup, and he could envision Cherry's hair spread out on the bench seat as she lay under him. It had been close to nine years ago, and yet the memory was as vivid as if it had happened yesterday.

He could almost hear the sounds of the bullfrogs through the open windows of the truck. Almost smell the plumeria-scented lotion that she loved to wear. Almost feel the rough fabric of the seat covers as it scratched his bare hip with every stroke as he moved in rhythm with the woman beneath him.

Except she hadn't really been a woman. She'd been a girl, and he'd been just a boy.

A stupid boy who made stupid decisions based on his dumb ego and his own selfishness.

Well, he wasn't a boy now. He was a man, and he knew how to control his ego and make smarter decisions.

Most of the time.

And Cherry was most definitely a woman.

"Earth to Taylor. You gonna take this plate, son, or do you just want me to hold it for another ten minutes?" Russ held the plate out to him.

He grabbed the plate, heat warming his neck. "Sorry, Dad, I was thinking about something else."

"Uh-huh." He gave a light-hearted chuckle as he fixed himself a plate. "So, Cherry, have you heard anything about the diner? Do they know what the damages are?"

"I haven't heard much. I kind of put Stan in charge while we've been up at the hospital." She looked over at Taylor. "I was hoping we could go over there tomorrow and take a look at the place."

Taylor nodded. "Sure. I'd like to see how bad it is too. What do you think, Sam? Do you want to go over and check out the diner?"

The boy shrugged, his attention focused on twirling the loose strands of spaghetti around his fork. "Sure. Can I get a chocolate shake? Cherry always makes me a shake when we visit the diner."

"I don't know what kind of shape the kitchen will be in, buddy," Taylor said. "But I bet we can find a chocolate shake somewhere in town tomorrow."

"I hate to put you out," Cherry told him. "I'll try to see about getting my car towed tomorrow, too. I just haven't had the energy to call anyone about it."

"I already took care of it."

"What do you mean you took care of it?"

"I had the guys over at Westside Garage tow it in. They said the alternator was shot, and they were gonna put in a new one this afternoon. It should be ready by tomorrow."

She gave him an icy glare. "Why would you do that without even checking with me?"

Whoa. "What's wrong? Why are you upset? I thought I was helping. In fact, I kind of thought it would make you happy."

"It would have made me happy if you would have talked to me first."

She rubbed her hand across her forehead as if her head ached. "It's just with the cost of the fire damage and the diner being closed, I don't know if I can afford to replace the alternator right now."

"Don't worry about that. I already took care of it."

She raised an eyebrow at him. "I don't need you to *take care* of anything else for me."

He raised his hands in surrender. "All right. Listen, it's no big deal. Dan owed me a favor, and he said he had a spare alternator around. Besides, he loves tinkering around on those old bugs. So don't worry about it."

She glared at him, and he could tell she was trying to keep her tone light even though she spoke through gritted teeth. "It is a big deal to me. And I'd rather you not tell me what to worry about and what not to worry about."

"All right. Let's all simmer down now," Russ said. "I think we can probably save this argument until after dinner. And when Sam and I aren't around."

"It's okay, Russ," Sam said around a mouthful of spaghetti. "My dad told me sometimes married people argue and that it's okay. It doesn't mean they don't love each other, they just disagree. And since they're getting married, we know they're gonna argue sometimes."

Russ had been lifting his fork to his mouth, the tines full of sauce-covered noodles, and his hand stopped in midair.

He cocked an eyebrow at his son. "I must have missed the engagement announcement. I hadn't heard that you two were getting married."

Sam reached for the basket of rolls. "Yeah, they're called fiancés. That means they're getting married."

A light-hearted twinkle lit Russ's eyes as he regarded his son. "This is certainly exciting news, son. When's the big day? I want to be sure to get it on my calendar."

Taylor busied himself with taking a roll and spreading it with butter, his eyes focused on the task instead of his father. "We haven't actually set a date yet. We'll let you know."

His dad chuckled softly. "Yes, you be sure to do that." He grinned at Cherry, who was suddenly extremely engrossed in her meal. "I've always wanted a daughter."

"I've always wanted a monkey," Sam said, releasing the tension as the adults broke into laughter. "What's so funny? Don't you think it would be cool to have a monkey as a pet?"

Taylor shook his head. The laughter felt good after the stress of the last few days. "Yes, I think it would definitely be cool to have a monkey."

He grinned at Cherry, and his insides did a funny little twist when she grinned back.

And suddenly having a pet monkey seemed easier than having a fake fiancée and taking care of an eight-year-old broken-hearted boy.

Chapter Seven

Now what were they supposed to do?

Cherry hadn't thought about the sleeping arrangements until they'd finished tucking Sam into bed in the guest room later that night.

Pulling the door shut behind them, she and Taylor stood in the hallway, awkwardly looking at each other. He graciously offered to sleep on the sofa.

"Don't be ridiculous," she told him. "It's your bed. I can sleep on the sofa."

Russ walked out of the kitchen, a cup of tea in his hand. "Cherry, don't be silly. You don't have to sleep on the sofa on my account. I'm not that old-fashioned. You all can sleep in the same room. Heck, you are engaged to be married after all."

He chuckled as he headed for his bedroom. "Good night."

Left with little choice, they stepped into Taylor's

bedroom. He'd brought in the Walmart bags from the motel and laid them on the bed.

Cherry sighed and dug through the bags for a toothbrush and toothpaste. "You know what? I don't care where I sleep. I'm so tired I could fall asleep standing up."

Taylor opened a dresser drawer and handed her a gray T-shirt. "Just in case you wanted something clean to wear to bed."

He really was thoughtful. She brushed her teeth and stripped out of her clothes. She needed to get some of her own things from her apartment tomorrow.

Would everything in her place smell like smoke? How much stuff would be ruined or smoke-damaged? Add that to her list of things to worry about.

She sighed and pulled the soft T-shirt over her head, the hem coming to just below her rear. She could worry about those things tomorrow.

Tonight she had something else to worry about.

Like the six-foot-three hottie on the other side of the door whom she was supposed to go crawl into bed with.

Taylor sat on the edge of the bed wearing a white T-shirt and a pair of gym shorts. He looked up as she stepped out of the bathroom.

"It's all yours." She tugged the ponytail holder from her hair and shook her hair loose.

His eyes went soft as he watched her hair fall, and something inside her went into tingle over-drive.

Suddenly conscious of the short T-shirt and her bare legs, she pulled back the comforter and slipped into the bed. "The bathroom's all yours if you want it," she repeated.

He shook his head as if coming out of a spell. "Oh yeah.

No, I'm good. I already used the guest bathroom to brush."
He stood and looked around uncomfortably, as if he were
unsure quite what to do next.

Pulling his T-shirt over his head, he gave Cherry a great
view of his muscled chest.

She swallowed, her mouth suddenly dry.

He switched off the lamp. The bedroom window was
open, the light from the moon illuminating the room, and a
soft breeze carried the scent of summer.

Lifting the corner of the comforter, he slid into bed,
lying down on his back and looking up at the ceiling.

Even with six inches between them, she could smell the
masculine scent of his aftershave and the faint minty scent
of toothpaste.

The smell of toothpaste made her think of his mouth.
His lips. Kissing him.

Stop.

Stop thinking about his lips.

Stop thinking about kissing him.

She hadn't kissed him in close to nine years. Would he
still taste the same?

Would his lips feel the same against hers?

Did he still do that funny thing that drove her mad
where he sucked lightly on her bottom lip?

He took a deep breath and shifted, as if trying to find a
comfortable spot. He settled again, this time his arm closer
to hers, and she could almost feel her skin heating from the
nearness of him.

Five minutes ago, she'd been so tired she could have
fallen asleep leaning against a wall.

Now she was in a soft bed, with a pillow beneath her

head (a pillow that smelled like him), and she was wide awake.

All of her senses were on guard, every nerve ending alert for the slightest movement. For the brush of his skin against hers. For his foot grazing hers as he shifted.

Every thump in her chest echoed in her ears, and she tried to take a settling breath.

Could he hear how hard her heart was beating?

Calm down. It's just Taylor.

She'd known him since they were kids. They used to sit next to each other on the school bus. Their sides had touched thousands of times. He'd held her hand every day for her entire senior year.

He'd also held her face as he tenderly kissed her. He'd held her waist as they'd danced at prom. He'd held her back as he'd moved against her in the darkened room of her grandparent's basement.

And he'd held her heart.

She'd given her heart, her body, her soul to him.

And he'd taken them, then left her behind.

Driven off in that old blue pickup. The pickup where they'd first made out. First made love.

And where they'd made Sam.

"Did you ever think about me?"

Geez, did she really just say that?

Out loud?

"All the time." His voice was clear, not carrying any trace of sleepiness.

Was he wide awake next to her, conscious of her every movement?

She turned toward him, lying on her side.

His eyes were open, still staring at the ceiling.

"Why didn't you ever call me?" Her voice was soft, barely above a whisper. Almost as if she didn't really want him to hear her question.

As if she were afraid to hear his answer.

He rolled onto his side, facing her, and she read the pained expression on his face, even in the dim moonlight of the room. "I wanted to. I started to. Lots of times. But I didn't know what I would say, so I chickened out."

Sheriff Taylor Johnson spent time in the military, carried a gun, was a policeman and a sheriff. And he was afraid of calling her? Of hearing her voice on the other end of the phone? She had a hard time believing that.

"You don't seem like much of a chicken to me. Why would you be afraid to talk to me?"

He shrugged.

The muscles of his arms flexed with the movement, and she wanted to reach out, to run her fingers across the hardened flesh of his bicep. "I guess I was mostly afraid that you wouldn't want to talk to me at all. I was an idiot. A stupid kid. I was so full of myself and thought I knew what I wanted. Thought the military was going to be my ticket to freedom. You know I wanted out of this small town so bad."

"And was it? Your ticket to freedom?"

"I don't know. The military taught me a lot. A lot about myself. About what I wanted out of life. What kind of man I wanted to be. But it was also really lonely. You wouldn't think it would be. I was surrounded by people all the time. And most of the guys in my unit were great. But you could have six guys in a room with you, laughing and belchin' and talkin' about getting laid, and you could even be laughing along with them, and still feel like you were all alone."

He sighed and reached out his hand, lightly pulling a strand of her hair through his fingers.

She tried not to shiver as his slightest touch sent a wave of sensation down her spine.

She held her breath, waiting for his next words, the dark room offering a sort of safety net. A protective shield around them where they could talk about the past.

Talk about the hurt.

His voice was deep, deeper than it had been when they were kids.

He twirled her hair around his fingers as a slow smile spread across his face. "God, I love your hair. I used to lie awake at night just thinking about your incredible hair. And your freckles."

She rolled her eyes and let out her breath.

"I know you hate them, but I loved them. Remember how I used to try to connect them into a dot-by-dot picture?" He chuckled.

She laughed with him. "Yes. You were an idiot."

His laughter died. "Yeah, I was. I was an idiot. But I figured it out too late. Then I didn't know how to fix my mistakes. The only thing I knew how to do was to move forward. To stay the course. I had made my bed and I needed to lie in it. I knew I'd screwed up, and I didn't deserve you. And I knew by the time I got out of the service, you'd have moved on. I felt like I'd blown my chance. Plus you were pretty pissed at me when I left. That was a hell of a fight that last day, and I honestly didn't think you'd ever speak to me again."

"Yeah, that was a hell of a fight." Memories of that day

filled her mind. They'd both said things they probably didn't mean.

She knew now that her anger had come more from her issues with her mom walking out on her when she was a kid than they had to do with Taylor leaving or him wanting to join the military.

Their fight was full of teenage drama, and she cringed at some of the hateful words that she had thrown at him. "I'm sorry. I was hurt."

"I'm sorry, too."

As they spoke, their bodies seemed to have drawn nearer together, as if they were magnets being pulled closer by an invisible magnetic field. She could feel his leg a hair's length away from hers.

He reached out.

Her breath caught.

He skimmed the back of his knuckles softly down her cheek. "You're so beautiful. Sometimes it hurts to even look at you."

Emotion swelled in her throat.

Could this be real?

Could Taylor be here, touching her face, so close that she could stretch out her fingers and touch him?

He leaned closer, his breath warm on her face.

The scent of his aftershave filled her senses.

His thumb traced the edge of her bottom lip, and she wanted to weep for the sheer pleasure of his skin against her lip.

Closer.

His hand cupped her face drawing her nearer still.

She couldn't breathe.

Couldn't move. Frozen in anticipation of the taste of him.

His lips grazed hers. Softly. Deliciously slow, as if savoring their flavor.

He pulled back. Just a fraction.

Testing.

Teasing.

His mouth against hers.

The sweetest brush of a kiss.

And she shattered.

Something inside of her broke apart, and she fell. Her senses reeling, cartwheeling in a ferocious spin of emotion.

She couldn't think. Didn't want to.

Just wanted to feel.

To taste.

To kiss the lips of the man she'd dreamed about for nine years.

She touched his face, kissing him back. Softly once.

Again.

More.

She pressed her lips against his, kissing him harder, feeling the passion building inside and trying to control its release.

She felt his hand dive into her hair, as he filled his fingers with it.

Cradling her head, he drew her face closer, feasting on her mouth.

He shifted then his body was on top of hers, the delicious weight of him pressing her into the mattress.

Her leg wrapped around his, drawing him tighter against her as she returned his kisses. Met his desire with a fervor of her own.

His hand slid under her shirt, and his fingers grazed her waist.

She moaned against his mouth, her breasts tightening against his chest.

Every nerve ending in her body was on fire. Her muscles taut with anticipation of the next feeling. His next touch.

The bare skin of her stomach pressed against his, and she couldn't get enough of his touch. She wanted to freeze this moment. This fraction of time, in the dark, in this bed, with his hands on her body and his lips crushing hers.

She didn't want this moment to end. Pulling back, she looked into his eyes. Eyes that she knew so well yet not at all. She searched for answers.

Listened for him to tell her they might have another chance.

Instead, the terrified screams of a child filled the air.

Chapter Eight

Taylor raced for Sam's bedroom, his heart pounding in his chest, as he heard Sam scream again. Cherry was practically on his heels as she ran behind him.

He flung open the door, the light from the hallway shining on the small figure tossing in the twin bed.

The sheets were tangled around Sam's legs, and his head was damp with sweat.

Cherry pushed past him, calling the boy's name as she reached his side. "Sammy, it's okay. Wake up, sugar."

Sam blinked awake, his eyes filled with terror.

He clung to Cherry's arms. His breath hitched in his chest as he tried to speak. "I was having a nightmare. We were in the car, and the truck was coming right at us. I could feel it crash into us."

"Shhh. It's okay now." Cherry pulled him into her arms and cradled the boy against her chest. Her eyes looked frightened as she peered up at Taylor. "It was just a bad dream."

Sam pushed against her, his face contorted in pain. "But it wasn't a dream. It was real. It really happened. The truck really hit us, and my mom and dad are really dead."

He stood in the middle of the room, frozen, not knowing what to do to help, his gut twisting for this little boy who'd just screamed from a nightmare.

A nightmare that had really come true.

The only thing he knew to do was try to be there. He crossed the room and sat on the bed on the other side of Sam.

The boy threw his arms around Taylor, his sweaty hair damp against his chest. He rubbed his hand along Sam's back.

He didn't know a lot of eight-year olds and wasn't sure if the boy was small for his age or not, but he sure seemed small to him. His hand practically covered the boy's entire back.

He didn't know what to say.

How could he tell him everything was going to be all right when he didn't know if it would be? "I'm sorry, Sam. I'm really sorry."

The boy took a deep shuddering breath and clung to his chest. Taylor looked up at Cherry.

She looked as lost as he felt, her eyes round with sorrow.

Sam reached back and squeezed her hand.

They sat like that for several minutes. Taylor softly stroking the boy's back while Cherry gently held on to his hand.

Sam's breathing settled, and his muscles relaxed.

"How about you try to go back to sleep now?" she quietly asked.

"Will you stay in here with me?"

"Yes, of course." She shifted so Taylor could set the boy's head back down on his pillow, then she lay down on the bed next to him, cradling his small body against hers.

Sam settled against the pillow, his eyes closing in fatigue. He struggled awake, looking around the room. "Where's Taylor?"

He reached out and took Sam's hand. "I'm right here, buddy. I'm not going anywhere."

Not letting go of Sam's hand, he laid down behind Cherry, spooning against her back.

She set her hand on top of their joined ones.

"Everything okay in here?" Russ stood in the doorway of Sam's room, his voice low.

Taylor nodded. "Yeah, Dad. Thanks. You can go back to bed. Everything's okay."

He heard the click of the latch as his dad pulled the door shut and felt Cherry relax against his chest. He laid awake and listened as her and Sam's breathing evened out as they fell asleep.

Yeah, everything was okay.

For now.

Cherry pushed open the door of the diner. It was still early the next morning, and she would normally have filled dozens of orders by now.

But today, the diner sat empty, a fine layer of soot still visible on every surface. An acrid scent of smoke filled the air.

A ball of panic blossomed in her chest at the thought of the work ahead of them and how much it was going to cost to do the repairs.

And having her only source of income out of commission fed the intensity of the panic.

"Wow, this place is dirty," Sam said, in his usual matter-of-fact tone.

He pushed past her and ran up to the counter. After brushing off the seat, he climbed onto one of the stools then spun toward her. "Hope the shake machine still works."

"Don't worry, I haven't forgotten about the chocolate shake." Taylor stepped into the diner, a tool box clutched in his hand. "I've never seen this place so empty."

"It's not totally empty, dude." Stan pushed through the kitchen doors. His hair stood on end and a smudge of soot covered his cheek, but danged if he wasn't a sight for sore eyes.

Cherry grinned and crossed the room to throw her arms around her friend. "I am so glad to see you. Do you know how bad the damage is yet?"

"Nah. The insurance adjustor came out yesterday and took some pictures. He said he'd be by with a quote, but we were okay to start clearing stuff out and cleaning up. Most of the damage is contained around the stove. Except for the smoke and water damage. Oh, and the big hole that burned through the ceiling. I think everything up there and in here is covered with soot. That's what I've been doing the last few days, just cleaning the kitchen."

She poked her head into the kitchen and could see the evidence of his work. The dishwasher was humming, and he had a sink full of bubbly water stacked with dishes. One side of the kitchen gleamed, the other was still blanketed in soot. It looked like a before-and-after picture. "Wow, you have been working."

"Hey, little dude." Stan offered Sam a high five.

Stacy had been bringing Sam to the diner since he was small, and Stan had a soft spot for the boy.

She'd called Stan the day before to fill him in the car accident and tell him about Sam.

Stan put a comforting hand on Sam's small shoulder. "Sounds like we're going to be seeing you a lot more around here. Sorry about your parents. That sucks, man."

Sam nodded and fiddled with the hem of his shirt. "Yeah, it sucks."

Her heart broke for him.

She knew as a parent she should probably tell him not to say "sucks," but in this case, it did suck.

It sucked really bad.

Stan gestured to the kitchen. "Do you want to help me in the kitchen? You can wash some dishes, and I'll even let you pick the tunes."

"Okay." Sam slid off the stool and followed Stan into the kitchen.

"We're going to go up and check on my apartment, Stan. You good here?"

"Totally. As long as my man here picks some good tunage." He scrolled through his phone. "Sam, you want to hear my playlist for 'Good tunes' or 'Happy music'?"

"Um, let's do happy music," Sam said, pulling over a stool and dunking his hands into the water filling the big kitchen sink.

It looked like Stan had it handled. The melodic notes

of a Jack Johnson song filled the air, and Cherry turned to Taylor. "Can you help me check out my apartment? The fire department said I couldn't go up there, but since you're a volunteer fireman, maybe it's okay if just you go in?"

Taylor nodded. "Let's go see." He set down the tool box and held the door open for her.

They walked around the side of the building and climbed the stairs to the apartment over the diner. The back door of the kitchen was open, and she could hear Stan's music wafting out into the alleyway.

Taylor pulled the yellow caution tape from the door, and she handed him her house key. He unlocked the door and pushed it open.

The thick smell of smoke filled the air. She peered into the apartment and groaned. A huge hole sat in the middle of the floor and she could see down into the diner's kitchen.

The apartment opened into one big room with a kitchen along the wall. It had a large bedroom at the far end and a good-sized bathroom.

She was thankful she'd closed the door of her bedroom, hoping that kept out some of the smoke damage.

The same layer of soot and ash covered every surface up here, and she could see warps in the wood floor from the water damage.

Taylor held a hand against her arm. "Stay here in the doorway. I'll go in and see how bad it is. Is there anything you really need from in here?"

She sighed, too overwhelmed to think of everything that could be damaged or lost. "Mainly just some clothes. And my laptop. There's a photo album on the shelf of my bedroom that I'd like to have. And my jewelry box."

Taylor nodded and carefully stepped into the room. He took tentative steps, testing the floor before he put his whole weight on it.

The floor groaned and creaked under his feet.

She reached out to him. "Holy crud. Be careful."

"Don't worry. I'm taking it slow. I know what I'm doing." He cocked his chin and offered her a sly grin. "Are you worried about me?"

"No," she replied, trying to sound offhand. "I just can't afford to pay the medical bills if you fall through the floor."

"Uh-huh." His grin remained as he pointed to the closed door at the far end of the apartment. "Is that your bedroom?"

"Yeah. There should be a laundry basket on the floor, half full of clothes. Those are the things I probably wear the most."

He inched past the hole in the floor, sliding sideways with his back against the wall, then pushed open the bedroom door and peeked inside. "It doesn't smell quite so bad in here. Either that or I'm getting used to it."

He disappeared into the room and came back with the laundry basket. He set it on the floor of the open doorway. Cherry could see her simple jewelry box nestled in the clothes and the brown edges of the photo album sticking up out of the basket. "The photo album looks okay. What else do you want me to grab?"

"There's a backpack hanging off the closet door. Could you stick my laptop in there? And do you see my tennis shoes on the floor? The pink ones?"

He disappeared again, and she could hear him rummaging around the room. "Got the shoes and the computer."

"Do you see my cowboy boots in the closet? The brown ones with the teal inset? Can you grab those?"

His head poked around the doorway. "Really? Do you think you're going to need a pair of boots in the next week?"

"They're brand new. I just bought them." They'd been her one big splurge last month. She hardly ever bought anything for herself but had seen the boots in the window of Tate's Western Shop and had to have them. "Do you want me to come in and get them myself?"

He held up his hands. "No, stay there. I'm not sure how safe that floor is. I'm getting the boots."

"I think a pair of my favorite jeans are on the chair by my bed. Do you see those? And a pair of jean shorts should be on the floor."

"Found them." He dropped the boots, jeans, and shorts into the basket.

She chewed her bottom lip trying to think of what else she might need in the next few weeks. "I probably need a few things out of my dresser. Can you open the middle drawer there on the right? Just grab the stack of T-shirts on top?"

He pulled the drawer out, grabbed the top few shirts, and dumped them in the basket.

"And there's underwear in the top drawer. Just grab a handful."

He offered her a naughty grin as he pulled out the top drawer, and his eyes roamed over her underwear. "Do I get to pick the ones I want you to be wearing? I like these." He picked up a black lacy thong and twirled it around his finger.

Heat crept up her neck. No woman wanted a man poking around in her underwear drawer. "Just put some in the basket."

Laughing, he shuffled a hand through her panties. "Are you worried I'm going to find one of your toys in here?"

Um. No. She'd purposely not told him to go into the bottom drawer for that very reason. "My toys are none of your business."

He held up a red lacy bra. "Do you need some extra brassieres? I think we should bring this one."

She narrowed her eyes and looked around for something to throw at him.

"Um…just so you know, we can like, totally, hear you guys down here." Stan's voice came up through the hole in the floor.

"What's a bra-zeer?" she heard Sam ask.

"You'll find out soon enough, dude."

"But Taylor said they might have toys up there." Sam's voice sounded hopeful.

Her face heated with embarrassment, and she shook her head at Taylor, who was doubled over in laughter.

"Just get back to washing those dishes," Stan said.

"Are you done now?" she asked.

Taylor said nothing but held up another bra, this one sheer black lace. He wiggled his eyebrows at her.

"Just put some in the basket and let's go, you dork."

Still chuckling, he dropped a couple of bras into the basket. Hefting the backpack over his shoulder, he picked up the basket and carried it across the room, carefully easing back past the hole in the floor.

She slugged him in the arm as soon as he was close enough to reach.

He only laughed harder as they walked down the stairs and around to the front of the diner. She held the door and he walked in and set the basket on one of the tables.

Cherry picked up one of the shirts and wrinkled her nose. "Ugh. All of these clothes stink like smoke."

"Yeah, I know a few tricks from the fire hall for getting the smoke smell out, but we're probably going to have to wash them several times."

Hmm. He sure did say "we" a lot.

She wasn't sure if she liked it or not. If she could trust that he was really sticking around.

If she could trust *him*.

"I can help with that."

Cherry turned, a smile breaking over her face, as she recognized Charlie Ryan's voice. Charlie was one of the few women friends that Cherry had, and she stood in the doorway of the diner with her boyfriend, Zack Cooper, his fourteen-year-old daughter, Sophie, and her handsome ranch hand, Cash Walker.

Growing up in Broken Falls, she and Taylor had gone to school with Zack and Cash. Taylor and Zack had played on the same football team, and the three guys had been getting in trouble together since they were kids.

Cherry rushed forward to hug her friends. "What are you guys doing here?"

Charlie squeezed her shoulder. "We're here to help. We brought sandwiches, Sophie's mac-n-cheese, and four pairs of willing hands." She pointed at the basket of clothes. "I can take those clothes out to the house and wash them for you. I've heard hanging them out on the line to dry helps get the smell of smoke out."

"You don't have to do that. I can go over to the laundromat later."

"Nonsense. I want to help." Charlie cocked an eyebrow at her. "I'm not good at a lot of things, but I can work the washing machine, and it will make me feel better to know I helped."

A sigh of relief escaped her as Cherry smiled at her friend. "Okay. Okay. And thank you. That would be great."

Zack stepped forward to shake Taylor's hand. "Hey, buddy, looks like y'all have quite a mess here."

Cash clapped him on the shoulder. "We came to work. What can we do?"

Taylor gestured to the kitchen. "Most of the repair work needs to be done in the kitchen. I could use a hand hauling out the damaged stuff and replacing the dry wall. And we've got lots of stuff to wash and wipe down if Sophie wants to lend a hand."

"Taylor, you don't have to do this. Don't you have to work or something?" Cherry asked. Why was he being so nice to her?

"I'm fine. The office knows where to find me. I'm sure they'll call if a big crime spree spontaneously breaks out." Taylor led Zack, Cash, and Sophie into the kitchen, and she heard him introducing Sam.

Charlie gave her an appraising glance. "Why don't you want him to help you? He is your *fiancé* after all."

Cherry groaned. "Seriously? How in the hamhock do you know about that?"

"Who doesn't know about it? It's a small town, remember?" Charlie cocked an eyebrow at her. "I am a bit surprised that you didn't mention your engagement when we were at Taco Tuesday last week. That seems like an important bit of news."

Cherry picked at the loose polish on her thumb nail. "It just happened recently. I, uh, just haven't had a chance to tell you about it."

"I guess not. And it must be extremely recent, especially since I recall you complaining to me over margaritas last week that you hadn't been with a man in close to a year."

"A year?"

Cherry's head popped up to see Taylor standing by the counter.

That's just great.

Maybe another hole could appear in this floor and just swallow her into it.

Taylor pointed at his tool box. "I just came back in to grab my tools. Didn't mean to interrupt." He ducked his head sheepishly and grabbed the box.

Walking back toward the kitchen, shaking his head, he muttered, "Well, I'll be a son of a gun. A year?"

Cherry buried her face in her hands. "Thanks a lot, Charlie. I thought you were supposed to be my friend." Hearing no reply, she peeked out from between her fingers and spied her "supposed" friend doubled over in laughter.

"Sorry," Charlie sputtered between gales of laughter. "I couldn't have timed that better if I tried."

"Yeah, thanks. Now I won't feel so bad about putting you to work. Go grab a bucket and a sponge, and help me clean up behind the counter."

"Yes, ma'am." Charlie offered her a mock salute, still grinning. "And don't worry, we'll talk about this more later when we're alone."

Not if she could help it. Cherry suspected her friend knew her well enough to guess there was something fishy about the engagement, so the less she had to talk about it, the better. She just needed to keep Charlie's focus on something besides her and Taylor and their supposed engagement. In fact, she needed to keep her own thoughts off that subject as well.

It was easier to concentrate on something tangible. Like cleaning up the place.

Stan turned up the music, and the sweet thump of reggae music filled the diner.

The group worked together for several hours, then stopped to take a break for lunch.

Charlie and Sophie brought in a huge basket full of food and a cooler of cold drinks. They'd cleaned off a couple of tables, and they all shared the noon-time feast.

The kids had eaten quickly, and Sophie had taken Sam outside to play.

Sophie was a sweet teenager, and it warmed Cherry's heart to see her with Sam, getting him to laugh and play along with her silly jokes.

Cherry also loved seeing the adorable romance happening between Charlie and Zack.

Their relationship had been touch and go earlier this summer when Charlie had first come to town to take over her grandmother's farm, Tucked Away. But they'd worked things out, and it was obvious how in love they were.

The subtle caresses, the way they held hands as they sat at the table, the way Zack couldn't help touching Charlie when he was near her.

It warmed her heart to see her friends so happy. And if she were honest with herself, it made her a little jealous, too. She'd been loved like that once.

A long time ago.

It seemed easier not to think about it.

Not to think about the guy that couldn't get enough of her then left her behind.

But she couldn't ignore it. Not when that guy was sitting across the table from her, nibbling on a chocolate chip cookie.

Her eyes went to his mouth, and she envisioned him nibbling like that on her neck.

He laughed at one of Cash's stories, then looked her way and caught her staring at him. He grinned, almost as if he knew what she was thinking.

Thank goodness he couldn't actually read her mind. Otherwise, he'd know that her thoughts switched between alternately wanting to kill him and wanting to jump his bones and lick his chest.

Geez. Did it suddenly get warmer in here? "We better get back to work." She stood up from the table.

Dunking her hands in some hot water might help stop her from having visions of the night before and any thoughts of licking his anything.

Either that, or maybe she should try dumping cold water on her head.

"Look what we found. Can we keep him?" Sam stood in the doorway of the kitchen, a scruffy brown dog in his arms.

Oh great. She did not need this.

"Sam, where did you get that dog? And put him down. He's filthy."

Sam's delighted expression deflated, and a little pain hit Cherry in the heart. "We've been playing with him out in the alley. He doesn't have a collar, so I don't think he belongs to anybody."

"He seems pretty skinny, and his coat's awful dirty. I think he's been outside for a while," Sophie said. She stood behind Sam, looking like a willing accomplice.

"Bring him over here. Let me take a look at him." Zack, a veterinarian, was undaunted by a scruffy animal. He held his arms out for the dog.

Sam clutched the animal protectively to his chest.

Sophie nudged him forward. "It's okay. I told you my dad's an animal doctor. He won't hurt him."

Sam trudged forward and handed the dog over to Sophie's dad.

Zack ran his hands along the dog's body then pulled back its lips and inspected its teeth. "He looks like he's less than a year old, and he's probably a little under-nourished." The dog leaned across Zack's arm and licked Stan's hand.

Stan offered Cherry a sheepish grin. "I might have seen him hanging around the alley the past few days. I'm not saying I've exactly been feeding him, but the little dude did seem hungry, and if a few scraps fell out of the bag on the way to the dumpster, then that wasn't really my fault."

"I can take him over to the clinic and check him out," Zack offered.

Everyone looked at Cherry.

Really?

She looked down at Sam's face.

"Please, Cherry," he begged. "He doesn't have a home or anyone to take care of him."

He wasn't just pulling on her heartstrings, he was engaging in an all-out tug-of-war.

How could she refuse him when she knew Sam was probably connecting even more with the dog because he was an orphan, too?

Well, sort of. Sam actually did still have a mom. He just didn't know it.

And neither did anyone else.

Including his father.

But did they really need to take in a stray dog that looked like it was probably infested with worms?

The dog tilted its head at her, its brown eyes peeking out from under tufts of matted fur. She had always been such a sucker for a stray.

She looked to Taylor for help. "You know we're staying out at Taylor's. You'll have to ask him before we bring a dog into his house."

Sam ran over to Taylor and threw his arms around his legs. "Please, Taylor. Can I please keep him? I'll feed him and walk him and take care of him. And he can even sleep with me."

Ugh. Not before he had a bath.

"And I don't even need a chocolate shake. Not if I can keep this dog."

Taylor laughed and grinned down at the boy, and Cherry knew she'd lost her only ally.

"Sure. But let's give Coop a chance to look him over and make sure he's okay first."

"Thank you. Thank you." Sam squeezed Taylor's legs then rushed over to the dog. "Did you hear that, boy? You get to come home with me."

"After Zack checks him out," Cherry said. "And you give him a bath."

Why did she have to sound like the grumpy voice of reason? She was usually the one who dove head-first into bad decisions.

Was this what it was like to be responsible for another human being? To make the hard decisions that no else wanted to.

Was this being a mother?

Zack, Sophie, and Sam took the dog to the vet clinic, leaving the rest of them to resume the work of cleaning and repairs.

Stan, Cash, and Taylor retreated into the kitchen. Charlie filled another bucket with hot, soapy water and went to work cleaning off the red vinyl booths.

Cherry found some glass cleaner and sprayed the windows next to where Charlie was working. "So, did I do the right thing? Should I have said no, or is it okay I let him keep the dog?"

Charlie shrugged. "How the heck should I know what the right thing is? I'm in charge of a whole farm full of animals and sometimes I almost forget to feed the cats. Good thing Cash is around and always giving them scraps."

Cherry sunk onto the seat of the booth that Charlie had just wiped down. "He's seemed so sad the past few days. He doesn't actually cry. Which kind of freaks me out. Like shouldn't he cry?"

Charlie shook her head. "I don't know. People grieve in different ways."

"Did you see the way he was smiling when he brought that grubby mutt in here? Like he'd just won first prize in a contest. He looked so happy. I couldn't say no." She twisted the ends of the paper towels between her fingers. "And Taylor was no help. He didn't even hesitate."

Charlie looked over her shoulder as if checking to make sure the men were still occupied in the kitchen. "It seems to me like Taylor has been helping you out a lot the last few days. How did that happen?"

Flecks of shredded paper towel fell onto Cherry's leg. "I don't know. I honestly don't know what in the hell-o has happened the past few days. It's just been a blur. I feel like I've been walking around in a dream." Tears pricked her eyes. "And a bad dream. Such a bad dream. I can't believe Stacy is gone. I have to be so strong for Sam, but I loved her, and I'm going to miss her so much."

"Oh honey. I'm so sorry."

Charlie squeezed into the booth next to her and wrapped her arms around her shoulders. "You're stronger than you think." She nodded toward the kitchen. "And it seems like you're being offered some pretty broad shoulders to lean on."

Cherry rubbed her eyes, willing the tears back. "Yeah, they are pretty broad, but I don't know how much I should lean on them. That didn't get me very far in the past."

"What happened with you two? I mean, I know you were an item in high school, but you never talk about him."

"What's to say? We were high school sweethearts, and then we weren't. Taylor left, and I stayed. End of story."

"Yeah, right. I'm a writer, remember? There's always more to the story. Come on, spill it."

Cherry blew out a breath. "Taylor and I started dating the summer between our sophomore and junior year. We'd known each other forever, and I'd had a crush on him since seventh grade. We were a perfect couple. We made each other laugh, and we didn't really ever fight. Not over anything important. We were together all the time. I thought we really loved each other. I know I really loved him."

"So, what happened?"

"Taylor's mom had cancer, and she died in the middle of our senior year. Something changed in him, and all he wanted to do was get out of Broken Falls. Out of Montana. We'd always talked about leaving together, but I had my grandparents to take care of and the diner. He enlisted in the military without telling me, and then one day, he just told me he was leaving. We got into a huge fight, but it was too late. He had to go. And he did. He just left. Drove off. And I didn't hear from him again until earlier this year when he came back to town as the sheriff."

"But you were just kids."

They had been kids, but they'd made grown-up choices that had grown-up consequences.

"I know. But there's something about your first love. And I really thought he was the one."

Maybe she still did. But how could he be the one?

How could she ever trust him again?

Charlie narrowed her eyes and twisted her mouth in that funny, thoughtful way she had. "Hmmm. Something tells me there's more to this story."

Oh, there's more all right.

And he's over at the vet clinic washing mud and gunk off a mangy orphaned dog.

But she couldn't tell Charlie that. She couldn't tell anyone that. Especially Taylor.

Something changed last night.

When he'd kissed her, she felt like they might actually have a chance. A chance at a future.

But not if he learned the truth. If he found out that she'd lied to him all these years. And gave Sam away without telling him.

Charlie was right. There was more to the story.

A lot more.

But one thing Taylor would not put up with was being lied to.

Chapter Nine

"He is kind of cute." Taylor eyed the scruffy dog squirming in Sam's lap. "What do you think you want to name him?"

Sam squinted up at him, a thoughtful expression on his face. "I don't know yet. I feel like it's a pretty big decision, and I don't want to rush it."

"Good thinking." How could such a young kid already be so dang smart?

"No dogs at the table." Cherry walked in from the kitchen, a plate of pork chops in her hand. His dad followed behind her, his oven-mitted hands holding bowls of mashed potatoes and gravy.

His dad must be showing off. Or trying to impress Cherry. They usually only ate this good on Sundays.

Sam put the dog on the floor, and it curled up next to his feet.

Cherry took her place next to him, and Taylor picked up

her hand to say grace.

It was the first time he'd gotten to hold her hand all day.

It felt good in his. Right.

His dad said the blessing, and they all dug in.

He'd worked up an appetite after the full day of hard work at the diner, but they'd accomplished a lot.

Russ plopped a spoonful of potatoes on Sam's plate then passed the bowl to Cherry. "So Sam, tell me about this dog."

"Well, Dr. Cooper, I mean Zack, said he thinks he's about a year old so he's really still a puppy. We gave him a bath, and Zack gave him some shots and made sure he didn't have fleas or worms or anything. Although I don't know exactly how you would have worms."

"Worms are not really a great topic for the table," Cherry told him as she spooned gravy onto his pile of potatoes.

She was really good with him. Sam was lucky to have someone that really loved him as his guardian.

"Oh. Okay. Sorry. So anyway, Zack also said that except for being kind of skinny, he seemed to be in pretty good shape. And Zack helped me give him a bath so he's all clean, and you don't have to worry about him getting your house messed up."

How many times was this kid gonna mention Zack's name? Like he was the Greek God of Veterinarians?

Hmmm. Were those tiny seeds of jealousy rumbling around in his gut?

Did he want to be the only hero in Sam's life?

Nah.

It takes a village right?

Except maybe *he* wanted to be the head of the village. Not Dr. Zack.

"I'm not worried about him getting anything dirty. But how do you know he isn't somebody's dog?"

"Zack said the same thing. But I know he isn't. He's an orphan—like me."

Cherry's eyes widened. "How do you know what an orphan is?"

He gave her a look that said she was the clueless one. "If you're a muggle and your parents have died, you're an orphan. Just like Harry Potter. Even though he turned out to not be a muggle. But maybe it was magic that brought me this dog. Or maybe an angel. I just know I was supposed to find him today."

Taylor watched the mix of emotions play across Cherry's face as she listened to Sam talk. Her eyes went from amused to proud. And then to pained.

He hated to see her hurting.

"Zack said we could put up signs at the vet clinic asking if anyone knew whose dog he was. But if no one claimed him in the next few days, then I could adopt him. Just like my mom did with me."

Cherry's fork clattered to her plate.

A strange look crossed her face, and Taylor couldn't read her expression.

"What do you mean just like you?" she asked.

Sam tilted his head at Cherry. "My mom and dad told me that I was adopted. That God gave me to them because one of his angels couldn't keep me. I don't think it was a real angel, though."

"No, I suppose not." Cherry's voice was soft.

She must not have known.

But she and Stacy were so close. Surely her cousin would

have told her.

"They said someday if I wanted to meet my real mom, that they would help me." Sam pushed his pork chop across his plate. "But I guess I won't ever find out now."

A stilted hush settled over the table.

What was anybody supposed to say to that?

Russ cleared his throat. Leave it to his dad to come up with something. "Well, if it's meant to happen, you'll still find a way to meet her. These things have a way of working themselves out." He smiled down at the boy. "In the meantime, we need to come up with a name for this mutt."

Sam grinned, the topic of the dog outweighing his adoption. "Yeah, I kind of like Max or Jack. Or maybe Bumblebee. What do you think?"

"I think maybe you should sleep on it. Some of the best answers I've gotten have come after a good night's sleep," Russ said.

Sam turned to Cherry. "You won't need to sleep in my room tonight. I'll have Max, Jack, or Bumblebee to sleep with, and he'll help keep the bad dreams away."

"You sure you want that dog in your bed with you?" Cherry asked.

"Of course I do. He's already my best friend."

She looked toward Russ. "Is that okay with you?"

Russ shrugged. "Fine by me."

It was fine with Taylor, too.

Because that meant Cherry would be back in his bed again tonight. Just thinking about her lush body lying next to his made his heart race.

How far would things have gone last night if Sam hadn't had the nightmare?

How far might they go tonight?

Two hours later, he and Cherry stood at Sam's bedside. She'd tucked him in, and the dog lay curled against Sam, his head resting comfortably on Sam's pillow.

Considering the dog had probably spent the last several weeks sleeping in an alley, he must have been in doggie-heaven about now. A full stomach and a cushy bed seemed to equal one happy dog.

And one happy boy.

Sam couldn't stop smiling at the mutt, and it warmed Taylor's heart to see him so happy. He knew the dog wouldn't fix everything, but he sure offered a great big canine Band-Aid.

Cherry leaned down and kissed Sam's forehead. "Good night, Sam. I adore you."

The dog tipped his head up and snuck a quick lick against Cherry's cheek. She laughed. It was good to hear her laugh.

"The jury's still out on you, Max-Jack-Bumblebee." She ruffled the dog's furry head. "But you're definitely growing on me."

Taylor stepped to the door and held it open for Cherry. "Good night, buddy. We'll be right down the hall if you need us."

"Okay, good night." Sam was already turning away and cuddling in to the dog's body.

"That dog sure seems to make him happy," he said as they walked into his bedroom. He pulled out his dresser drawer and handed Cherry another T-shirt. Charlie had taken her clothes to wash, and she still didn't have much to wear.

Cherry held the shirt up and grimaced. "Do you seriously

expect me to wear this?"

The blue and yellow shirt had a bobcat on the front of it surrounded by the insignia of Montana State University. "It's from MSU and has a bobcat on it. No self-respecting Griz fan would be caught dead wearing this."

"Oh yeah. I forgot you were a University of Montana fan and loyal to the Grizzlies." He hadn't really forgotten. They'd been rival fans all through high school and used to tease each other about it.

She narrowed her eyes at him, and he couldn't help but grin. "You did not. You handed me this shirt on purpose."

He shrugged. "You don't have to wear it. I'm fine with the alternative of you coming to bed not wearing a shirt at all." He held her gaze, knowing his eyes held the threat of a dare.

"I'd rather wear nothing than wear the colors of MSU." She pulled her shirt off and dropped it on the floor.

Holy crap. He never thought that would work.

What the hell was he supposed to do now?

He stood frozen in place as Cherry turned off the bedroom light and walked slowly toward him. The light from the bathroom spilled into the bedroom, giving the room a soft glow.

The bedroom window was open, and the faint scent of rain filled the room. His attention was focused on the luscious redhead coming his way.

Her hair was loose and curled around her shoulders. In the dim light, her skin was creamy white. He couldn't tear his eyes away from her and her half-naked body.

Her lush breasts pushed out of the top of the white lacy bra she wore, and he ached to fill his hands with the weight of them.

Cherry stopped right in front of him and looked up, her expression full of a naughty challenge.

"I think those pants have a little MSU on them," he teased. "Maybe you ought to get rid of those, too."

Without saying a word, she unzipped her pants and let them drop to the floor.

He swallowed, his throat suddenly dry.

She stood before him in only her bra and panties, and he suddenly had no idea what to do. Where to put his hands.

He wanted to touch her so bad, but he didn't want to spook her. Something in him told him that she wasn't as brave as she was acting. Even though he wanted to pick her up and throw her on the bed, he knew he had to go easy.

He cupped her cheeks gently between his hands. She closed her eyes, and he nearly came undone.

She was so beautiful. He almost couldn't stand it.

Leaning down, he softly kissed her, his lips grazing hers. She moaned against his mouth, and sensation rippled through his body.

She tasted the same. Kissing her lips felt like coming home.

He ran his fingers lightly down the sides of her arms and grinned at the gooseflesh that pebbled her skin.

The rain beat against the window, the drops falling harder now.

Cherry's teasing bravado was gone. Her eyes were now vulnerable and full of desire.

He held her gaze as he knelt before her, then closed his eyes as he rested his cheek against her bare stomach. He heard her slight intake of breath as he laid a soft kiss on the spot right below her belly button.

Starting at her ankles, he ran his hands up the insides of her legs, slowly, caressing her skin as he moved closer to her center. Sliding his fingers under the elastic band of her panties, he slowly drew them down her legs, leaving her wearing only her bra.

And that seemed like still too much. He needed to see her. All of her.

He rose and skimmed his hand along her waist and around to her back.

Dipping his head, he kissed the soft tops of her breasts as they pushed up above the lace cups of her bra.

He found the clasp and released the hooks. He hadn't realized he was holding his breath as he slid his fingers under the straps and slowly, torturously pulled the straps down her arms and let her bra fall to the floor.

He took a step back, releasing his breath, and just looked at her.

She stood naked before him, and he knew by the look in her eyes that she was baring more than her body to him.

"You are more beautiful than I ever could have dreamed."

Her face broke into a shy smile, and the feelings tinkering around inside of his heart multiplied by ten.

All he wanted to do was make her smile.

Well...and also make her moan. And gasp. And make her claw at the bedsheets as she cried out his name.

She raised her arms and wrapped them around his neck, her flirtatious smile back. Nipping at his neck, she ran her tongue along his throat.

Okay, forget that earlier thought. She could make *him* moan.

Her breath was warm against her ear. "It seems to me that now you have entirely too many clothes on."

He couldn't agree more. He took a step back and stripped off his clothes. He wore a chain around his neck, a small gold key dangling from its center. Pulling off the chain, he bent to unlock his bedside drawer and pulled it open.

His holstered sidearm lay inside the drawer next to a pile of bullets and a box of foil-wrapped condoms. He grinned over at her. "I keep all my protection in this drawer."

She laughed and pushed him onto the bed. Climbing on top of him, she straddled his waist, pressing her hands against his chest. "Do you think you need protection against me?"

A streak of lightning lit the room, silhouetting her naked body in a flash of blue light. Her hair was a wild mess of curls around her shoulders and her breasts hung free, full and ripe.

She looked like a goddess, sitting on top of him, and everything in him ached with need. With a fierce desire to kiss, to touch, to taste every part of her.

Yes. He was definitely going to need protection.

And although he intended to take advantage of several of those gold packets of protection, there was nothing in that drawer that could protect the actual part of him that he worried was in the most danger.

His heart.

Chapter Ten

Cherry rolled over and hit solid muscle.

Bright morning sunlight poured into the bedroom, and she gazed at Taylor's face. His eyes were closed, and his breath still held the steady rise and fall of sleep.

He was so damn handsome. He'd always had the most gorgeous thick eyelashes. It wasn't fair how great his eyelashes were.

She'd always thought that saying about a guy having a chiseled chin was ridiculous. But really, that was the only way to describe Taylor Johnson. His entire face looked like it could have been chiseled out of the finest marble.

A light layer of stubble covered his cheeks, giving him a rugged look, and she wanted to reach out and run her fingers along the short blond whiskers.

She wanted to just lie like this. To watch him sleep and soak in his beautiful face. Memorize every new feature. Every nuance that the last nine years had given to his appearance.

He had a little scar on the left side of his chin that she didn't remember. She'd have to ask him about that. Hear the story of how that happened.

There were so many things that had happened in the last decade.

They had lived completely separate lives from each other.

She wanted to hear everything. Every story. She wanted to get to know him again. To learn everything about him.

Before he was gone.

Before this fake engagement and this perfect little pretend life came to an end. Because this couldn't last. This would eventually have to end.

And she would have to go back to her real life. A life without Taylor. And this lovely soft bed.

And that amazing thing that he did with his tongue last night.

"What's that grin all about?" Taylor's eyes were open, and he smirked at her as if he knew exactly which part of the previous night she was replaying in her head.

She smiled back, already feeling the heat of a blush creeping up her neck. "Um, I was just thinking about that thing, last night, you know, when you did that—"

He chuckled. "Yeah, I know exactly what thing you're talking about." He ran his fingers lightly down her bare arm, sending delicious shivers up her spine.

Before they'd fallen asleep the night before, she'd put the dreaded MSU shirt on after all and a pair of Taylor's drawstring gym shorts. They were too big, but she didn't want to have to worry about being covered up if Sam had another nightmare and she had to run into his room again.

"Taylor. Cherry. Get up. I need your help." Sam burst through the bedroom door and jumped on their bed.

Cherry sat up, her eyes searching his small body for injuries or blood. "What's wrong? Are you okay?"

Sam tried to catch his breath. "It's not me, I'm fine. It's Rex."

"Who's Rex?"

"My dog. I named him after my favorite dinosaur." He slid off the bed, grabbing her arm and pulling at her. "Come on. He got into the cow pen, and I can't get him to come out. Those cows are too big, and Taylor told me to stay out of the corrals."

Taylor was out of bed and pulling on a T-shirt. "It's okay, Sam. The cows won't hurt the dog." He stuffed his feet into the pair of sneakers lying on the floor at the end of the bed.

"They might step on him." Sam was already at the bedroom door, waiting impatiently as Cherry slipped on her flip-flops. "Come on."

They followed Sam outside and across the driveway.

Sure enough, the dog was racing around the cow pen, barking and trying to herd the cows. Where he was trying to herd them to was a mystery.

The rain the night before had turned the pen into a muddy mess, and the dog kicked up little flecks of mud as he ran.

Taylor stood at the fence and whistled. "Here, boy. Come 'ere, Rex."

The dog completely ignored him.

"What should we do? He's gonna get trampled." The alarm in Sam's voice was almost heartbreaking.

Taylor chuckled as he crawled between the fence railings. "I guess we're gonna get muddy." His foot made a squishy sound as his tennis shoe sunk into the thick mud. He crossed the corral and shooed the cows back.

They looked at him with boredom in their eyes, but some of them lumbered toward the other side of the fence.

"Come here, pup." Taylor held out his arms and tried to cajole the dog to him.

Rex obviously thought he had a new playmate and raced back and forth across the corral at top speed.

"He's coming your way. Grab him," Taylor called out.

Now that most of the big heifers were across the corral, Sam seemed less afraid and followed Taylor's lead as he climbed through the bars of the fence.

"Be careful," Cherry said. She stepped up to the fence, trying to sidestep the majority of the mud.

The little dog raced toward Sam, barking playfully and having a great old doggy time. He stopped a few feet in front of the boy and flattened his chest on the ground, declaring Sam his alpha dog, but also challenging him to a chase.

Sam moved sluggishly through the mud, trying to reach the dog.

Rex ran around behind him and stopped in front of her, his pink tongue lolling out the corner of his mouth.

She stuck her head through the bars and reached for the dog. Rex took that moment to do a full body shake, flinging flecks of black mud across her face, hands, and chest.

"Aahhh. Gross." She looked down at her mud-flecked chest then up at Taylor and Sam who wore matching grins. She narrowed her eyes at Taylor. "What are you laughing at? These are your clothes."

He chuckled. "They'll wash. And that color of mud looks good on you."

Everything looked good on him. Even wearing mud up to his shins, he still looked hot.

She kicked off her flip-flops and crawled through the fence. Thick, cold mud squished up between her toes and she grimaced. "Ewww."

Sam's eyes were wide with surprise, like he couldn't believe she'd just stepped into the muddy pen.

She smiled at him. "What? I was already muddy." She clapped her hands. "Now let's catch that silly dog."

Sam laughed. A wonderful, free laugh filled with joy.

He raced across the pen, chasing the dog. Rex barked and sprinted between the three of them, running circles around them and eluding their attempts at capture.

He circled close, and she thought she had him. She reached forward, but the dog slipped through her arms, and she lost her balance. Tumbling forward, her arms pin-wheeling, she fell face-first into the mud.

She could hear Taylor's gleeful whoops of laughter and Sam's uncontrollable giggles.

"I think I hurt myself," she said, waving Taylor over. "Can you help me up?"

Taylor's laughter died as he rushed across the pen to her side. He reached out his hand. "Are you okay? What did you hurt?"

"My pride." She grabbed his outstretched hand and pulled him down into the mud.

"No, you didn't," Taylor said, his teeth extra white against his muddy face. He grabbed her around the middle and pulled her onto his lap then tipped them both into the mud.

Sam shrieked in delight and ran forward, jumping onto the dog pile.

The actual dog ran in excited circles.

The next few minutes turned into a frenzied mud fight, the three of them laughing and flinging handfuls of mud at each other as they ducked and dodged and tried to crawl away.

She felt hunks of mud stuck to her hair. Any other day, she would be mortified. But today, she couldn't be happier. She was having the time of her life.

And so was Sam. It was so good to hear him laugh and see him play. It was worth every smear of mud on her body, including the glob she could feel in her ear.

Blissfully happy, she laughed as she grabbed a handful of muck and threw it at Taylor.

The sound of a car engine had them all looking up as a brand new black Chevy Denali drove down the ranch's driveway.

Oh. Shit.

Not just *oh shit*. But HOLY shit.

Cherry recognized the car right away.

It belonged to her cousin Reed, and her heart sank at the thought of getting caught sitting in the mud in front of her cousin.

The car came to a stop, and all of her happy feelings deflated like air from a balloon.

Her day had been going so well.

She hadn't seen or heard from the Hill family since the funeral the weekend before. They had all sat together in the long front pew of the church. Sam had looked so small, his legs swinging from the pew as he sat between her and Taylor. The words of the minister had seemed faint and far away as Cherry's mind raced with memories of her cousin.

The ladies from Stacy and Greg's congregation had put together a potluck in the basement of the church, and Cherry'd suffered through hugs and tearful words of sympathy as she waited for the day to be over. All she'd wanted to do was go home and sleep.

But she had Sam to take care of now so she'd soldiered through the day, leaning on Taylor for support. And he had been a rock. He'd never left her or Sam's side. Sam had been so precious, quietly sitting through the service. He'd fallen asleep right after, and against her great aunt's wishes, she'd had Russ take him back to the ranch. She didn't care if it made them mad, they were always mad at her for something anyway.

She'd put all of her focus on getting through the day and getting home to the ranch. To the place that made Sam happy. And her, too. At least until this moment.

The back door of the Denali opened. Her Great Aunt Bea emerged, and her day went from bad to worse.

"What in tarnation is going on here?" her aunt asked as she pressed her cane to the ground.

Cherry gave Taylor a panicked look.

They scrambled out of the mud and slogged to the fence railing, their previous joy gone, replaced by a feeling of dread.

She could tell that even Sam and the dog felt the shift.

The boy quietly followed Taylor as they crawled back through the fence, and the dog stuck close to Sam's heels.

Reed and Olivia had emerged from the big SUV, and

the three Hill family members were standing in a row, all wearing matching expressions of disdain.

They were all dressed in their Sunday best, and Cherry had a sinking feeling they had just come from church.

Due to the diner's long hours, she didn't always make it to church every Sunday, but she and Stan tried to work out a schedule where they could take turns. With the fire and everything happening with Sam, she hadn't even realized it was Sunday.

And evidently, this had not been the Sunday to skip.

Olivia wore a crème-colored designer dress and had her arms crossed across her chest. Clad in her standard black old lady dress, Aunt Bea's sour face looked like she'd just tasted something bad.

"We thought we would just stop by on our way home from church today," Olivia said, raising a hand to pat down her perfectly coifed hair.

Stop by? Yeah, since Taylor's ranch was just a mere hour and a half out of their way.

"Yes, we spent our morning worshipping in the Lord's house." Aunt Bea nodded her head at their muddy bodies. "It doesn't look you all made it to church this morning."

"We're going tonight," Taylor said without missing a beat. "The evening service is more contemporary, and we'd thought Sam would enjoy it more."

Oh my gosh. She could have kissed Taylor Johnson right on the mouth.

Oh wait, she had, last night. Several times.

And also on the... Well, now probably wasn't the best time to be thinking about that. Not with her pious aunt currently peering down her morally supreme nose at her.

As if he were a Supreme Court Judge, Reed stepped forward and glanced down at Cherry with a barely-disguised look of scorn. "We just came out to make sure Sam was doing okay and to check on the state of the environment that he was living in."

"They have these things called telephones. You could have called first."

A sneering smirk covered his face. "I'm glad we didn't. This way we got to see Sam in his natural environment."

Natural environment? What was he talking about? "He's a child, Reed, not an animal at the zoo."

"You could have fooled me." Bea said, her voice full of contempt. "It looks like animals were exactly how you were behaving. Just look at yourselves."

Cherry looked down. Thick smears of mud covered her bare legs, and chunks of mud stuck to her clothes. Bits of hay dotted the dark mud, and she could feel a glob of the muck hardening across her cheek, like a redneck facial treatment.

If the state of Sam and Taylor were any indication, then she must have looked terribly filthy, too. Sam's blond hair stuck up in mud-filled spikes, and Taylor's arms were covered in the brown gunk.

In retrospect, it probably wasn't a good idea for Sam's cast to get that muddy. That was going to be a booger to clean.

"Look, we were trying to catch the dog, and we got carried away. We were just having some fun." The explanation sounded weak even to her ears.

Most people would look at the rag-tag muddy group and bust out laughing. But not the Hills. And not when they were looking for ammunition to take Sam away from her.

"Well, I guess we got the information we came for,"

Reed said and turned toward the car.

A flicker of hope blossomed in Cherry's chest. Maybe this would be okay. Maybe they would see that she was making Sam happy. "You're leaving?"

"Of course we are." Olivia stepped forward. "And we're taking Sam with us." She reached out for Sam's arm but looked like she couldn't quite figure out where to grab.

"No. I don't want to go with you." Sam shrunk against Taylor's leg.

"Listen here, young man, you'll come with us now, and I don't want to hear anything else about it." Bea leaned forward, her eyes set in a hardened glare.

She reminded Cherry of the wicked old crones in so many fairy tales. Except she didn't have a poisoned apple or a cauldron of brew. But for all Cherry knew, she would make Sam do all the housework and would lock him in a dungeon at night.

She couldn't let that happen. They were not going to take Sam away. "He's not going with you."

Aunt Bea turned her menacing gaze toward her. "Don't smart talk me, missy. This was all a mistake in the first place. Stacy never should have set you up as the guardian. You can't even take care of yourself."

Reed held out his hand. "Come on, Sam."

The boy held on to Taylor's leg. "No, I don't want to go."

"I'm not asking."

"He said he doesn't want to go." Taylor stepped forward, gently pushing Sam behind his legs. "I think we established before that Cherry has the law on her side."

Reed sneered up at Taylor. "I think she has one law man on her side." He lowered his voice to a commanding tone.

"Sam, I'm not messing around here. Get in the car."

"No. I'm staying." Sam's voice was shrill with alarm, and Rex must have picked up on his distress because the dog whined then circled close to the boy. He dipped his head, and his lips pulled back in the slightest of snarls.

Reed took a step back. "Hey, tell that dog to calm down."

"He's my dog," Sam said. "And I'm not going anywhere without him."

Olivia bristled. "You are not bringing that muddy mutt in my car." She had always talked with her hands and waved them wildly around as she spoke, which set the dog into a frenzy.

Rex must have thought they were either playing or that Reed and Olivia posed a threat because he raced wildly around them, nipping at Olivia's heels. She shrieked at the dog, hopping around and trying to kick her foot at it.

"Rex, come here, boy." Sam must have known the dog's behavior would not help his case, and he ran after the dog, trying to grab its skinny body. He passed by Olivia, leaving a big smear of mud across the side of her dress.

Olivia screeched in horror, and the more she hopped around and the shriller her voice became, the more the dog raced about and barked.

Taylor leaned down, making a grab for the dog. "Dang it." In his haste to snatch his body, he got his hand too close to his head and as the dog barked, his teeth grazed Taylor's hand.

"That mongrel bit you," Olivia cried. "It probably has rabies."

"It's nothing," Taylor muttered as he wiped his hand on a semi-clean spot on his shirt. Cherry grimaced as she saw the red smear of blood he left behind.

"He's not a mongrel." Sam finally caught the dog and plopped to the ground, cuddling the furry creature in his lap.

Rex settled down and licked the boy's face.

Bea's face wrinkled in disapproval. "Make that mutt stop licking your face. That is disgusting."

"He's not disgusting. He's my best friend." Sam's voice took on the shaky quality that Cherry recognized as him trying not to cry.

Reed opened the back door of the car. "Sam, I'm serious. Let go of that dog, and get in this car right now."

"That boy is not going anywhere." A new voice joined the mix, and the frenzy calmed at the sound of Russ's deep and authoritative tone.

The group turned as one to watch Taylor's dad walk down the front steps of the porch. "He's staying right where he is. Come over here, Sam." He held out his arm, and Sam ran to him and threw his arms around his waist. Rex followed and lay down next to Sam's feet.

It warmed her heart the way Sam had bonded with Russ.

Of course, she was the only one that knew Russ was actually the boy's grandfather. What would Russ think of her if he knew the truth?

If he knew that Cherry had given away his grandson and never given him a chance to get to know the boy. She shuddered at the thought.

But right now, she was just thankful for Russ's presence. Something about him spoke of strength and calmness. She recognized the same qualities in Taylor as she inched closer to stand by his side.

"Who the hell are you?" Reed asked.

"I'm Russ Johnson, Taylor's dad. This is our ranch." He narrowed his eyes at Reed, not the least bit intimidated by the lawyer. He scolded him as if he were a teenage boy. "And I'd appreciate if you didn't swear in front of the boy."

Reed huffed with indignation, obviously not used to other men telling him what to do. "Look, Mr. Johnson, I don't know who you think you are or what right you think you have to even be a part of this conversation, but Sam is my nephew. He's my family."

Reed's condescending tone did nothing to rankle Taylor's dad. Russ smiled at him as if they were just having a friendly, neighborly chat. "Well, he's about to be part of my family, too. Once these kids get married."

"Yeah, right. If they're even really engaged." Olivia's voice held a snide tone of disbelief. She turned to Cherry. "We've been asking around, and no one in town seems to have even known you two were dating, let alone engaged."

Without a moment's hesitation, Russ spoke up before Cherry had time to formulate a response. "I've known about it for months. They reconnected before he came back to town. Why do you think he's here? Do you know anyone who would take a small-town sheriff job if he didn't have something bringing him to the town?"

Olivia seemed to mull over Russ's explanation. "Then why doesn't anyone else know about it? We can't find one person who has seen them together."

"You know how small towns are. Everybody in everyone else's business. They were keeping it quiet until they knew if they were really serious. They didn't want to get the rumor mills started until they were sure."

Taylor took her hand. "And now we're sure."

She listened to these two men talk about their engagement so easily, she almost believed it herself. If she weren't the one they were talking about, she would have completely bought their story.

Unfortunately, Olivia wasn't as easily swayed. She pursed her lips as she scrutinized Taylor and Cherry. "Then why don't they tell everyone now? If they're so serious, after all."

Her grip tightened on Taylor's hand, but she didn't have to worry. Russ came to the rescue again.

"They were just about to. They're throwing an engagement party in town next weekend. They've been planning it for weeks."

They had?

"Yeah, we've had the band scheduled for a month now," Taylor said.

Geez, these guys were so good, she caught herself wondering what band they had booked.

Wait. There was no band because there was no party.

Well, I guess there is now.

Bea had been unusually silent. She stood against the SUV watching the group talk. "If you have been planning this big party, why had we not received our invitations? We *are* your family, you know. Or weren't you planning on inviting us?"

Olivia narrowed her eyes at Cherry. "Yeah, it's funny that you've been planning this so-called party for weeks but no one in our family knew anything about it."

"I'm pretty sure I heard my mom talking about it on the phone with Cherry." The group all turned to Sam as he spoke up.

Why that little fibber.

Did he know this was all a lie, and he was just playing along because he knew it would help to keep him with Cherry?

Or had he maybe heard her and Stacy talking about some other party or event, and Sam just assumed it was the same thing?

"We were getting ready to send out the invitations when the accident happened," Taylor said. "We've actually been considering postponing the event."

"Oh, by all means, don't postpone on our account," Bea said. "We'd be happy to come to this engagement party. Wouldn't we, Reed, dear?"

Reed nodded. "Yeah, we would. We'd love to come to this party and celebrate the happy couple. Where did you say you were having it again?"

"Here at the ranch. Next Saturday night. About six," Russ said.

"We'll see you then." Reed opened the door and helped Aunt Bea into the back seat. "And that crazy dog better be gone or tied up somewhere because I don't want to see it again. You better get that bite looked at. Who knows what kind of diseases that mutt could be carrying."

Sam pulled the dog closer to him, and Russ put a comforting hand on the boy's shoulder.

Reed and Olivia climbed into the SUV and slammed their doors. The car pulled a U-turn then took off down the driveway, leaving the mud-splattered group in the dust.

Taylor put an arm around her shoulder. "You okay?"

She smiled up at him. "I am now that they're gone." She crossed to Sam and knelt in front of the boy. "Are you okay,

Sam?"

He nodded. "I don't want to go anywhere with them." He put his arms around her neck and hugged her tight. "I want to stay with you."

She looked over Sam's shoulder at Russ and Taylor. "Well, it looks like we've got a party to plan."

Chapter Eleven

Taylor swung the hammer and pounded the last nail in. He'd been working on replacing the drywall in the diner's kitchen for the last two days.

Zack and Cash had stopped by to help the day before. They'd hauled away the rest of the debris and cleaned out the space where most of the fire damage had been.

The griddle top was shot, but Cherry had to wait for the insurance money to come through to get a replacement.

A lot of the work was labor and cleanup of the smoke and water-damaged area. One of his deputies had shown up to help him haul a load to the garbage dump, and his dad had stopped in that morning with fresh sheets of drywall.

One of the great things about small towns was the way that everyone pitched in to help.

Cherry had been working in the front of the diner, and a steady stream of women from the town had dropped by to help clean or bring food.

Stan worked at restocking and getting the kitchen back in order. He supplied the positive attitude and always had upbeat music playing in the back.

Sam and Rex ran between the front of the diner and the kitchen, usually taking care of odd tasks that someone had given them.

Sam was learning where things went, and Cherry had shown him how to run a few of the appliances behind the counter, like the coffee pot and soda machine.

His main job was to make sure the coffee pot stayed full. He'd found an order pad and took drink orders from anyone helping with the repairs in the diner. He was turning out to be a pretty good waiter.

He'd told Cherry he was practicing so he'd be able to help her once the diner was re-opened.

The boy had a goofy grin but was smart as a whip, and Taylor caught himself smiling more when the boy was around. He hadn't been around that many kids before, but something about Sam touched his heart, and the kid was really growing on him.

It was probably just because he'd lost his own mom as a kid, and Taylor connected with the child who had lost a parent too young.

He could hear Sam telling a joke to Cherry. The rich peal of her laughter floated on the air and made him smile.

That woman had a great laugh. Actually, she had a great everything.

He grinned as he thought about the night before with her. Having Cherry in his bed every night had turned out to not be so bad.

Especially now that Charlie had brought Cherry her

own clothes. Charlie had used some special detergent she got from the fire department to get the smoke smell out. And she'd washed everything twice and hung it outside on the line to dry.

Cherry seemed more at ease in her own clothes. She didn't have much, but they were her things, and they fit better than anything of Taylor's. Especially her jeans.

Yeah, her jeans fit really well.

And he'd been right about that red lace bra. It was definitely his favorite. Especially when it was lying on the floor of his bedroom.

Cherry and he had been each other's first in high school, and he remembered a lot of fumbling, frenzied teenage sex with her. Which was amazing to a teenage boy.

But what they had now was *beyond* amazing. Cherry's body was all lush curves and soft skin that smelled like soap and fancy lotion.

And lord have mercy, that hair.

Visions of her hair spread out on the pillow filled his head, and he thought she looked like a red-haired angel. A naked red-haired angel.

Okay, maybe an angel wasn't the best description. Because she certainly wasn't an angel in bed.

Full of fiery passion, she displayed a fierce hunger for him. As if she were starving and he were her last meal. The way she kissed him? Damn. Almost as if she were tasting him, devouring him. Feasting on him.

And lord help him, he loved it.

He matched her hunger, meeting her every need with a lust of his own. His appetite for her seemed to be insatiable, and he couldn't get enough of her.

The sex with her was wild and intense, and he loved the way she fought to keep her passionate sounds quiet so they wouldn't wake up Sam or his dad.

The night before they'd barely made it into the bedroom before he'd had to have her.

She'd closed the bedroom door, and he'd pressed her back against it, taking her mouth in an onslaught of kisses.

He'd lifted her legs, wrapping them around his waist as he held her against the door. He filled his hands with her lush bottom. She squirmed against him, driving him crazy with desire as she clutched at his back.

He couldn't get her out of her clothes fast enough, and he'd ripped the collar of the T-shirt he'd been wearing as he jerked it over his head.

All he'd wanted, all he'd needed, was to have her naked and underneath him, her bare skin pressed against his.

"You doing okay? You want me to get you a soda or some tea?" Cherry stood at the doorway of the kitchen, interrupting his thoughts, and he felt a blush creeping up his neck.

She must have seen it, because her lips curved into a naughty grin. "What were you thinking about?"

He smiled. "The same thing I'm thinking about right now, babe." His eyes traveled over her body, skimming her curves.

She wore a pair of khaki shorts and a tight blue Henley T-shirt. The T-shirt hugged her breasts perfectly, and the top button was open, teasing him with an occasional glimpse of her cleavage.

All Taylor wanted to do was rip open that T-shirt and bury his face in her breasts.

These were the kinds of crazy thoughts that had been filling his head the last few days.

He'd never spent so much time thinking about tearing the clothes off a woman and tossing her on the bed.

"Are you just going to stand there and eyeball my boobs, or are you going to tell me what you want?"

He took one step forward and wrapped an arm around her waist, drawing her close to him. He leaned down, inhaling her scent as he laid a trail of kisses along her neck. "You, woman," he said into her ear and was rewarded with her quick intake of breath. "You're what I want."

She tilted her head up and pushed him into the kitchen, away from the eyes of the women from the Methodist church who had brought over ham sandwiches and were polishing everything to a bright gleam.

"Then take me." Her hands were in his hair, and her lips crushed his. She pressed against him, and he ran his hands down her back then filled them with her curvy behind.

His brain turned off, and his body took over, his every instinct filled with having this woman.

Her lips were so soft, and she tasted faintly of lemon meringue pie. She kissed him with a fevered passion, and he couldn't get enough of her. Couldn't get close enough. Couldn't touch enough. Taste enough.

His hands slid under her shirt and up her rib cage. Her skin was so smooth, and he groaned against her mouth.

His hands cupped her ample breasts, and he could feel her pert, tight nipples through the fabric of her bra as he grazed them with his thumbs.

She gasped at his touch, at the contact to the sensitive area, and her back arched into him.

He lifted her to the countertop, and she wrapped her legs against his waist.

This woman was literally going to kill him. He wanted her so bad.

His manhood bulged against his jeans, and he felt like he might explode. What was it about this damn red-haired woman that sent him into such a tailspin?

What was she doing to him that he was ready to take her on the counter of the diner, with six women from the Methodist church within earshot?

"Are you gonna need me to bring in those extra two-by-fours, dude?" Stan pushed through the kitchen doors then held his hands up at the sight of him and Cherry in mid-makeout. "Sorry, dudes."

Taylor stepped back, and Cherry yanked her shirt back into place.

Stan looked at Taylor, and a grin split his face. "Nah, dude, I don't think we're gonna need those two-by-fours. It seems like you got plenty of wood already in here." He busted up at his own joke, bending forward and hooting with laughter.

Taylor ignored the chuckling cook, adjusted himself, then helped Cherry down off the counter. "Sure, some iced tea would be great." He grinned at her, his breath still coming in ragged gasps.

She smiled back, that secret smile that lovers shared. "I'll grab it for you right now. One iced tea coming up."

"You better make it with lots of ice, please," he called after her. He watched her bottom wiggle as she walked out of the kitchen then looked up to see Stan shaking his head.

The diner cook chuckled. "Dude. You got it bad."

Boy, did he.

"Here's your iced tea." Sam pushed through the swinging door, carrying a tall glass. Rex followed at his heels. "And Cherry told me to tell you she put in lots of extra ice. Not sure why." The boy crinkled his forehead as he looked at Taylor. "Were you hot or something?"

"Dude."

"Get back to work, Stan. Cherry's not paying you to stand around all day," Taylor ribbed the cook good-naturedly. He took a big drink of the cold tea.

"Cherry's not paying me at all," Stan said. "Is she paying you?" A wicked grin crossed his face. "Never mind, don't answer that."

"I'm getting paid," Sam said. He pulled a handful of dollar bills out of his pocket. "Cherry said I could keep any tips I made." He lowered his voice conspiratorially. "One of those ladies from the church gave me five dollars, and all I did was bring her a root beer."

Taylor smiled down at the boy. "Remember that lesson. Always be nice to people, and you never know how you will be rewarded. Sometimes you'll be graced with a smile or a kind word, and sometimes it will seem like nobody notices at all. But other times, you might end up with a new friend or a new job."

"Or a five-dollar bill." Sam grinned.

The boy's smile made Taylor happy. "How's old Rex doing? Not getting into any trouble I hope."

Sam patted the dog on the head. "No way. He's doing perfect. Cherry said I can't have him in the diner once it opens, but he can be in here while we're working on it."

Cherry had taken Sam and Rex to the local dog groomer

the day before, and they had scrubbed and shampooed the dog again and given him a haircut.

Without the matted and gnarled fur, he was a pretty cute dog. His brown eyes were expressive, and it was obvious how much he adored Sam.

Which seemed to be just the medicine the boy needed. Cherry had confessed the night before that she was worried that the dog would give the Hills one more piece of ammunition to use against her keeping Sam.

He wished the dang thing hadn't bitten him right in front of them. It wasn't even a bite really, just a scratch. And it was more his fault than the dog's for getting his hand in the way when the dog was all riled up. He'd been around animals his whole life, and this dog didn't seem dangerous to him at all.

If he were worried at all, he wouldn't let it near Sam.

But the sweet temperament and the devotion in the dog's eyes told Taylor that Rex would never hurt the boy. In fact, he had a feeling that dog would do anything to protect him.

He knew the feeling.

Something about Sam just inspired him to want to protect him. To keep him safe.

He felt a pang of guilt about the fake engagement and knew it probably wasn't fair to Sam to give him the idea that he and Cherry were *really* getting married.

But the ends outweighed the means if it meant that Sam got to stay with Cherry.

Taylor liked the boy, cared for him.

And just because he and Cherry had a fake relationship (well, semi-fake; she certainly wasn't faking the night before) didn't mean that he couldn't still have a relationship with

Sam.

"Hey, Sam. I was thinking. I have tomorrow morning off and wondered if you'd be interested in going fishing with me in the morning."

"Yeah! I always wanted to go fishing. My dad was gonna take me up to Chouteau Creek." A look of despair crossed Sam's face.

"It's okay. You can talk about him."

He watched a myriad of expressions cross the small boy's face as he went from sad to angry to controlled.

Such a young boy shouldn't have so much control over his emotions. He should be able to cry if he needed to, or get mad. The kid should be able to punch something or break something.

Taylor certainly had when his mom had died. He'd broken a lot of somethings. Including a certain redhead's heart.

He'd been young and stupid and had no idea how to control his anger and grief. How did Sam have such a handle on his feelings at such a young age?

Or maybe he didn't. Maybe he just needed the right outlet. Maybe Sam needed a safe way to get some of his anger out.

He'd have to work on some ideas to help with that.

For now, he could start with taking the boy fishing.

"You know you gotta get up early to have the best chance at catching some fish. You okay getting up early tomorrow?" Taylor asked.

"Sure. Can Rex come, too? I bet he's always wanted to go fishing."

Taylor laughed and ruffled the boy's hair. "Yeah, sure. Rex can come. We'll put together some fishing gear for you tonight, then we'll be ready to take off at first light."

"All right. I can't wait. I'm gonna go tell Cherry." The boy's face lit with a grin as he pushed through the kitchen doors.

Taylor smiled at Sam's huge grin. And he felt like a hero.

He just hoped he could live up to the boy's view of him.

Chapter Twelve

Cherry pulled in to the driveway of the Tucker farm. Everyone in town knew it as Tucked Away and had loved Gigi Tucker, the older woman who had owned this land forever.

Earlier that summer, Gigi had passed away and left the farm to Charlie, her granddaughter. A granddaughter that she had never met but had been searching for most of her life.

Cherry had met Charlie when she'd first come to town, and the two had quickly become good friends. Sometimes people just connect, and that's how it'd been with Charlie.

Talking to her was easy and comfortable, and Cherry was thankful for the woman's friendship.

And thankful for the help she'd given her since the fire. Helping clean up the diner had been great, but washing her clothes and getting the stink of smoke out of them had been the biggest boost to her demeanor. Just wearing her own clothes again had made her feel more in control.

And now, as if doing her laundry hadn't been enough, she was going to ask her friend for another favor.

A big one.

She needed Charlie's help planning a pretend party to make a fake engagement seem authentic enough to help her to keep her real son.

How did she get herself into these messes?

Cash stepped out of the barn, and she waved as she got out of the car. "Hey, Cash."

He sauntered over and pulled her into a hug. The man was all muscle and smelled like a cross between hay and aftershave. "Hey there, darlin'." His voice was smooth and sexy like it could melt butter. And hearts.

And he'd melted plenty of hearts in town. With his dark wavy hair and ice-blue eyes, he was the object of many women's fantasies. And he ate it up—flirting with all of them. And they all loved it, young and old.

Charm oozed out of his every pore, yet he always seemed sincere. And fun. He could coax a smile out of anyone, yet still had a way of making every woman feel like they were gorgeous and sexy.

"So I heard you and that bum, Taylor, are gettin' hitched." He narrowed his eyes and gave her a naughty grin. "Does that mean I missed my chance with you?"

She laughed. "You missed your chance with me back in sixth grade when you picked Sarah Jean over me to be on your kickball team."

He clapped his hand to his forehead. "When are you ever going to get over that stupid kickball game? We didn't even win." He slid a dusty rock toward her with the toe of his cowboy boot. "How 'bout we start a game now? You'll be the first pick on my team."

She looked around the farmyard. "Who are we gonna play against? The goat and a couple of chickens?"

He shrugged. "Sounds like we'd have a pretty darn good chance of winning if we did. That old goat stinks at kickball."

"Nah, it's more fun to hold it against you."

A loud swear word worthy of a sailor came from the open door of the farmhouse, and Cherry turned toward the sound. "Charlie in the house?"

Cash chuckled. "Yeah. I think she's baking. That's why I'm out here, out of the line of fire."

She gave him a playful shove. "I guess we'll have to take a raincheck on that kickball game."

"You know where to find me." He waved and headed back toward the barn. "Tell Taylor he still owes me a beer."

Grinning, she climbed the front porch steps and pulled open the screen door.

She found Charlie in the kitchen with her arms elbow-deep in a wad of dough. She looked like she'd declared war on a bag of flour, the white powder lying in a thin coat on every surface.

"What in the hamhock are you doing?" Cherry asked.

Charlie blew her bangs off her forehead. She had a chunk of flour-covered dough stuck to her cheek. "I am trying to make freaking homemade bread."

"Why? They have perfectly fine loaves of bread that you can buy at this thing called a store. It's really not even that expensive. In fact, I'm flat broke, and even I can afford to buy a loaf of bread."

Her friend gave her a look of exasperation. "I was talking

to Zack the other day, and he told me this story about how his mom used to bake homemade bread and how much he loved it. Even his teenage daughter can make bread. It can't be that hard, can it?"

"I don't know. Ask Sophie, if she's the one who knows how to make it. I've never attempted it. Because I am not a pioneer woman. And I'm not ashamed to use the modern convenience of a store."

"Quit giving me a hard time, and get in here and help me knead this freaking dough." Charlie scooted over to give her some room.

"All right. Calm down." Cherry crossed to the sink, washed and dried her hands, then dipped them in the flour and grasped a hunk of the firm dough. "Is it supposed to be this hard?"

"That's what she said."

"Seriously?" Cherry giggled with her friend. "Actually, I heard that kneading flour is supposed to be a sensual experience."

Charlie laughed. "There is nothing remotely sexy about squishing around a hard ball of dough, making a giant mess, and spending two hours on a task that may still result in failure." A grin crossed her face. "Okay, that could describe a sexual experience."

The two friends collapsed into giggles.

Cherry bent forward, wheezing in laughter. She waved a flour-covered hand in front of her face as she tried to catch her breath. "Oh my gosh, that wasn't really even that funny, but I needed that so bad."

Charlie sobered and narrowed her eyes at her friend. "How are you holding up? For real? I know this has all got to be a lot, the fire, losing your cousin, and trying to take care of Sam. Are you doing okay?"

"No. But I have to be. I don't have a choice. The diner is my only means of support, so I have to do what it takes to get it up and running as soon as possible. I'm so busy, I don't have time to grieve for Stacy, so I just don't let myself think about her or Greg. I put all of my focus on Sam. He needs me, and I can't let him down."

"That must be hard, though. I know I'm adjusting to the role of mother in Sophie's life, but we're gradually working up to it. You became an instant mom. Just add water, and you've got a son."

She'd become an instant mom all right, but it wasn't water that had been added. "That part's okay. I've known Sam since he was born, and I *truly* love him. I've always loved him. I want to take care of him. That's why I'm so worried about the Hills coming in and trying to take him away."

"Why would they do that?"

"They think I'm not capable of taking care of him. Like I don't have the means or the money and that my cousin Reed and his snooty wife would do a better job. He's a hot-shot lawyer so they have buckets of money lying around."

"It takes more than money to raise a child," Charlie said, resuming her position at the counter and pressing down on the ball of dough. "Otherwise there wouldn't be so many rehab centers full of rich people's kids."

"Yeah. I know. But money helps. Especially if you have none. They know I run the diner, and they're using that against me. They say I won't have time for him, and they don't think I can take care of him as a single woman with no dependable means of income."

"Ahhh." A look of understanding passed across Charlie's face. "That's where Taylor comes in. Being engaged to the town sheriff gives you income, a man of the house, and a more respectable position in their eyes."

Cherry said nothing as she picked at a speck of hardened dough on the side of the counter.

"Don't worry. Your secret's safe with me. And it's really not that hard to believe."

"Well, my family isn't convinced."

"Why not? Half the town knows you were high school sweethearts. It's not that far of a stretch to imagine that you got back together or that he came back to town for you. It shouldn't be too hard to convince them it's a real engagement."

A sly grin crossed Cherry's face. "Welllll, some parts have gotten a little more real lately."

Charlie's eyes widened. "Oh my gosh. You little vixen."

"Hey, it's not all my fault. We're staying out at his farm and sleeping in the same room. You try lying in bed next to a man who looks like Taylor Johnson and see how real it gets."

Charlie held up her hands and a fleck of dough went flying. "No judgment here. I think it's great that you're finally getting lucky. And I knew something seemed different about you. For a woman who should be seriously stressed, you seemed to be in a very good mood the last few days."

"He is a pretty good stress reliever." Cherry giggled.

"So, what's the big deal? You like each other. You get along. Why not just go along with the scheme? People can stay engaged forever. It just needs to last long enough to convince your family and let all this stuff with Sam die down. Then if you want, you can always have an amicable breakup."

"That's the problem. My family is already pushing us to prove that our relationship isn't fake. And I don't have years. I don't know if I even have weeks. Reed and my Aunt Bea have money. They can take this to court. And besides, Taylor isn't the most reliable person to have a pretend long-term relationship with. He's not very good at sticking around."

"He seems like he really cares about you."

"He's seemed like that before. I just can't count on him to stay."

"Maybe he's changed."

Maybe he had.

It seemed like he had.

But Cherry couldn't risk putting all of her faith in a man that had deserted her when times had gotten tough before. Because raising an eight-year-old boy was definitely going to lead to some tough times. "I want to believe he's changed. I want to believe in him. But it's tough."

"At least he's trying."

"I know. Trying's the easy part. Staying is the hard part. Right now, things are good. Actually, they're great. He's sweet and thoughtful. He's so good with Sam. And the nights with him are amazing." She arched an eyebrow at her friend. "I mean seriously, a-mazing."

Charlie laughed. "I can imagine. So, again, what's the big deal? Why don't you enjoy it while it lasts?"

"Because all I can think about is that it won't last. I think part of why sex with him is so great is because I'm afraid that every time is going to be the last time. So I give it everything I have. Every moment, every touch is even more intense because I'm afraid it's going to be the last chance I have to touch him. That I'll wake up in the morning, and he'll be gone."

She pulled a hunk of bread dough from the mound and curled it in her fingers. "I can let my body get involved with his, but I can't let my heart into the mix. I can't go through the pain of losing him again. And honestly, I'm worried about letting Sam get too close to him and then watching Sam lose another person in his life."

Charlie rested her floured hand on top of Cherry's. "Maybe you just need to give him a chance. If he's willing to go along with this whole scheme, then it doesn't sound like he's planning to take off."

"Go along with it? It was his idea." Cherry sighed. "And it was his idea to have the party, too. His and his dad's."

"What party?"

"Our engagement party. That's the main reason I came out here. Although dissecting my sex life and mushing around some bread dough has been fun." She grinned at Charlie. "The Hills were at the ranch a few days ago, and Olivia claimed she hadn't found one person in town to collaborate our engagement. Russ told them we were just about to announce it, and somehow it ended up that we're having an engagement party out at the ranch on Saturday night."

Charlie laughed. "Wow. Well, I love parties. I hope I'm invited."

"Invited? I came out here to ask if you'd help host it. I have no idea how to throw a party like this. I can manage the food, but every time the diner has catered an event, I'm the one that stays in the background. The person that no one notices. The one that quietly goes around making sure there's enough wings and fried cheese sticks. I don't know how to be the center of attention."

Her friend grinned. "Well, I do. And of course I'll help. We'll get Sophie, too. She'll love it. We're going to throw an engagement party the likes of which Broken Falls has never seen."

The sun rose over the edge of the horizon as Taylor drove the truck down the old dirt road. This had been the spot where his dad had first taken him fishing when he was a kid.

Sam peered over the edge of the dashboard. "Is that it?"

"Yep." He parked the truck and pointed through the trees to a small cabin. "And that's my grandpa's hunting cabin. It's pretty rustic, but we used to come up here in the summer and spend the weekends. It's a good place to get away from all your troubles and when you need time to think."

Sam nodded, his face serious, as if he knew all about having troubles and needing time to think. "Neat. Can we go look at it after we're done fishing?"

"Sure." He reached for the door handle of the truck. "You ready to catch some fish?"

"You bet I am." He bounced in his seat, his energy apparent. Rex, who had been lying in the seat next to him, now stood, his tail wagging at a feverish pace.

Taylor grabbed the gear from the back of the truck, and they walked to the bank of the creek. This part of the creek had a lot of great rocks for sitting and watching a fishing pole.

Tall trees lined the banks and offered shade against the late summer heat. Even though it was barely dawn, he felt the heat building in the air.

He pointed at the wooded hills on the other side of the creek. "I grew up around here and spent a lot of time exploring these hills. Have you done much hiking?"

Sam shook his head.

"Well, I'll tell ya, I think hiking is medicine for the soul. Sometimes when I'm stuck on a problem or trying to figure something out, I just get outside and go for a hike. There's nothing like clean air and being in the woods to clear your head. There's even a little cave up there."

"There is? Cool. Can we go check it out?"

Taylor grinned. "I doubt we'll have time to hike up there today, but I'll bring you back later this summer. We can pack a lunch and hike up there. How's that sound?"

Sam smiled up at him. "Cool."

"Good, it's a plan then." He clapped his hands together. "All right now. We better get back to task here. These fish ain't gonna catch themselves."

Sam giggled.

They'd stopped for a carton of night crawlers on the way up, and Taylor peeled back the lid of the Styrofoam carton. "Reach in there and grab a worm. Make sure you get a good one."

Sam wrinkled his nose at the wriggling worms. "How do I know which one is a good one?"

"Ahh, just get one that looks good and fat. And extra juicy. The fish love those."

Sam laughed as he reached in and plucked a slimy worm from the dirt. Pulling it free, the worm stretched and snapped, and its lower half sucked back in to the dirt. "Oh no. I broke it."

"Nah. Don't worry about it. The fish like half-worms just

as much." Taylor gave him a wink, and Sam's expression of alarm eased.

He showed the boy how to thread the worm's body onto the hook. Sam watched intently, his face a mixture of awe and disgust.

A ribbon of brown goo exploded from the side of the worm.

"Oh gross. Did you see that? It pooped. The worm pooped. That was sick. And cool." Sam giggled.

Taylor laughed at the myriad of faces that Sam made and at the way the boy laughed at the simplest things. "You ready to throw it in?"

He showed the boy how to cast and set the line, then propped the pole between two rocks. He'd put a bobber on the end of the line and told Sam to watch for it to go under the water.

Sam settled in against a rock. Rex lay down next to him, his head in the boy's lap. Sam looked over at him. "I like this. Fishing is good."

He chuckled and set about getting his own pole ready.

Yes, fishing was good.

And this was a good choice.

Fishing was easy. It didn't take much effort, and the serenity of the water soothed even the stormiest of souls.

He set his line and snuck a glance at Sam.

They had securely wrapped his casted arm in plastic that morning. Sam twisted a blade of grass between his fingers as he watched his line and casually rested his unbroken arm on the dog's back. He seemed at peace.

Then his expression changed. A wild look of surprise covered his face as he looked up, his eyes wide. "The bobber!

It went down. Did you see it? It bobbed."

"Grab your pole! Start reeling it in." He jumped up and crossed to the boy's side. He put his hand on the end of the pole but tried to let Sam do most of the work. The cast on his arm made it a little awkward, but the boy managed with a bit of Taylor's help.

Sam wound the line in, his little body squirming as much as the fish on the line. "I got it. I got one!"

"You sure did." He lifted the pole and grabbed the small fish on the end of the line. He pulled the hook from its mouth and passed the fish to Sam.

Sam held it reverently in his hands. "My first fish."

He couldn't help but grin. He remembered the first fish that he'd ever caught. And it was in this same creek. His dad had brought him here to teach him to fish, too.

He pulled his phone from his pocket to get a picture. "Hold that fish up, and I'll take your picture. We can send it to Cherry later."

Sam held the fish up, a huge grin on his face, and Taylor snapped a picture.

"All right. Now we gotta put him in the basket. Then I'll show you how to clean it, and we can take it home tonight and you can have him for supper."

The boy wrinkled his nose. "I've never eaten a fish before." He beamed up at Taylor. "But I'll try it."

He chuckled and showed Sam the basket that he'd staked to the side of the creek. He helped him to drop it in, then eased the basket back to float in the water and keep the fish cool.

"You did it. Caught your first fish." He clapped Sam on the shoulder. "How does it feel?"

The boy's smile faltered, and Taylor watched as his face crumpled in dismay.

Sam's bottom lip trembled, and he covered his face with his hands as he began to cry. His small shoulders shook as he sobbed into his hands.

"Hey. Hey now. It's okay." Taylor sank to the ground and pulled the boy into his lap, cradling him against his chest. "It's okay to cry."

"I miss my dad." Sam clutched Taylor's shirt in his small hands and cried into his chest. "I miss them so much."

"I know you do." He rubbed Sam's back, his heart breaking for the child. Sam often acted so mature that he sometimes forgot just how young he was. And thinking back, he couldn't remember seeing the little boy let loose and cry yet.

Taylor said nothing, just rubbed his hand in small circles on the boy's back and let him cry it out.

Sam clung to him, his sobs coming in hard gasps as he released the pain and grief that he must have been bottling up inside since the accident. His crying finally tapered off, and he took big shaking gulps of breath, trying to calm down.

Sitting up, he swiped his arm across his tear-stained cheeks. "Sorry."

"There's nothing to be sorry about, buddy. Sometimes a guy's just gotta cry and get all that stuff out."

Sam peered up at him, a questioning look on his face. "Do you cry sometimes?"

"Yeah, I do." Geez, this kid was killing him.

The pain on his face felt like a physical punch to Taylor's gut, and he just wanted to take the pain away. Make him smile again. "I don't know if I told you this, but my mom died when I was a kid, too."

"She did?"

"Yeah. I was older than you. I was in high school. And my mom wasn't in a car accident. She was sick. She was sick for a while. So I had time to say goodbye to her. But it was still hard. Really hard." He touched Sam's cheek. "And I still miss her."

"You do?"

"Of course I do. She was my mom. Sometimes I miss her so much that it still makes me cry." He smiled at Sam. "It's okay to cry. And it's okay to miss them. They were your parents."

Sam shrugged. "But they weren't my *real* parents."

"Hey. Come on now. They sure as heck were your real parents. They were the ones that raised you, that taught you to walk, that sung you to sleep. And they were the ones that changed all your stinky diapers."

That earned him a small smile from the boy.

"I'm serious. Your mom and dad adopted you because they wanted you. They wanted a baby to pour all their love into. They *were* your real parents."

"But what about the mom and dad that gave me away. They must not have wanted me." Sam's voice was small, and he couldn't meet Taylor's eye.

"You don't know that, Sam. There are all sorts of reasons why someone might give their baby up for adoption. A lot of times it is because they can't take care of a baby, and they want to give their child a chance at a better life. Maybe your parents loved you so much that they sacrificed their own chance at getting to raise you. Maybe they gave you up so you could have a life with parents that could do a better job of taking care of you."

Sam tipped up his chin, finally looking into Taylor's eyes. "Do you think my real mom would ever want to meet me?"

Taylor shrugged. "I don't know. I know I'm sure glad to have met you."

"I asked Cherry about her, but she doesn't seem to want to talk about it."

"Well, remember your mom was Cherry's cousin and her best friend. Maybe it's just hard for her to talk about it."

"Do you think *you* could help me find my real mom?"

"Me? Why me?"

"Because you're the sheriff. And you know lots of people." Sam's eyes were filled with hope.

"You watch too much TV." Taylor hated the way the look of hope changed to one of disappointment.

He didn't really think this was any of his concern, and he sure didn't want to upset Cherry by nosing around in her family business.

But they *were* engaged, sort of, and he did care about Sam. It might not hurt to ask a few questions. "I guess I can look into it. Usually those records are sealed so no one can get into them, but I can give it a try."

Sam's face lit with a smile. "Thanks, Taylor. I know you can find out. You can do anything."

Taylor nodded at his pole. "Apparently I can't seem to catch a fish as well as you. How about we set our lines again and have a snack?"

Rex barked his approval.

Later that night, he and Cherry lay in bed together, her lush body snuggled against his side.

Cherry ran her fingernail down his chest. "Sam couldn't stop talking about going fishing with you today. He had a great time. How about you? Did you have fun?"

Taylor grinned down at her. "I have never regretted a day spent fishing."

She playfully swatted his arm. "You know what I mean."

"I know. Of course I had fun. Sam's a great kid. I really like hanging out with him."

"Me, too." Her voice held a wistful tone.

"Did he tell you that he cried today?"

She pushed up on one elbow, alarm in her eyes. "No, why? Did he get hurt?"

"No, he caught a fish."

"I don't understand. Why did that make him cry?"

"Because evidently, his dad had always promised to take him fishing."

"Oh."

"Yeah. We talked a lot about his parents today. I told him it's okay to talk about them. He wasn't sure if he could because no one else was talking about them, and he didn't want to get in trouble or make anyone sad."

Cherry's eyes filled with tears. "Poor baby. I am so not good at this. That's why I wasn't talking to *him* about it. Because I didn't want to make him sad."

"It's important to talk about them. He needs that. I can remember when my mom died, and no one would talk about her or even mention her name. But all that did was make me feel like there was something wrong with me, because I thought about her all the time. I missed her so much, and

I needed to talk about her. Not all the time. I'm not saying that. But if something makes you think of Stacy or Greg, just tell him. Especially if it's a good memory or something that makes you smile. Does that make sense?"

She nodded. "I did it all wrong back then, too, didn't I? I should have talked to you more about your mom."

Her face looked so sad, it tore at his heart.

He tipped her chin up and gazed into her eyes. "Hey, listen, we were kids. We didn't know what the hell we were doing. Sometimes I still don't. We both could have handled things differently. But we can't change the past. We can only move forward. We only have control of this moment. The one we are in right now."

Cherry snuggled against his chest. "I like the moment we're in right now."

He grinned. "I know a way to make you like it more." He leaned down to kiss her and was rewarded with a soft moan against his lips.

Had he just missed an important chance to talk about their past? Should they wrestle these demons now and bring the past out? Shake the dust off the rugs and clear the air of all the muck and pain that they caused each other all those years ago.

He pulled back. "Cherry."

She smiled up at him, a dreamy look in her eyes. "I love it when you say my name. I have the lamest, silliest name, but when you say it, it sounds sexy."

A grin crept across his face. He lowered his voice and sang in a low, sweet tone. "She's my cherry pie. Tastes so good, make a grown man cry." He leaned in and nipped at her bottom lip.

She shook her head and grinned. "I'm ashamed to admit that I sort of secretly love it when you sing that song to me."

He nuzzled against her neck, softly kissing the sweet, tender spot below her ear. "You want me to keep singing?"

"I just want you, period." She wrapped her arms around his neck. The movement pressed her breasts together and up, and all thoughts of song lyrics fled from his brain.

Chapter Thirteen

Cherry woke to an empty bed and the sound of power tools coming through the window. What was Taylor up to now?

She heard Rex bark and figured Sam must be up as well. Throwing back the covers, she climbed out of bed and stretched.

Over the last week, she'd been using muscles that she hadn't used in a long time. Her body was sore, but in a good way. A really good way. Time spent in bed with Taylor was better than any yoga session.

They'd been getting along so well. Tonight would be the real test.

The engagement party.

She'd been so caught up in trying to get the diner up and running and taking care of Sam that when Charlie offered to take care of the party, she let her.

She had no idea what Charlie had planned or how many

people were coming. How many people would she have to convince that she and Taylor were a real couple? And that they were planning to get married?

"Hey, Charlie," she called to her friend as she stepped out onto the front porch.

Charlie turned and waved, looking gorgeous as always in jeans, a sleeveless white top, and pink cowboy boots. Her long blond hair was pulled into a high ponytail, and she held a clipboard.

A clipboard? Really? To have a few people out for a barbeque?

Cherry crossed the yard and peered down at the clipboard. The page was full of notes and checked tasks. "How's it going? This seems like a lot of work for just a few people."

"A few people? Half the town wants to come. I've already had over a hundred people let me know they're planning to show up."

"A hundred people?" Yeesh. Small towns. No one wanted to miss out on anything.

"I know. It blows me away how different small towns are. But everyone loves you, and nobody wants to miss out on a party."

And how many people were coming just to see if she and Taylor were a real item?

That thought made her stomach hurt.

She watched a couple of guys from the fire department grab a piece of plywood from the back of a pickup and lay it on the ground next to several others. "What are they doing?"

"Building a dance floor."

"A dance floor?" This shindig was getting carried away.

But the thought of dancing with Taylor made her pulse

race a little. Being twirled around the dance floor in his strong arms.

They hadn't danced together since prom nine years ago.

Memories of the high school dance came flooding back. The flowing pink dress, the tons of bobby pins that Stacy had stuck in her hair to give her the perfect updo, the way Taylor had looked heart-breakingly handsome in his tux with the pink cummerbund that exactly matched the color of her dress. Dancing for hours in his arms, laying her head on his shoulder during slow songs, and laughing as they bounced around to the fast ones.

Then after, listening to the radio as Taylor laid her back on the bench seat of his truck. He'd made her a mix tape of their songs and to this day, she couldn't hear a Tim McGraw song without being right back in that truck.

And without thinking of Taylor and that night. The night that changed everything.

The night they'd made Sam.

"Earth to Cherry." Charlie waved a hand at her.

"Sorry. I missed that."

"I could tell. You were suddenly a million miles away."

A million miles and nine years ago away.

"I said that Taylor's dad is getting his old band together to play for tonight. I've never heard them play, but Zack said they used to be quite popular. They played local bars and county fairs. Some people probably don't even care about you and Taylor. They may just be coming out to hear Russ's band, Wishbone."

Great. The more attention diverted from her and Taylor the better.

This party was becoming much bigger than she'd first

imagined. A lot of people were going to a lot of trouble to help them celebrate a fake engagement. "This seems really extravagant. Who's paying for all of this?"

"There's not that much expense really. A lot of people are bringing food and the band is free. The guys from the fire hall love Taylor so they're setting up the dance floor and hauling out hay bales to sit on. I think Russ is covering the decorations. I was talking to him earlier, and I think he's hoping things work out with you and Taylor."

He's not the only one.

Wait. Don't even go there.

She couldn't let herself hope for something real with Taylor. Yeah, the sex was pretty real. But she couldn't count on him. Couldn't trust that he wouldn't start to feel trapped in this small town and take off again. It was easier to not let her heart get too involved. Keep a safe distance. Keep it physical.

Except, if she were being honest, she'd have to admit that it was already too late.

Taylor and Sam walked out of the barn, the dog following closely on their heels. Sam held a hammer in his hand, and Taylor carried a red tool box. A leather tool belt slung low on his hips, and the snug black T-shirt he wore clung to his muscled chest and arms.

Holy hot-ness. A friggin' tool belt.

"Cherry. Do you see the party?" Sam came running up to her. "Taylor's been letting me help. We're building a dance floor and a stage for the band. Isn't that cool?"

She smiled at his enthusiasm. "Yeah, buddy. It's pretty cool." She glanced at Taylor and caught him smiling down at Sam, and her heart fell.

Yeah. Way too late.

"This party is becoming a little bigger than I thought it would be," she said to Taylor.

"It's Broken Falls. The whole town loves a party." He leaned down and spoke softly into her ear. "The more people that are here, the less doubt there will be about our engagement."

She tried to ignore the delicious shivers that his warm breath on her neck were causing. He was right, of course. "I know. I'm just pouring all of my savings into repairing the diner. I don't have a lot of extra to put into such an extravagant party."

"Don't worry about that. Everyone is pitching in, and my dad's band is playing for free as long as we feed them. We had too much meat in the freezer anyway. This is a good excuse to get it cleared out for fall."

He had an answer for everything.

"Okay, well I've got to go in to the diner today and get some work done. I feel bad leaving you here to take care of this, but I've got to get the restaurant open as soon as I can."

"It's all good. You go take care of the diner. Sam and I will take care of the party." He held up his hand and earned a hearty high-five from the boy.

"Are you sure? You don't need to do that. Sam can come with me into town."

"I want to stay and work on the party. Please, Cherry," Sam pleaded with her.

"All right. Text me if you need anything."

"You go into work," Charlie said. "We've got this handled, and Sophie's bringing over some lunch later so we'll get your men fed."

Her men?

How she ached for that to be true.

But she had work to do and didn't have time for silly fantasies about a white picket fence life. Or a life with a hot cowboy, an adorable boy, and a mangy, orphaned dog.

Her day flew by as she worked at the diner, cleaning up, reordering inventory, and trying to get the restaurant ready to open. She had to wait for the new stove to come in and for the rest of the repairs to be finished, but there were plenty of things she could do.

Thoughts of her dwindling savings account drove her to keep working.

Her back hurt, but she'd accomplished a lot that day and felt good as she pulled the VW into the driveway of the ranch. Taylor's friend had come through and repaired the little car. She'd picked it up the day before, and it ran better than it had in years.

Driving down the lane, she was amazed at the transformation of the ranch. The area in front of the barn had been turned into a dance floor and stage. Hay bales circled the dance floor, and strings of lights hung from the open barn doors.

The big front porch had long tables covered with red-checkered tablecloths waiting for casserole dishes and plates of desserts. A big smoker sat to the left of the porch, and the smell of grilled meat filled the air as she climbed from the car.

Excitement filled her.

She was always working and didn't often have time to attend many of the town's events. But she loved them. She couldn't believe this party was for her.

To celebrate her engagement.

Her *fake* engagement.

Her excitement came crashing down.

How could she do this? How was she going to get through this night?

"Hey there."

She looked up to see Taylor standing on the porch, a gorgeous smile on his face.

A smile just for her.

The screen door slammed, and Sam came running out and flew down the stairs.

His little face shone with excitement, as he grabbed her hand and pulled her toward the house. "Come on, Cherry. You gotta get ready for the party. People are gonna be here in less than an hour."

She could do this.

She had to.

Laughing, she let Sam pull her up the porch steps. "Okay, give me thirty minutes, and I'll be ready. Just let me take a shower."

Taylor offered her a crooked grin. "Need any help?"

Yes. She needed someone to soap her up. Because looking at him made her want to get dirty. Really dirty. And Taylor was just the guy she wanted holding the soap.

Her mouth went dry at the thought of his naked body, soapy and slick, sliding against hers.

She looked up at him.

His grin had deepened, and he raised an eyebrow at her. "I can tell you're thinking about it. Your neck just went red."

Stupid pale skin. Always gave her away. "I think I've got it. This time."

He chuckled. "I got you something. It's on the bed. Charlie helped me pick it out."

She gave him a quizzical look. "You got me something? What is it? Why?"

"Because I wanted to. Now go get ready before you're late to your own party."

She hurried into Taylor's bedroom.

She couldn't bring herself to call it *their* bedroom. Even though she was sleeping in it every night.

On the bed lay a gorgeous dress, and she gasped at the sheer beauty of it.

And the thoughtfulness of the man who bought it for her.

The dress was made of a flowing material and the various shades of blue and green made her think of the colors of the sea.

It was an A-line design and had a halter style bodice which was ideal for her figure. She ran her hand across the soft fabric and imagined it against her skin.

It was perfect.

Thirty minutes later she stepped on to the porch. The dress fit perfectly, and she wore her thick red hair curly and loose around her shoulders. She had on the cowboy boots that she'd made Taylor get out of her closet.

A few guests had started to arrive, and Russ was working with a group of older men to set up the band.

She took a deep breath. She could do this.

Hearing Taylor's boots on the porch behind her, she grinned as a pair of strong arms wrapped around her waist. She leaned back against his hard, muscled chest.

"Lord have mercy, you are one beautiful woman, Cherry

Hill." His mouth was near her ear as he pulled her close, and his words sent a thrill down her spine.

"Thank you." She couldn't look at him. She was afraid if she did, she might shatter into a million pieces.

Her heart ached with want, and she knew if she looked into his blue eyes, she'd be lost.

It was enough to feel him. To have him near. To have his arms around her. "Thank you for the dress. I love it. It's perfect."

He squeezed her. "You're kind of perfect."

She closed her eyes.

No, she wasn't.

She was so far from perfect, she wasn't even in the ballpark. But she knew tonight had to be perfect.

They had to convince the town that they were really engaged.

She turned around, staying in the circle of his arms and peered up at him. "Are you ready for this? Ready to try to persuade half the town that we're really engaged?"

"I'm not sure. Maybe we ought to practice." He leaned down and pressed a tender kiss on her lips. His hands tightened on her waist, and he kissed her again, this time a little less on the "tender" side and more on the "I want you right now" side.

The rest of the world fell away whenever he kissed her.

It was just the two of them, and she circled his neck with her arms and kissed him back. Her breath caught as he sucked at her bottom lip, and she wanted to forget the party.

Forget everything and just throw this man down on a bed somewhere and have her way with him.

And then let him have his way with her.

Twice.

"Well, you've got me convinced." Charlie's voice interrupted them. She sounded amused as she walked up onto the porch, a Crock-Pot in her hands.

Cherry pulled away from Taylor, straightening her dress. "We were just, you know, practicing."

Charlie laughed. "Well, it looks like you've got it down to me." She hefted the Crock-Pot. "I brought meatballs."

Taylor took the Crock-Pot from her hands and set it on one of the food tables. "Sounds great. I'm going to go help Dad with getting the band set up." He lightly slapped Cherry on the butt as he passed by. "Save me a dance."

The two friends turned to watch Taylor cross the yard. He wore snug Wranglers with cowboy boots and a soft blue western shirt.

"Damn, that is one fine piece of Montana cowboy," Charlie said. "How have I gone my whole life without knowing how hot cowboys actually were?"

Cherry laughed. "Well, you're here now. And by the way, thanks for the dress. I love it."

"It looks gorgeous on you. But don't thank me. It was all Taylor's idea. He saw it in the window of the Lady Bug Dress Shop downtown and wanted to get it for you. He knew you didn't have many of your own clothes because of the fire. He called me to make sure he got the size right, but otherwise, that was all him."

Hmm. Taylor Johnson was just full of surprises.

The screen door slammed, and Sam and Rex came rushing out. Sam wore new jeans, a blue western shirt similar to Taylor's, and a new pair of brown cowboy boots.

Another surprise.

She pulled the boy into a quick hug. "Sam, you look great. Where did you get these new clothes and the boots?"

"Taylor. He took me into Tate's Western Store today and got me these." He stuck his foot out showing off his new boots. "He said we needed to look good for the party tonight. Aren't these cool? They're just like Taylor's."

Cherry grinned. "Yes, they are pretty cool." It seemed that Taylor'd had a busy day. And was evidently quite a shopper.

What other surprises did this man have in store for her tonight? She swallowed, and her body heated at the thought.

But first, she had to make it through this party.

Within an hour, the ranch was full of people. Laughter and country music filled the air as more people poured in, carrying lawn chairs and hot dishes. The tables on the porch filled with food and baked goods.

Taylor stayed by her side, holding her hand or resting his arm around her shoulders. The night air was still warm, and dusk settled in. The lights from the barn cast a warm glow over the whole scene, and Cherry let herself relax just a little. Let herself enjoy the moment.

Russ's band had warmed up and were belting out country tunes. Zack was gliding Charlie around the dance floor, his arm secure around her waist. Sophie and Cash were swing-dancing in the middle, and the teenager laughed as Cash twirled her around. It was a party atmosphere, and Taylor grabbed her hand and pulled her to the dance floor.

His dancing skills had improved, and he pulled her into a quick two-step, his hand firm on her back as he guided her around the dance floor. He spun her, pulling her in and out of his arms in time to the music.

She threw back her head and laughed.

A pure laugh. A laugh of joy. A joy she hadn't felt in weeks. Not since Stacy had died.

Looking across the dance floor, she could see Sam and Rex next to Russ.

Taylor's dad sat in a chair on the side of the stage, picking the banjo on his lap. Sam danced and laughed as Russ made silly faces at him and sang along to the song.

Sam seemed happy, too. It was so good to see him laugh.

Taylor guided her toward the stage as the song ended. "Hey, Dad, can you play that one by Tim McGraw? The one I told you about?"

Russ nodded and traded his banjo for a guitar. He led the band in the opening notes, and Cherry's heart tumbled.

Had Taylor really just asked his dad to play *their* song? The one from high school? Had he remembered all these years? She searched his face for a clue.

"What? You didn't think I forgot our song, did you?" He winked at her and glided her around the dance floor.

She didn't know what to think.

On the third time around, he grabbed Sam, pulling him into their dance.

He let go of her and swung Sam around, then showed him the basic steps of the two-step. Then he pulled Sam between them, and the boy moved his feet with theirs as Taylor taught him the steps. "Quick, quick, slow, slow."

"You're getting it," Cherry said, laughing as Sam collided with her feet.

Sam giggled and laughed as he tried to keep up with the steps. "I'm dancing. Can Rex dance with us, too?"

Taylor chuckled. "I don't know if dogs are any good at

dancing." His laughter died, and he stopped as he looked out to the driveway.

"What's wrong?" Cherry turned to see her cousin's black Denali coming down the driveway.

She'd prayed that Reed and Olivia would've changed their minds and decided not to make the drive down for the party.

Her prayers had not been answered.

The truck parked in the driveway, and the Hill family emerged. They'd brought Aunt Bea, but it looked like they had left Susan, Stacy's mother, at home.

Of course, Bea wouldn't skip this. She wouldn't want to miss a chance to embarrass or humiliate her great niece.

Taylor took her hand. "Well, we better go face the music."

Cherry held back. "But I like this music so much better."

He grimaced. "Yeah, me, too. Maybe they won't stay long."

Yeah, not the way her luck had been going lately.

Although she was just dancing in the arms of a hunky cowboy, so her luck couldn't be all bad.

She took Sam's hand, and they crossed the yard together. The three of them.

Almost like a family. If even for a little bit.

Reed had the hatch of the Denali open, and he pulled a red bicycle from the back end and set it on the ground.

"My bike," Sam cried. He dropped her hand and took off running for the bicycle.

Well played, Reed.

"Hey, sport," Reed said, as Sam reached for the handlebars. "We stopped by your house and picked up your bike." He looked up at Cherry. "He loves riding that dang bike. I thought he might want to have it out here to ride around."

Wow. He was actually thinking of Sam and wanted to do something nice for him. Her heart softened a little to her cousin. "Thanks for bringing it. That was nice of you."

Sam was already off, riding the bike in circles around the guests, the dog yapping at his heels.

"I'm not a bad guy, Cherry. And I really do care about Sam." He laughed as he watched the boy racing down the driveway, his casted arm stuck out awkwardly as he held the handlebars. "I just want what's best for him." He turned his eyes back to Cherry, the cold look of condescension back. "I just don't think that's you. Even if you are back together with the sheriff here."

And there he was. The bastard.

How could she have let her guard down, even for a second, and believed that Reed had anything but his own best interests at heart?

"Things do look pretty cozy here," Olivia said, eyeing Cherry and Taylor's joined hands.

Taylor's voice was cordial, yet held just a hint of steel. "Welcome to our engagement party. There's plenty of food, and the music is great. Please stay and enjoy yourselves." He held out an arm to Bea.

She grudgingly took his offered arm and let him lead her toward the porch. "Oh, we are planning to stay, but it's yet to be determined if we will actually *enjoy* ourselves."

Cherry's cousins followed her aunt, and she let out her breath.

She watched them grab plates and fill them with food. Her family was well-known and several people approached them to say hello.

Taylor was the perfect host, pouring on his down-home

charm as he pointed out dishes made by the locals and noted which ones he thought were the best recipes.

After they all had full plates and were settled in, he ambled back toward Cherry. He leaned down and laid a soft kiss on her lips. "See, no problem. I'm going to win those bastards over yet."

She laughed. "You do love a challenge."

He put an arm around her, and she let herself relax into his comforting embrace. Maybe it was going to be okay. Maybe this was all going to work out.

She looked across the yard at the people laughing and having fun, including her cousins. "Everyone seems to be having a good time."

"And several folks have congratulated us on our happy upcoming union. I haven't had anyone question me or even act the least bit suspicious."

Maybe they weren't suspicious because they could see the way she really felt about Taylor.

It wasn't hard to pretend to be in love with him.

And she was never very good at hiding her emotions anyway. Maybe they could see that she really did care about him.

Maybe they could see what she was trying to hide.

Even from herself.

Her thoughts were interrupted by the sound of a loud truck.

She looked up to see an old red pickup kicking up dust as it raced down the driveway.

Right toward where Sam was riding his bike.

Chapter Fourteen

Taylor looked up at the sound of the truck engine. He recognized the piece of crap truck as belonging to Leroy Purvis, whom he'd heard had recently been released from jail.

What the hell was he doing here?

The truck was coming in way too hot, and Taylor's heart froze as he saw Sam riding his bike across the driveway.

"Sam! Get out of the way!" Taylor raced toward the boy.

Purvis must have finally seen Sam, because he suddenly slammed on his brakes.

The truck skidded in the soft dirt toward the boy on the bicycle.

He barely registered Cherry running beside him as he ran. All he could focus on was the heavy pickup sliding toward the small boy.

The boy that had stolen a piece of his heart. That he had fallen in love with the first day that he met him. The boy that he would do anything to protect.

He reached Sam just as the truck came to a shuddering halt a mere foot from the boy's bike. He grabbed Sam and lifted him out of harm's way. "You okay, buddy?"

Sam nodded, his eyes wide with fright. "I'm okay. That just scared the crud out of me."

Taylor laughed and hugged the boy to his chest.

Cherry caught up to them and threw her arms around them both. "Oh my gosh, Sam. Are you hurt?"

Taylor handed Sam to Cherry. "He's okay. But that bastard Purvis isn't going to be."

He strode to the side of the truck and wrenched the pickup's door open. Reaching in, he grabbed Leroy Purvis by the scruff of his shirt and yanked him from the cab. "What the hell do you think you're doing? You could have killed that boy."

Leroy fell to the dirt. He scrambled backward. "Look, I didn't see him. I'm sorry, all right." His voice held the unmistakable slur of a man who'd been drinking too much.

"No, it's not all right. You're drunk." Taylor hollered for one of his deputies. "Hicks, get over here."

The band had stopped playing, and the party-goers stood quietly watching as the deputy hurried toward him. Zack and Cash moved to the edge of the crowd as if ready to step in if Taylor needed them.

Russ had dropped his guitar and raced to Sam, and out of the corner of his eye, Taylor could see his dad comforting Sam and Cherry.

Leroy staggered to his feet, holding his hands out in front of him. "Look, I said I was sorry. I don't want no trouble. I'm just here for my wife. Emma! I know you're here."

He looked out over the guests. His face lit with recognition so he must have spotted her.

Taylor turned to see a brown-haired woman in a faded red dress at the edge of the dance floor. Emma Purvis. Except he'd known her as Emma Frank. He recognized her from high school, and he seemed to recall she'd been a few years behind him.

Hicks stood by Taylor's side. He tilted his head toward him and spoke quietly. "Purvis just got out of county for beating Emma up last month. He roughed her up pretty bad. She filed for divorce while he was in jail."

Leroy called again for Emma, but she stayed by the barn.

An older man came striding forward, and Taylor was pretty sure he was Emma's dad, Clyde. "Leroy, you need to get the hell out of here and stay away from my daughter. You ever come near her again, and I'll kill you myself."

Leroy glanced from the sheriff to Emma's dad, and Taylor recognized the look in his eye. The look of a caged animal.

He knew nothing good would come of a mean drunk when he felt cornered. "Now, let's all settle down. Leroy, I'm going to suggest that you go with Hicks here. He's gonna take you back to the station and give you a little time to cool off."

A little time to cool off—in a cell.

Taylor did not abide by anyone drinking and driving, and he didn't need a sobriety test to see Purvis was well past the legal limit.

But right now, he just wanted to get the guy into the back of Hicks's squad car.

He took a step closer to Leroy.

Leroy backed up, panic creeping into his expression. "I told you I don't want no trouble. You all just need to stay back."

Taylor advanced another step.

It must have been one step too many because Leroy reached behind his back and pulled a gun from his waistband.

He waved it wildly in Taylor's direction. "I said stay back. Don't nobody come near me. I just came for my wife. Emma!"

Taylor took a small step to the side, putting himself between the gunman and his family.

And he knew in that instant that Cherry and Sam were his family. They meant everything to him. And he wasn't about to let some piss-ant drunk do anything to harm them.

He kept his eyes trained on Leroy and lowered his voice to a soothing tone. "Let's all just calm down now. Leroy, there's no need for a firearm. Why don't you just set that gun down, and we'll talk about this."

Leroy's eyes were wild, and he pointed the gun directly at Taylor. "I've tried talking, and ain't nobody listening to me. I told you I don't want any trouble. I didn't want to have to use this."

"Nobody's making you use it at all." Taylor didn't take his eyes from Leroy, but he was quickly assessing the situation. Calculating the distance between Leroy and the truck and registering the type of gun he was brandishing. It was a small caliber handgun.

He lowered his voice so only Hicks could hear. "I may need to borrow your gun."

Hicks took a slow sideways step toward Taylor. He heard the deputy flip the snap open on the holster on his hip before he raised his hands toward Leroy. "Listen now, Mr. Purvis, we know you don't want any trouble, and neither do we. Why don't you just do like the sheriff asked, and put the gun down?"

Good man. He knew his deputy was creating a distraction and had raised his arms to allow Taylor easy access to his gun.

Out of the corner of his eye, Taylor saw Emma's dad take a step closer to Leroy. He swung the gun wildly toward his ex-father-in-law. "Get back, old man. She's my wife, and she's coming home with me."

Clyde Frank's eyes narrowed and his voice shook with rage. "Over my dead body."

"You asked for it."

A shot rang out.

Clyde fell to the ground.

Screams filled the air.

The next few seconds happened in a blur. Taylor had already been reaching for his deputy's gun.

He pulled it from the holster and fired a shot at Leroy Purvis.

A spray of blood dotted Leroy's face as his expression turned from surprise to pain, then he crumpled to the ground.

A single second of silence was followed by a pandemonium of screams and chaos.

"Take care of my family," Taylor instructed Hicks as he raced toward the fallen body of Purvis.

He knew he'd shot him in the shoulder so the likelihood he would die from the shot was minimal.

But he still held the gun in his hand, and that was

Taylor's immediate concern. Taking advantage of Leroy's drunken reaction time, he rushed forward and kicked the weapon away from him.

Despite his yowls of pain, Taylor flipped Purvis over and pulled his arms behind his back. He knelt down, placing his knee into the center of Purvis's back.

Hicks rushed up beside him and passed him a set of handcuffs. "Cherry and Sam are with your dad." He waited for Taylor to handcuff Leroy, then hauled him to his feet.

"You shot me, you bastard. Somebody get a doctor." Leroy's words were slurred, and he pitched forward.

A crowd had gathered around the truck, including Cherry's cousin, Reed.

An older man pushed through the crowd. "Let me take a look at him."

Doc Genrich had been their family doctor for as long as he could remember. He was also the bass player in his dad's band. "Thanks, Doc. But maybe you should take a look at Clyde Frank first."

Doc waved a hand in Clyde's direction. "He's fine. Leroy's so drunk, his shot missed Clyde by a mile. I heard it ding off the smoker. Clyde just fell to the ground so Leroy wouldn't shoot at him again."

"All right." Taylor stepped back and let Doc examine Leroy.

The doctor pulled up Leroy's blood-stained T-shirt revealing a stomach soft with flab. His shoulder was spotted with blood, and a gunshot wound was visible under his collarbone.

"Somebody grab me a clean towel or some paper towels," he said.

Zack must have been thinking the same thing because he'd already crossed to the porch and grabbed a big stack of napkins. He handed them to the doctor who pressed them to the wound to stop the blood flow. Then he checked his back where the bullet exited.

Dropping the shirt, he clapped Leroy on the shoulder. "You're gonna live, son." He turned to Taylor. "Good shot. The bullet went clean through. I've got my bag in the car. I can bandage him up until you can get him to the hospital."

"I don't want to go to the hospital. I don't want to go anywhere. Not without my wife." Leroy struggled uselessly against the stronger deputy's hold.

"I'm not your wife anymore." Emma stood at the center of the crowd. The handcuffs on Leroy's wrists must have given her the courage to come forward.

Her dad stood at her side and held an arm around her shoulder. After almost getting shot, Taylor wasn't sure if Clyde was offering comfort or seeking it.

"You'll always be my wife. I love you, Emma." Leroy's voice was pitiful and whiny.

"You gave up that right when you busted my face and shoved my head through the shower door for not cleaning it well enough." A gasp was heard in the crowd of town's folk. "I did love you once, Leroy, but you don't have the right to hit me. Or anyone. I filed for divorce because I don't want to be married to you anymore. In fact, I don't ever want to see you again."

"Come on, Em. You don't mean that."

"I sure as hell do mean it. That's why I filed a restraining order against you and changed my phone number and moved to another town. How did you even know I was here?"

Taylor had been watching Leroy's face, and he was shocked to see his eyes flicker to Cherry's cousin, Reed.

What the hell was that about? Why would Reed have anything to do with this loser? Let alone put a woman's life in danger by revealing her whereabouts?

Unless that was the whole point.

Could Reed have hoped to create an incident at the engagement party? Surely even he wouldn't sink that low.

Would he?

Taylor glanced at Reed, but the other man avoided his eye.

"She's made it clear she doesn't want to see you, Purvis," Taylor said to Leroy. "My deputy is gonna take you over to the hospital, but make no mistake, you are under arrest for breaking the restraining order, driving under the influence, attempted murder, and whatever else I can come up with. Hicks'll read you your rights on the way to the hospital." He nodded at his deputy. "Get him out of here."

Hicks hauled Purvis toward his car, and Taylor made his way toward Cherry and Sam. All he wanted to do was wrap his arms around them and hold them tight. Make sure they were okay.

But his hands and his shirt were covered in blood.

His dad stood with Cherry and Sam, one arm around each of them. They stepped forward to hug Taylor, but he raised his hands to stop them.

He looked into Cherry's eyes. "As much as I want to wrap you both in my arms right now, I can't. I'm covered in this bastard's blood. I don't want this filth to touch either of you."

"Maybe you should of thought of that before you

brought them into your life." Reed had followed Taylor and tried to step between him and Sam. "It's pretty clear that you live a dangerous lifestyle. You just shot a man. How can you possibly think Sam would be better off with you than with us, where he would be safe and far away from firearms and criminals?"

Taylor turned to face Reed. "You're a lawyer, Reed. You *are* a criminal."

Reed gestured to Taylor's clothes, obviously ignoring the jab at his profession. "Look at yourself. This is supposed to be a party, and you're covered in a man's blood. A man that you just shot."

Taylor noticed that he kept emphasizing the fact that he just shot someone. "That man had a gun and fired at a civilian."

"My point exactly. I plan to file a motion next week for full custody of Sam. I plan to cite this flagrant display of violence and let the judge know that firearms are kept and used in your home."

"Don't be an idiot. Firearms are kept in ninety percent of the homes in this county. In fact, the judge goes deer hunting with my dad, so I'm fairly certain he has a gun in his home, too."

"Not one that he shot a man with."

Taylor sighed. "Reed, I'm an officer of the law. Of course I have a gun. But my dad and I both keep our firearms locked in a gun safe. We're both very conscientious gun owners, and we would never put Sam at risk."

Cherry had been silently standing by, but now she took a step in front of Taylor.

Like she was the one protecting him. "Reed, you didn't

want me to have Sam when you thought I was a single woman on my own. Now you don't want me to have him when we have someone actually protecting us. Make up your mind. Besides, I feel safer with Taylor than anywhere else."

A tiny burst of pride filled him at her words, and he didn't want to let her down.

And he sure as hell didn't want her to lose Sam because of him.

He looked around the yard.

Some people had already left, but most were sticking around, probably hoping to catch more action. Small towns did love their gossip, and he knew the story of their engagement party was going to make the rounds by morning.

At least people would be talking about them being engaged. So that was good.

But they didn't need to add a family squabble and a custody fight to the list of things that happened at the party.

He took a deep breath to calm the anger that he felt toward Cherry's family. "Listen, this is supposed to be a party to celebrate the woman I plan to marry. We've still got a lot of food left, and I don't believe I've heard the band play my favorite song yet. So, as far as I'm concerned, we are finished with this conversation. You all can either stay and enjoy the party or feel free to leave now."

Reed narrowed his eyes at Taylor as if he wanted to say more but was wisely keeping his mouth shut. He gestured to his wife. "Come on, Olivia. We're going home."

Olivia literally tipped her nose in the air. "Fine. I didn't even want to come to this party." She took Bea's arm and walked her to the truck.

Why did they have it out for Cherry so bad?

The Hill family climbed into their vehicles and drove down the driveway.

Russ clapped a hand on Taylor's shoulder. "You all right, son?"

"Yeah, I'm good." He looked down at his bloody shirt. "I just need to get changed."

His dad nodded and winked at him. "You did good today. You protected your family and the people of this town. You've got nothing to be ashamed of. Don't let that high-falutin' jerk-wad make you feel any less about it."

"Thanks, Dad."

"You go on and get cleaned up. I'll take Sam with me, and we'll get his bike picked up and put away. Then we'll get the music fired up and get this party going again."

Taylor nodded and headed up the steps of the porch.

Cherry followed him. "I'll come with you."

She followed him into the house and his bedroom. Their bedroom. He shut the door and stripped off his shirt as he stepped into the bathroom.

He turned the faucet on and rubbed his hands under the flow. The blood had dried to a tacky rust color, and the water pooled red in the sink as he scrubbed his hands and arms.

Cherry reached for a washcloth and held it under the water. She wrung it out then used it to gently wash away a spot of blood that had smeared against his cheek.

He pumped liquid soap into his hands and rubbed the lather up his arms. Splashing water on his chest and face, he tried to wash away the blood and cool his heated temper. "Damn it. I just wanted this party to go off without a hitch. I wanted your family to see how good you were with Sam. That you're the right person to raise him."

That we're the right people to raise him.

Where had that thought come from?

He knew where. He'd been thinking it all night. He wanted Cherry and Sam to be part of his family.

But had he blown it tonight with the stupid scene with Purvis? He grabbed a towel and scrubbed furiously at his arms and chest. "Why did that idiot have to make a scene tonight? At our party? And why is your cousin such an asshole?"

Cherry laughed. "I've been wondering that all my life." She leaned against the counter as he dried off, then stepped into the bedroom to find clean clothes.

He dug through his closet for a clean shirt. "But he's an extra a-hole when it comes to you. Why does your family have it in so bad for you?"

"Also a mystery. I think it's mainly because of the diner. And because of the close relationship I had with my grandparents. They always kind of doted on me, and it caused a huge stink when they just gave me the restaurant."

"Your cousin has a high-paying job. Reed's a lawyer, for goodness sakes. What the hell would he want with a diner in Broken Falls? Did he want to run it?"

She laughed. "Of course not. He hasn't worked there a day in his life. He only wanted it because they gave it to me. But not Stacy. She loved it as much as I did, and she was thrilled for me when I took it over. Gram taught us to use the soda fountain when we were kids, and we used to invent new drinks and try to get the customers to sample them. Gramps was always our guinea pig. He'd try anything we made."

Her voice wavered a little with emotion, and she stared

down at the washcloth still in her hands. "It didn't have anything to do with the diner. It was that I got something that he didn't. Something of value. He thought we should sell it and split the profits. Stacy was the only one who supported me in running the place. She used to bring Sam down and help out. She'd set his baby carrier on the counter and make malts. She was the only one who understood that the diner was more than just a restaurant to me. It was our grandparents' legacy."

She looked up at him, and her eyes held a plea for him to understand. "I want Sam to have that. I want him to know the place that our grandparents made. I want to teach him how to make malts and share the secret recipe for the BFFC Cherry Bomb soda."

"The what?" Taylor had pulled a clean shirt from the closet and was buttoning it up.

"The BFFC Cherry Bomb soda. It was my and Stacy's invention. BFFC stood for Best Friends and Favorite Cousins. It was silly but it was special. And I want to share that with Sam."

He wanted her to share it with him, too. He liked to hear her talk about her family and her past.

He remembered going in to the diner to see her when they were in high school. He'd even helped out a few times when they were short-staffed. The diner had always represented family to him and to the town. And to Cherry, too.

It was good to hear Cherry talk about Stacy and laugh about memories of her.

"I'd like to try one of those, too." He stepped closer to her and wrapped his arms around her waist. She tipped her face up to look at him, and he offered her a sly grin. "You know Cherry is my favorite flavor."

He dipped his head and kissed her softly. "Mmm-hmmm. Cherry definitely tastes the best." His lips hummed against hers, and desire sparked in his gut.

Well, actually lower than his gut.

Lifting her hair, he laid a line of kisses along her neck. She smelled so damn good. And her skin was so soft. Holding her against him was just what he needed.

He didn't want to think about her asshole cousins or that idiot Purvis. He didn't want to admit that shooting a man tonight still had him a little shaky. He just wanted to lose himself in her kiss.

He traced her lips with his thumb and tried not to think about the way his hand shook slightly.

But she noticed.

Cherry reached up and held his cheeks between her hands. Her eyes searched his. "Are you really okay?"

He had been. He'd been keeping it together.

But the look of concern—of love, maybe—in her eyes was enough to have him come undone.

He pulled her tight against him, burying his face in her neck, against the silky strands of her hair. "I don't know what I would've done if Sam had been hit by that truck. Or if anything had happened to you. I saw that guy pull out a gun, and all I could think about was protecting you and Sam."

"And you shot a guy tonight."

"Yeah, there's that, too." He laughed, trying to ease the tension in his chest. Lighten it up, make a joke out of it.

As a police officer, he'd seen some pretty terrible things, and sometimes the easiest way to distance himself from the reality of a situation was to make light of it, no matter how serious it was. Or there was always the deflection route. Turn the conversation to another topic.

He was good at that one, too. "Hey, don't worry about me. It's not like I killed him. It's always a little scary when I have to pull my gun, but I don't feel bad for shooting a wife-beating drunk in the shoulder." He jostled her against him. "How about you? You okay? I'm sorry your party got ruined."

She laughed. "I don't care about the party. I care about keeping Sam. And tonight was about convincing the town that we're really engaged and in a real relationship. I think we did that. If nothing else, that kiss on the porch should have convinced a few people."

It had sure convinced him that this was something real. And that he wanted to make it real.

Not just to him, but to her as well.

How could he make her see that he still cared about her? That he always had? "Listen, Cherry, I wanted to tell you—"

"Hey, you guys, aren't you coming back out to the party?" Sam stood in the doorway of the bedroom. "Russ said he's making homemade ice cream, and it's almost done."

He released Cherry from his arms and turned to the boy. They would have time to talk later.

And they *would* talk.

He scooped Sam up into his arms. "Hey, buddy. I love homemade ice cream. We better get in line so we don't miss out."

He held his hand out to Cherry. She didn't say anything else, just smiled up at him and slipped her hand into his. He squeezed it a little tighter than normal.

As the three of them headed back outside, his words

echoed in his head.

He didn't want to miss out.

Not just on the ice cream, but on a chance at a real relationship with Cherry. A real life with her *and* Sam.

A chance at having a real family.

Chapter Fifteen

Cherry leaned forward as Taylor's truck pulled up to *their* spot at the lake. She hadn't been up here in years. The lake was still beautiful. Funny how in the moonlight it looked just the same.

The party had broken up around eleven, and several people had offered to stick around and clean up. They'd made quick work of gathering trash and taking down the lights. The guys from the fire department would come out tomorrow to take down the dance floor.

They'd borrowed some tables from the church, and Taylor wanted to run them in to town so they'd have them for after the service tomorrow. Russ had offered to put Sam to bed and suggested Cherry ride along to keep Taylor company.

He was so obvious. She could see right through his flimsy attempt to give her and Taylor more time together.

But she loved Russ, and she loved him for wanting to see her with his son.

And really, keeping Taylor company wasn't too difficult of a task.

They'd unloaded the tables, and Taylor had asked her if she wanted to go for a drive.

She hadn't expected him to take her to the lake. The spot they used to park when they were teenagers.

The very spot they'd made Sam.

He rolled down the windows, and a soft, warm breeze blew through the truck. She could hear crickets chirping and the gentle lap of the water against the shore. The sounds of a summer evening.

Taylor sat back in his seat and pulled her into his lap.

Just like he used to.

It felt so familiar to be in his arms. So right. She leaned against the door and reached up to touch his face.

A face that had filled her dreams, her memories. She ran her finger along his chin line, the rough stubble of his whiskers rough against her skin. "You didn't use to have whiskers."

He laughed. "I didn't use to have a lot of things. Like a working brain." He reached for her hand and held her fingers to his lips. Lord have mercy, the man had amazing lips. "I'm sorry, Cherry."

"What for?"

"For leaving like I did. For leaving you behind. For not calling after I left."

His words brought the memories of that summer back to her, and she swallowed at the emotions building in her throat. "We were stupid kids. We both made mistakes."

She'd pulled her hair up into a ponytail earlier, and he tugged at the elastic band, releasing her hair around her shoulders.

The simple gesture sent sensual shivers down her spine.

He brushed his hand through her now loose hair. "I was a stupid kid. I can look back now and see all the dumb things I did. But at the time, I was just so caught up in my own head. My mom died, and I didn't know how to handle that. And I didn't know how to handle the depth of my feelings for you. Looking back now, I think I was probably afraid of how close I was to you and afraid to lose someone else that I loved so much."

"I made mistakes, too." Now was the time. She had to tell him.

This was the moment to tell him about Sam.

He slid his hand under her hair and cupped her neck.

He pulled her to him and laid a soft kiss against the corner of her mouth. "Babe, I'm not a kid anymore. I can't promise that I won't make stupid mistakes once in a while, but I still care about you. I think about you all the time. When I'm with you, I want to be touching you and when I'm not, all I think about is when I'm going to be with you again."

He pulled back and looked into her eyes. "When that guy pulled that gun this afternoon, all I could think about was keeping my family safe. *My* family. You and Sam *are* my family now. I know it hasn't been very long that we've all been together, but it just feels right when we are. I love that kid. I don't want us to have a fake relationship."

What was he saying? "You don't?"

"No. I want us to have a *real* relationship. A real shot at making this family work. I want you back in my life. For real."

Now. She had to tell him now.

She had waited years to see him again.

And in her deepest most secret part of her heart, she had wished that he would come back for her. Come back and tell her he still loved her.

Now he was here.

She was in his truck at their spot on the lake. In his arms with his lips on her skin. Saying the things she'd waited years to hear him say.

What if she told him about Sam and it ruined everything? Family was so important to him. What if he felt betrayed that she'd never told him? Never even given him a chance to decide.

What if he hated her for giving his son away without even telling him?

But he was the one who left. That had been his choice.

And Sam was here now. It felt like they actually had a chance at making this work.

If they were a family, he would be like Sam's dad anyway, so maybe she didn't need to tell him.

Maybe he never had to know the truth. Especially if finding out the truth could mean that she would lose him again. And maybe this time forever.

But she had to tell him the truth. How could they start a real relationship with this big of a lie between them?

She had to tell him.

She took a deep breath. "But Taylor, I need to tell you—"

"Shh." He held his fingers to her lips. "No buts. I don't want to hear all the reasons that this can't or shouldn't work." He leaned in and kissed her. Softly, then with more urgency.

He pulled back. His hand still cupped her neck, and he pulled at the bow that held her halter top up.

The straps loosened, and her top fell down her front. He

trailed his fingers across her neck and down her chest.

His touch was soft, and her nipples pebbled with yearning.

Pulling her bra down, he released her lush breasts. Dipping his head, he twirled his tongue around one ripe bud, then sucked it gently into his mouth.

She arched her back, giving herself to him, all thoughts of anything besides this man and his lips on her skin forgotten.

His hand slid down her waist, across her hips, and lightly brushed the skin of her legs. Gooseflesh rippled across her skin as he slipped his hand under her dress.

Her body simmered, and she ached with want and need, moaning softly as his fingers trailed closer to her center.

She couldn't focus on anything but him. His mouth and the attention he was giving her breasts, sliding her taut nipple between his lips, teasing, sucking, and nipping at their swollen tips.

She squirmed against his hand as he cupped her bare bottom, running his thumb along the thin strap of her thong panties.

Gripping his shoulder, she bucked against him as his fingers explored, caressing, squeezing, gently spreading her thighs apart. Her arousal unbearably sweet as he finally reached her tender core.

She moaned his name as his fingers began to move in slow, sweet strokes.

Then he kissed her, taking her mouth in an onslaught of hungry passion.

His hand increased the pressure and pace, and she clutched at his back, digging her fingers into his muscled shoulders.

She arched into him, increasing the friction as the

tightness inside of her continued to build. He picked up the rhythm until she cried out against his mouth, bliss filling her as she came undone in his arms.

She sagged against him, her breath ragged. He kissed her forehead, and she grinned up at him. The sweet, sly grin of a naughty vixen.

She wasn't finished with him. Not even close.

Switching positions, she pulled her leg across him so she straddled his lap.

Starting at the top, she unbuttoned his shirt, dipping her head to kiss his chest. The cramped space of the truck cab constricted her movements, but she had enough room to scoot back and unzip the fly of his jeans.

He grinned up at her, a slow, sexy smile that had everything inside of her revving up for round two.

He pulled a foil packet from his pocket, ripped it open and covered himself with the condom.

This night seemed unreal.

She was in a truck with Taylor Johnson, her dress around her waist and her breasts bare as she straddled his waist. A warm breeze floated through the truck, caressing her already swollen and tender nipples.

Taylor noticed and leaned forward, sipping at one of the tight buds. She arched back, and he lifted his hips, pushing his jeans and briefs down.

She sucked her bottom lip between her teeth, as she felt his hardness brush against the bare skin of her thighs.

"You are so beautiful." His words escaped his lips, as he pressed a kiss against her collarbone. His hands moved along her back, caressing, tickling, sliding lower until they were under her dress and cupping her bottom.

He kissed her neck, her breasts, her lips, sucking and nibbling her skin, murmuring sweet words of want and desire. Her breath came in soft pants, as he lifted her hips then brought her down, joining them in sweet union.

He moaned against her mouth. "I want you, Cherry. Like nothing I've ever wanted before. I've been lost without you. Nothing ever felt right or complete after I left. Leaving you was the biggest mistake I ever made."

His words thrilled and moved her.

He spoke between kisses, his words coming out between harsh breaths as his hips moved in rhythm with her. "You filled my dreams, my fantasies. I swear to you, I could remember every moment we were together. I could remember the smell of your hair, the sound of your laugh."

She stopped moving and took his face between her hands, tipping it up to look into his eyes. "I remember, too. I couldn't believe it when you came back. I wasn't sure you would even want to see me."

"I wanted to see you. To touch you. To kiss you. I had hoped that you would at least be willing to talk to me. But in my heart, I wished that you would maybe give me another chance. I never imagined I would get you and Sam. Or that I would have you in my arms again. Or in my bed."

She grinned, then leaned down toward his neck and sucked his earlobe between her teeth. "Or in your truck."

He laughed. Then moaned at the delicious torture she caused by kissing his ear like that.

She leaned back, feeling brazen and sexy as she gave him a full view of her bare chest. Her long red hair felt wild and curly as it fell down her back and across her shoulders.

He reached up and cupped her cheek. "I need you, Cherry.

You make me crazy and happy and hot as hell. I want you back. Say you'll come back to me. Tell me that you're still mine."

She leaned forward, her hair tickling his chest. Her hips began to move in a slow, tortuous rhythm as she looked into his eyes. "Yes. I'm still yours. I always have been, and I always will be. My heart has always belonged to you, Taylor Johnson."

"Damn straight it does." He slid his hands down to grip her waist. His pace picked up as he moved beneath her. Her breath came in quick pants, and her nails dug into his skin as she clutched his back.

He buried his head in her neck, and she abandoned all thoughts as she lost herself to him. Drowning in his scent, in the feel of his skin, the taste of him on her lips. She cried out in pleasure, her soft moans reaching a crescendo as she tumbled over the crest of ecstasy.

She shuddered in his arms, sending another surge of heat through him, and he lost all control. He clutched her waist as his body let go in release.

She sagged against him, and he brushed her hair from her neck and laid a soft kiss on her neck. "You make me happy, woman. Like I just want to whoop and holler. Holler from the rooftops that this gorgeous woman is mine."

Grinning, he leaned close and sang softly in her ear. "She's my cherry pie. Tastes so good, makes a grown man cry."

She smiled as she nuzzled against his neck, feeling happy as well. Except for the small twinge of guilt that lay deep in her heart.

Would he still claim her as his if he found out the truth? If he found out that Sam was really his son and she'd never told him?

Chapter Sixteen

The next afternoon Taylor walked into the county hospital and asked the receptionist where to find Leroy Purvis.

She tapped at her computer keyboard. "He's in Room 105. Do you know where that is?"

"I'll bet I can find it. Thank you, ma'am." He tipped his hat then headed down the hall.

He'd had a weird feeling all morning about that look that had passed between Leroy and Reed and figured it wouldn't hurt to have a visit with the patient.

Leroy had the television on, and Taylor walked in just in time to hear him yell a wrong answer at Alex Trebek. He should have taken "Dumbasses for $100." That's a category he might have a chance in.

"Hello, Leroy."

Purvis looked up at him, a sneer on his slack face. "What are you doing here? Come to finish the job?"

"Nope. Looks to me like you've got that about covered."

The guy did look terrible. His skin had a sickly pallor, and his five o'clock shadow had passed five a few days ago. His eyes were red-rimmed and blood shot and had the glassy look induced by pain medication.

A morphine pump sat next to his bed, and Taylor assumed that was his medication of choice. A bandage covered Leroy's shoulder, and a silver handcuff linked his wrist to the railing of the hospital bed.

The room smelled like a bad mixture of alcohol, antiseptic, and body odor. Besides being shot, Leroy was probably detoxing as well.

"I just came to ask you a few questions."

Purvis narrowed his eyes. "Do I need a lawyer?"

Oh brother. This guy watched too many police shows. "Do *you* think you need one?"

"Hell no. I ain't done nothin' wrong. I'm the one that got shot." Evidently he hadn't been watching them closely enough.

His voice had that loopy quality of medication. Taylor thought he might have come at the right time to get information if Leroy had recently taken his pain meds.

"I'm not here to talk to you about that. I just got to wondering how you knew Emma was out at my ranch last night. I know you just got out of lock-up. It sure didn't take you long to find her."

He shrugged. "That wasn't no big deal. My lawyer told me."

"So you do have a lawyer?"

"Yeah, well he's court-appointed."

"Even so, I find it hard to believe that your lawyer told you where to find your ex-wife knowing full well that she had a restraining order against you."

"Well, not exactly like that. But Hill told me he was going to a big party in Broken Falls and that the whole town was supposed to be there. I knew Emma would probably go running back to her dad's place, and they wouldn't miss something like that."

"Did you say Hill?"

"Yeah, Reed Hill. That's my lawyer. Ain't you listening? He told me it would be a good idea for me to steer clear of the place, just in case Emma was gonna be there."

I'll just bet he did.

Reed — that sneaky bastard.

He would have known telling Purvis to stay away was just the thing to get him to show up and cause a scene at the party.

Taylor hoped that he hadn't known Purvis would bring a gun. Reed couldn't be that much of a jerk. He wouldn't put his own family in danger.

"Well, that's about all I needed to know. I'll let you get back to your show. It sounded like you almost had that last one." Taylor tipped his hat and backed out of the hospital room.

Leroy turned back to his show, holding out his good hand and giving Taylor the finger. "Thanks for shooting me, asshole."

Taylor shook his head as he walked down the hospital corridor. What an idiot.

But he did give him a valuable piece of information. Now to figure out the best way to use it against Reed and his threats.

On his way out, he passed the cafeteria and noticed Doc Genrich sitting at one of the tables, his white-haired head tipped down as he concentrated on a chart he was reading. A half-eaten piece of coconut cream pie sat on a plate on the table in front of him.

He looked up as Taylor stepped into the cafeteria and waved a hand in recognition. "Hey there, Sheriff. Join me for a piece of pie?"

Taylor shook his head. "No thanks. I've got to get back to the station, but I wanted to ask you about something. Get your advice on a case I'm working on."

"Sure, son. Have a seat." Doc gestured to the chair across from him. "What's on your mind?"

Taylor pulled out the chair and dropped into it. "Well, I'm working on this case where a child had recently found out he was adopted, and he wanted to find out who his birth parents were. Any advice on how I would go about helping this kid—this case, really—in locating the birth parents?"

Doc Genrich arched an eyebrow at Taylor. "Son, I may still seem young to you, but I was not born yesterday. And you're a terrible liar."

"I'm sure I don't know what you're talking about."

"I was out at the party last night, remember? And your dad and I have been friends for too many years to count. I've known you since you were a boy, so don't try fooling me. I know that Sam was adopted, but those records are sealed. Even using your badge won't help you with that one."

Taylor shook his head. "I knew it was a long shot. But Sam asked me to help him, and I really care about that kid." Taylor pushed back his chair to go. "Thanks for your help, Doc."

Doc held out his hand and rested it on Taylor's arm. "Don't go just yet. I wanted to ask you something. I saw you at the party with Cherry and Sam. You all sure seemed happy. What are your plans for those two?"

"I plan to marry Cherry. To be a family with her and Sam. To take care of them. You have known me a long time. And you know that woman was my first love and that I blew it with her by leaving all those years ago. I plan to make it up to her, every day for the rest of my life."

"You serious about that, son?"

"Serious as a heart attack." Taylor grinned. "Sorry, probably shouldn't joke about that in here."

Doc wasn't smiling.

His face held a serious expression, and he gave Taylor a discerning look. "You know as a doctor I took an oath to uphold confidentiality, to help my patients in a moral and ethical standard, and to do no harm. But in this instance, I almost wonder if I'm doing more harm by not saying anything."

"What do you mean? Do you know something about Sam's adoption?"

The older man sighed and rubbed his temples as if he were thinking over a hard decision. "I've known you and Cherry since you were kids. And I spent a fair bit of time with her that first year after you left. She had a pretty rough go of it when you left town."

He ducked his head. "I know. I was an idiot."

"About when was that that you left town? Would you say about eight, nine years ago?" The doctor gave him a pointed stare. "And about how old is that boy, Sam?"

Taylor swallowed. Mixed emotions and reactions were churning in his gut. What was Doc telling him? "About eight."

"Listen, Taylor, all I can say is that for a guy as smart as you were in school, you're sure not very good at math." Doc pushed back his chair and stood.

The doctor clapped him on the shoulder then left the room, leaving Taylor stunned and confused. What the hell? He couldn't mean that—

Taylor pulled out his phone and sent Cherry a quick text. *"When is Sam's birthday?"*

A few seconds later, his phone buzzed with a reply. *"February 18th. Why?"*

He typed back, *"No reason, just thinking about giving him a present."*

"You've already given him enough."

"Gotta go. See you tonight." He slumped back in his chair, mentally counting out the days. He may not be great at math, but he could subtract nine months. Sam had been conceived in May. Probably around the middle of the month.

He thought back to where he was in the middle of May nine years ago. He was finishing high school, thinking about the military, going to prom.

Holy shit. It couldn't be.

It had to be a coincidence. There were plenty of kids at plenty of proms in this state having unprotected sex.

Besides, she would have told him. She wouldn't have let him leave.

Although, he hadn't really given her a choice. And maybe she didn't find out until after he left.

He dropped his head into his hands. What the hell was he supposed to do about this? One thing had changed in Taylor over the years. He no longer made rash decisions. He thought things through, weighing the consequences of his actions or inactions.

He needed to think about this.

Figure out a way to find out the truth. There was no use getting everybody riled up until he knew for sure.

Cherry dropped her phone in to her pocket. *What the heck was that text about?* Why did Taylor want to know Sam's birthday? Was he really planning to get him a gift?

Could he have recognized Sam's goofy grin as the same one that shone from his face when he laughed at a silly joke? Or maybe he realized the blue of Sam's eyes were the same shade of the ones that looked back at him in the mirror.

Could he have somehow put the pieces together? Or was her own guilt of not telling him causing her to jump to conclusions?

No. No way.

A ball of panic filled Cherry's chest. What if Taylor found out? Found out that she lied?

Would he leave again?

Would he even say goodbye this time, or would she just go home to find him gone?

Stop it. You're being paranoid.

Stan called to her from the kitchen, asking about an insurance claim. She trudged into the back room, pushing down her fears and concentrating on the diner.

She needed to get this restaurant up and running. She needed to be able to take care of her and Sam.

Especially if they were going to be left on their own, with only her to help them survive.

Chapter Seventeen

"That was a good supper." Taylor leaned back and patted his stomach. He sat next to Sam on the front porch swing.

A full week had passed, and Cherry had taken Sam in to get his cast removed earlier that day.

Sam patted his stomach, imitating Taylor's movement. "Yep, Cherry sure does make good mashed potatoes. Those are my favorite."

"I can tell. I think you ate three helpings." He chuckled as Sam giggled.

The boy's laughter had this funny way of just plain making him happy. Making his heart feel full.

Maybe this was enough. Maybe he didn't need to know.

What if he found out it was true? That Sam was his son? Would they really just be able to go on like they were?

Could he forgive Cherry for lying to him? For keeping his son a secret all these years and not even giving him a chance to decide if he wanted to be part of his life.

He'd been thinking about it all week.

And thinking about it had caused an unsettled feeling and a tiny ball of anger to form in his gut. Why did she get to decide? Had she really robbed him of eight years with his own son?

He pulled a pack of gum from his pocket, stuck a piece in his mouth, then held out the pack to Sam. "Want a piece?"

"Sure." Sam unwrapped the gum and stuck it in his mouth. Rex had jumped up onto the swing and laid his head in Sam's lap, and he absently pet the dog's head.

The two had become inseparable. Sam didn't go anywhere without the dog. The boy chewed happily on the gum, content to sit with Taylor and his dog as he swung his legs under the seat.

Taylor studied his features. His eyes were blue, the same as Taylor's. But so what? Millions of people had blue eyes.

He did have the same white blond hair that Taylor'd had when he was a kid. But again, lots of kids had light blond hair.

He sighed.

There was no use speculating. No use getting angry or upset.

Not until he knew the truth.

He pulled the new evidence baggy from his pocket. "I think I heard Cherry say something about making a chocolate cake for dessert."

Sam's eyes widened, and he hopped down from the swing. "I think I heard that, too. We should go check."

He laughed and held out the plastic baggy. "You better give me that gum then."

Sam obediently spit the gum into the plastic bag in his hand. Taylor sealed the bag and stuck it in his pocket.

The boy was already too preoccupied with the dog and the suggestion that he might get cake that he either didn't notice or didn't care that Taylor had just stuck his piece of gum in his pocket.

"Why don't you head on in? I'll be there in a minute. Don't eat all the cake before I get there." He smiled as Sam raced for the front door.

Then he took his own piece of gum from his mouth and stuck it in another baggie.

He had a friend that worked in the lab, and he owed him a favor.

He'd drop these by in the morning and tell him they were for a case he was working on. His buddy would put a rush on the results if he told him it was important.

Not that he was in that big of a rush to find out the truth.

Part of him wanted to be Sam's dad. He already loved him and wanted to be part of his life.

But if he really was Sam's father, how could he then accept the terrible lie and betrayal from Cherry? How could they move forward with that between them?

No use worrying about it tonight. He would know the truth soon enough. And he knew his life would change either way.

Now all he could do was wait.

Cherry stepped from the bathroom and slipped under the covers next to Taylor. He lay on his side with his back to her and she snuggled up against him. His body was warm, and she wriggled against his back side.

Taylor didn't turn around. "I'm pretty tired tonight."

Hmmm. This was new. He hadn't been "too tired" yet. She tried not to let her imagination get away from her. Being "too tired" could mean any number of things. Like even that he *was* actually too tired. They'd had a lot going on lately. He should be exhausted.

There wasn't anything wrong with him being tired. It didn't mean anything.

Just because he was tired didn't mean he'd figured anything out or was upset with her. He didn't act mad. He just wasn't acting like his normal self.

Was she letting her own guilt make her paranoid? Probably. But then why did it seem like he kept looking at Sam during dinner that night?

She lay back on the pillow and listened to him breathe, waiting to hear his breathing even out in the steady sound of sleep.

It didn't.

For a guy who was so tired, he sure wasn't falling asleep very fast. He took a deep breath and let out a big sigh.

Oh boy. Big sighs never meant anything good.

Should she just ask him what was going on? What if she didn't want to hear his answer?

It was easier to miss out on one night of hot sex with him than to miss out on being with him entirely.

Chapter Eighteen

Taylor glanced into the mirror as he buttoned his shirt. He could see Cherry standing in the bathroom doing her hair in the reflection.

Damn, she was beautiful.

He could smell the scent of her lotion and shampoo. It had filled the room when she'd opened the bathroom door after her shower. He didn't know the exact scent. It was from one of those pink lotion bottles now scattered across his bathroom, but it was something flowery, and it smelled like her.

He watched as she fixed her hair. She wore a soft pink T-shirt and a pair of black satin bikini underwear. Every time she lifted her arms, a slim band of her stomach showed.

And every time he caught a glimpse of that bare skin, his gut clenched with want and desire. The rounded curves of her lush body had him wanting to fill his hands with her, to caress and stroke each luscious part.

It had been torture staying away from her the past two

days.

The first night he'd claimed he was tired. Last night he'd stayed at the station until late, taking over a shift and trying to get through the stack of paperwork that had been piling up on his desk.

He'd slipped into bed after midnight and listened to her soft, even breathing.

All he'd wanted to do was pull her against him and hold her.

Oh, who was he kidding? He'd wanted to rip her clothes off and make sweet, slow love to her. To kiss and feast on every part of her gorgeous body.

But he couldn't.

He wanted to forget about getting the lab results. Pretend that it didn't matter if Sam was his. If she'd lied to him. He hadn't heard back from his buddy yet, and he honestly didn't know what results he was hoping for.

"You okay?" Cherry had crossed the bedroom and stood behind him, her footsteps so soft on the carpet he hadn't heard her.

He turned and looked down at her. Into her stunning green eyes.

The eyes were supposed to be the windows of the soul, and he wondered what secrets were hidden behind the windows of Cherry's eyes.

They seemed the same to him. The same eyes he had been looking into since he was a kid. Eyes that were always full of understanding, of support, of love, of passion.

Now Cherry's eyes were full of questions. And pain. "I haven't seen much of you the last few days."

He ran a hand through his hair and blew out a sigh. "Yeah. I guess I've just got a lot going on. With work. And stuff."

She reached a hand up and laid it gently on his chest.

He closed his eyes. Just the feel of her hand caused ripples of longing to course through him. He placed his hand on hers then looked down at her. "Come here."

His words were soft, and he pulled her into his arms. He leaned down and buried his face in her neck. The smell of her hair surrounded him, and he breathed in her scent.

She laid a tender kiss on his neck, right under his jaw. The touch of her lips on his skin had him instantly hard, and he sucked in his breath.

He should push her away. Wait until he knew the truth.

It wasn't right to do this when he still had so many unanswered questions.

She pressed against him, her soft breasts squished against his chest, the pale crescents of her cleavage visible in the V-neck of her shirt.

Ah. To hell with what was right. He wanted this woman. He didn't care about anything else.

In this moment, all he cared about was getting his hands on her. Touching her skin, her lips, caressing the sweet curve of her rear.

He dipped his head and kissed her. Not lightly, but hard. An intense kiss filled with hunger and need. His hands ran down her back, cupping her butt, and lifting her up.

Her legs wrapped around him, her want matching his. She clutched at his back as she kissed his mouth.

Squeezing and stroking, he slid his hands under the silky bikini panties, dangerously close to her hot, sweet center. He turned and set her on top of his dresser.

Bending his knees, he laid a line of fervent kisses down her neck while his hands skimmed under her shirt. Tugging at her bra, he released her full breasts and assailed them with his mouth, kissing, licking, sucking at their tender tips.

She cried out, a quick whimper of need.

And he was lost.

Her hands gripped his shoulders as she arched her back. Her legs clamped around his waist like a vise, as she pressed her hips tight against him.

His phone rang.

He stopped and pulled back, gasping for breath.

Cherry sat on the edge of his dresser, her hair a curly wild mess around her face, her lips red and plump from being kissed. And kissed hard.

Her shirt was in disarray, and one of her bare breasts spilled over the top of the neckline.

She was the sexiest damn thing he'd ever seen.

The phone sat on the dresser less than a foot from his hand. The hand that had just been holding her against him.

It rang again.

He didn't want to look. He knew what it would say. *Please let it be the office. Let something be on fire.*

Hell, he'd take a homicide right now. Just please don't let it be the lab.

He looked down at the screen on the third ring, and so did Cherry.

The words *DNA Diagnostic Center* filled the screen.

He glanced at Cherry. A look of fear and pain filled her eyes. Her legs dropped from his waist, and she adjusted her shirt, covering herself up.

What if he didn't answer? He could let it go to voicemail. Then never listen to the message.

"You better get that," Cherry said, her tone flat and

emotionless.

He picked up the phone and accepted the call. "Yeah, hello. Sheriff Johnson here."

"Hey Taylor, I was just gettin' ready to leave you a message."

His friend's voice blared through the phone, and he was sure Cherry could hear every word. His tone was full of cheer and good humor. He had no idea he was about to wreck Taylor's world. "I got the results back on the case you were working on, and it's a match. The two samples are definitely related, so it's a yes for paternity. Hope that helps. Some poor bastard's either gonna be very happy or very shocked."

Shocked didn't begin to cover it. "Thanks. I owe you one."

His friend laughed. "Yeah, you owe me several. Next time I see you down at the Tavern, you're buying. Gotta go. See ya."

Taylor set the phone on the dresser. It felt like he'd been sucker-punched in the gut.

Then knee'd in the balls.

Twice.

Cherry stared at him, her eyes filling with tears. She didn't say anything, just stared, as if waiting to gauge his reaction.

He was waiting, too, not sure how to feel.

He had a son.

A son that he never knew about.

Because of her. His fists clenched at his sides, containing the anger that simmered below his surface.

The silence dragged on.

He tried to get control of his emotions. Think before he reacted. He looked into her eyes, wordlessly begging for her to give him some kind of response that made sense. That made all this go away. He shook his head in disbelief. "Aren't you going to say anything?"

"What do want me to say?"

"How about I'm sorry. You could start with that."

"I *am* sorry."

It wasn't enough. He needed to know why. "How about you tell me that you haven't been lying to me for the past eight years. Tell me that you didn't have our baby and give him up for adoption without ever even giving me a chance to know him. To have the option to take care of him. To take care of you both."

A single tear rolled down her cheek. "You were gone. You left me. How could I tell you when you were gone?"

That was it? That was her explanation?

He slammed his fist down on the dresser. "This is my fault? Seriously? That's what you want to lead with? That this is my fault because I left?"

She shrugged, her shoulders sinking inward.

"No. I don't accept that. You could have tried to find me. My dad could have tracked me down. Why didn't you even give me a chance?"

"I tried. I texted you after you left. I told you we needed to talk, and you said you needed time, then you never responded back to me."

He stared at her, shock coursing through him. "You *texted* me? And said we needed to talk? How the hell was I supposed to translate 'we need to talk' into 'I'm pregnant'?"

She shook her head. "I don't know. It sounds stupid when you say it like that. And it was stupid. I was a stupid kid. And so were you. I didn't know what else to do. You left. You made it clear that we were through, and that you were not interested in a future with me. I was alone, and I was scared. I was only seventeen."

"You're not seventeen now. You weren't seventeen when we walked into Sam's hospital room, and I met him for the first time. Why didn't you tell me then?"

Cherry covered her face with her hands. "I don't know. I was scared. I was in shock. Stacy was dead, and I couldn't handle that and taking care of Sam and dealing with telling you the truth."

"So, when *were* you planning to tell me? Never? Or maybe after we were married. After you'd already got your claws into me and committed me to marriage?"

"That's not fair."

"You're damn right it isn't fair.

"Besides, us getting married was *your* idea."

"Well it evidently wasn't one of my better ones." He sunk down on the bed and scrubbed his hand across his face. "Damn it, Cherry. Why didn't you just tell me the truth?"

He felt a lump of emotion building in his throat, and he didn't know if it was anger, fear, or sadness. Or a combination of all three.

What he did know was that he needed time to think. "Listen, I just need some time alone right now."

She pushed off from the dresser and sneered at him, her voice filled with disdain. "You're leaving? Why doesn't that surprise me?"

How dare she get mad at him right now? "I didn't say I was leaving. I said I needed some time to think. And I need to be alone to do that. Without you as a distraction."

That probably came out wrong but holy crap, how was he supposed to figure out how he felt about all this when she was standing around in her underwear?

She grabbed a pair of jeans off the bed and stuffed her legs in to them. "Fine. Sam and I will go out to Tucked Away and stay with Charlie. Or we'll stay at the motel in town. We sure as hell don't want to be *distractions*."

His stomach was in turmoil. He didn't know if he really wanted her to stay or really wanted her to go.

He couldn't seem to think straight. "Maybe that's best."

Her face fell.

She must have been wanting him to ask her to stay.

"Yeah, maybe it is best." She crossed to the closet and pulled out the laundry basket filled with her clothes.

Tossing it on the bed, she swept across the room, grabbing for anything that belonged to her and throwing it toward the basket. "I figured this wouldn't last. I knew you would do this."

"You knew I would do what? Find out I had a child? A son that the love of my life chose to get rid of before she ever gave me a chance to be in his life. What exactly did you know, Cherry? Because right now, I feel like I don't know anything. Especially you."

"Maybe you don't feel like you know me because you didn't stick around long enough to find out." She chucked a pair of flip flops into the basket. The ones that he had bought her.

Flashes of that day at the hospital came back to him. He had just wanted to help. He would have done anything for her.

This is what being a nice guy got him.

Well, screw that. "Lord, Cherry, cut me some slack. I was a kid. My mom had just died, and I was a mess. You and I had been fighting like crazy, and I just needed a way out."

The bed was filling with piles of her things.

How could she have so much of her stuff here in such

a short time? How could she have so completely taken up residence in his life?

He'd worked so hard to change his life, to not make rash decisions.

Except when it came to her. Then it seemed that he just jumped in with both feet. Jumped in without ever looking to see if there would be enough water below to catch him.

She turned to him, her eyes sparking with anger and the MSU shirt he'd given her to wear in her hand. "That's right, Taylor. *You* needed a way out. Well, so did I. You left me alone, and I was pregnant and scared. I had no money, no offers for college. All I had was a future working in a diner in a small town in the middle of freaking Montana. Stacy was my best friend. She had everything. Everything except a baby. I didn't know what else to do. It seemed like the best decision at the time. My baby would be raised in a loving home, and I would still get to see him. I didn't know what else to do because I didn't have you here to help me decide. Because you needed a way out."

She threw the shirt at him, and it fell at his feet. "Well, there's the door, Taylor Johnson. That's the easiest way out, and nobody is asking you to stay. All you have to do is walk out. Walk away. It's what you're good at it. So leave. Get the hell out of here. And don't worry, I'll be gone by the time you get back."

Anger and hurt bubbled inside of him. How the hell could she be this pissed at him? He was the one who should be pissed. And he had every right to be.

He narrowed his eyes at her. Pink bursts of color flushed her cheeks, and her hair was wild around her head. He'd seen her mad before, and he knew it wouldn't do any good to argue with her now.

Besides, if he didn't get out of here, he might say something he would regret later.

And right now, he was thinking a lot of things that wouldn't help anyone if he said them out loud. "Fine."

He grabbed his badge off the dresser and crossed to the bedroom door.

Waves of anger filled him. His voice rose as he turned back to her. "You can be pissed off all you want, Cherry. But you should save a little bit of that pissed for yourself. I'm not saying I did everything right, but you're the one who decided to give Sam up for adoption without giving me a choice to be in his life. I was his father. You should have at least given me a chance to do the right thing."

He turned his back to her and left the room.

His dad was standing in the living room as he crossed through, and Taylor held up his hand. The last thing he wanted right now was a lecture. "Not now, Dad."

He slammed the front door of the house and headed for his truck. He had to get out of there.

He needed some air and a minute to catch his breath and think this through. He had a son and an obligation to the boy.

And whether he liked it or not, he had an obligation to Cherry as well.

The Hill family was not going away, and if they found out Cherry had given Sam away once, they could use that against her to try to take Sam.

Too many thoughts were racing through his head. Too many emotions. He was mad and sad and overwhelmed.

He just needed to think.

To think about what the hell he was going to do now.

Chapter Nineteen

Cherry flung herself onto the bed. She landed on the piles of clothes she'd been tossing around.

She choked back a sob. *What the hell did I just do*?

Why did she always let her temper get in the way of her good sense? She could have just talked to Taylor. Like civilized human beings. He had every right to be mad. But so did she.

He said he wanted time to think. He didn't say he was leaving.

But she knew he was. She knew he wouldn't be able to take it. When times get too tough, that's when Taylor Johnson took off.

If she'd been smart, she would have insisted that she and Sam stay here. Insisted that they try to work it out.

But she'd never been known for making great decisions.

And now she was in a freaking fine kettle of fish. She'd told Taylor that she could go out to Tucked Away and stay with Charlie, but she'd never impose on her friend like that. She might not have a lot of money, but she still had her pride. Besides, she wasn't ready to talk about what happened with Taylor, and she knew Charlie would want to hear every detail.

Plus, this is what being a mom was about. It was about digging in and doing what she needed to do to take care of Sam. Having friends to count on was important, but she needed to do this on her own. Prove that she could take care of her son, without anyone else's help.

She and Sam would stay in a motel. There was only one in town.

With all the expenses of the fire, her one credit card was close to its max limit, but she could cover them for a week or so, then hopefully her apartment would be ready to move back in to.

What a mess.

How had she let her life get so out of control?

And how had she let herself believe that things could work out with Taylor? That they could be a family. A normal family.

Yeah, right. When had anything in her life been normal?

The only constant she'd had her whole life had been her grandparents and Stacy. And now they were gone.

Stacy was the smart one. She always had a solution for everything. Stacy was the one she went to when she was in trouble or had a problem.

Well, she had a whole mess of problems now. All she wanted to do was call Stacy and let her cousin tease her and joke her out of the disarray she had caused in her life.

But she couldn't call Stacy. She couldn't ever call her

again.

How could Stacy be gone?

The tears she'd been trying to hold back broke free. She pressed her face into Taylor's pillow as she let loose and cried.

She jumped as a small hand touched her shoulder.

"Are you okay, Cherry?" Sam stood next to her bed.

She hadn't heard him come in. Sitting up, she swiped at the tears on her cheeks, then held her arms open.

Sam scrambled into her lap. Rex jumped onto the bed and settled against her leg. The boy looked up at her, hurt evident in his blue eyes. "Are you really my mom?"

Pain squeezed at her heart. She didn't want to hurt Sam, but obviously he'd heard her and Taylor talking. It wouldn't do any good to lie now.

She nodded. "Yes, I am."

"And Taylor is my dad?"

She swallowed. "Yeah, he is."

He didn't say anything, and she could tell he was thinking it through. For only being eight years old, Sam had a way of reflecting over his circumstances that was wise beyond his years.

Cherry wished she had that skill. He must not have gotten that from her. "What do you think about that? Are you okay with it?"

He screwed up his face, and his eyes filled with tears. "I don't know. I love Taylor. He took me fishing. And I've always loved you. I want to be happy that you guys are gonna be my mom and dad, but I don't want to hurt my real mom and dad's feelings."

She couldn't speak over the emotion clogging her throat.

A look of pain and confusion crossed Sam's face. "Does that mean that they aren't my real parents anymore?"

"Oh, baby. Of course not." She pulled Sam into her arms and cradled him against her chest. "Stacy and Greg will *always* be your mom and dad. They loved you more than anything."

Sam's voice was soft as he asked her his next question. "Did you not love me very much then? Is that why you gave me away?"

Cherry's heart shattered.

She pulled Sam tighter against her. "No. That wasn't why. I gave you up because I loved you so much. I loved you more than anything else in the entire world. More than I loved myself. I *wanted* to keep you. But I knew that I couldn't. I couldn't give you the life I wanted you to have. I wanted to be selfish and keep you all to myself. But Stacy, your mom, wanted a baby so badly, and I knew that she would love you just as much as I did. And I knew if Stacy was your mom then I would get to stay in your life and be able to watch you grow up."

She tipped Sam's face up to hers, and the tears on his cheeks were like shards of glass in her already broken heart. "I loved you from the minute I knew you were inside of me. And I loved you enough to sacrifice my needs to make sure that you got a better life."

Sam's bottom lip quivered. Just enough to tear at her soul. "Are you able to keep me now? Or are you going to give me to another family?"

"Oh my gosh, no. I'm never giving you up again. Sam, I loved your mom, and I would give anything to have her back. But I believe in my heart that God has given me another chance to be your mom, and I am not ever letting you go again."

"But what about Uncle Reed and Aunt Olivia? They said that you aren't able to take care of me, and that I'm coming to live with them."

Anger flared in her that Reed and Olivia had talked to Sam behind her back. "I don't care what Uncle Reed and Aunt Olivia said, your mom and dad left instructions that if anything happened to them, that they wanted you to live with me. And I will fight with whatever I have to make sure that happens."

Sam's nose wrinkled. "Fight? You mean like you're going to punch Uncle Reed?"

She grinned. What she wouldn't give to punch Reed Hill right in his smug little self-righteous face.

Cherry jostled Sam in her lap and grinned down at him. "I might. I'll punch anybody that gets in the way of us being together."

Sam giggled, then his face sobered. "What about Taylor?"

Yes, she might like to punch Taylor right in the nose, too. "Oh honey, I can't tell you what's going to happen with Taylor right now. I never told him about you, so he's just trying to figure everything out right now, just like you. He has a lot to think about, and I hurt his feelings pretty bad."

"Can't you just say that you're sorry?"

Sometimes kids made it seem so easy.

If only her being sorry would be enough to take away the pain and the hurt that she knew he was going through. "I'm afraid that's not enough right now. Taylor just needs some time to think."

She lifted Sam off her lap and set him on the floor. "So,

we're going to go stay in a motel for a few days, just until my apartment above the diner is fixed."

"But I like it here."

An iron fist squeezed her heart. She liked it here, too. She liked it here in Taylor's home. In Taylor's bed.

In Taylor's arms.

But there wasn't anything she could do about that right now.

So she just had to suck it up and deal with it. Move on to Plan B. "I know, sugar. And maybe we can work it out for you to come back and visit Taylor real soon. But for now, we need to get your things together so we can get over to the motel."

The last thing she wanted now was for Taylor to come back and find her still here.

She followed Sam into his room and helped him to fill his suitcase with his clothes and toys. He hadn't brought that much with him and had only collected a few things since he'd been here.

Cherry was tempted to ask him to leave his rock collection here. But he had been so excited about finding each rock on the farm, and he'd explained to her and Taylor what made each rock special.

She drew the line at the dead frog carcass that Sam and Russ had found down by the pond last week. "Why don't we leave the dead frog here? In case Russ wants to see it some more."

Sam nodded, as if in agreement that Russ might actually be upset if they took the unique treasure with them.

Cherry pulled the guest bedroom door shut and wheeled Sam's suitcase into the living room.

Russ stood in the kitchen doorway, a steaming cup of fresh coffee in his hand. "You don't have to go."

She hated the sadness on Russ's face.

How many more casualties was she going to have to bear in this war of deception that she had started nine years ago. "Yeah, we do. Taylor needs some time to process all of this."

She looked down at Sam. "Hey, sugar, can you go in my room and finish putting all of my things into the laundry basket? Just put whatever's on the bed into it, okay?"

Sam shrugged. "Okay."

Cherry watched him go through the bedroom door, then she stepped closer to Russ. "Did you hear us arguing? Do you know?"

Russ huffed out a breath. "I've known since the night you brought him home. I'm Taylor's father, and that kid is the spitting image of Taylor when he was that age. I suspected it at first, but I knew for sure that night at dinner when Sam told us that he'd been adopted, and your face went white as a sheet." He took a sip of coffee before he spoke again. "I just wish you would have come to me. Back then. I could have helped."

She hung her head. "I know. I'm sorry. I was young and scared. I went to my cousin and my grandmother, and it seemed like the right thing to do at the time. I did the best I could."

Russ nodded. "I understand."

Cherry's voice barely broke a whisper and she couldn't look Taylor's dad in the eye. "Do you hate me terribly?"

Russ set down his mug and crossed the room. He pulled her into his arms. "Of course I don't hate you, girl. I love you as if you were one of my own. I'm disappointed in how things are turning out, but whatever happens, I want you to know that I love you, darlin'. And I love Sam."

Sam opened the bedroom door and pulled the overflowing laundry basket into the living room. "All right, I got everything off the bed. If you need anything else, you're gonna have to start a new basket."

Russ laughed and crossed the room to help Sam carry the full basket out to Cherry's VW Bug.

Cherry wasn't laughing.

The sad reality was that she didn't have another basket. She didn't have a basket, a bag, or a pot to piss in. She was flat broke and ready to engage in a war against her cousin.

A cousin who had money, power, and influence.

She'd never had money, but Taylor had helped to give her power and influence. And now he was gone. This was all up to her now. She was all that Sam had.

And she couldn't let him down. She fought back the tears that threatened to spill again.

She wouldn't cry, damn it.

Sam didn't need a crybaby for a mother.

He needed a warrior.

A woman of strength.

She pushed back her shoulders and took a deep breath. She could do this.

She might not have much more than the clothes on her back, but it was a strong back, and she wasn't afraid to work.

She had never been afraid of hard work, and she knew that hard work was what she faced now.

Heading for the front door, her woman of strength pep-talk playing in her head, she thought she just might have to punch someone yet.

Eight hours later, she wondered if the recipient of her punch was going to be the motel clerk. "What do you mean you're full?"

She was bone-tired after spending the day at the diner alternately cleaning up and spending hours on the phone with the insurance company.

Dark had settled in as she and Sam pulled into the hotel, and all she wanted to do was take a hot shower and crawl into bed. To close her eyes and forget about the fact that she wouldn't be lying next to Taylor tonight.

That she might not ever lie next to him again. But she couldn't think about that now. She needed to focus on her and Sam and getting them a place for the night.

The clerk couldn't have been much more than eighteen, and she looked at her phone more than she looked at Cherry. Her nails had been manicured, and her brunette hair fell in perfect wavy curls onto her shoulders and the ample amount of cleavage she was sporting. "What do you not understand about that? We don't have any rooms." She spoke in a slow, loud voice dripping with sarcasm.

Cherry wanted to take her phone and shove it down her pretty little neck.

She took a deep breath and tried to calm her frustration. "I understand what full means. I'm just surprised to hear that the motel is completely out of rooms."

"Well, my dad is renovating three of them and there's a rodeo or something in Great Falls, and so our other three rooms are full."

Her dad was the owner of the motel. That explained it.

Cherry couldn't figure out who else would hire this silly

twit to manage their front desk. "Look, can I just talk to your dad then?"

The girl shrugged. "Whatever. He's working on the rooms now. I think he's in room five or six. You can go over there if you want."

Cherry took Sam's hand and led him out the door. The motel was small, a sad U-shape of tiny rooms. It had been around forever, and Cherry was glad to hear the owner had plans to renovate. Anything that made the town more prosperous helped her business, too.

She and Sam trudged across the dirt parking lot, Rex following at their heels. They followed the sound of loud rock music, and she poked her head into the open door of room five.

A dark-haired man in his mid-forties stood on a ladder, using a small paint brush to trim the top edges of the wall. The paint was a soft khaki color and quite an improvement over the current dingy beige of the wall. He wore jeans, tennis shoes, and a paint splattered T-shirt with the remnants of a Van Halen logo on the front.

He waved and climbed down from the ladder. Still holding the brush, he turned down the little stereo that had been blasting the eighties rock. "Hey there. It's Cherry, right? From the diner."

Small towns.

She stepped into the room, careful to not disturb the tarp covering the floor. "Um, yeah, that's right. Cherry Hill. And you're…"

He gestured in apology to his paint-covered hand. "Mike. Mike Ferguson. I think you went to school with my little sister, Julie."

Cherry nodded. She remembered Julie Ferguson. When a graduating class had less than fifty people in it, you tended to remember all of them. "Listen, Mike. We're in a bit of a jam and we need a place to stay. I don't know if you heard about the fire at the diner?"

He nodded. "Yeah, I did hear about that. Glad to hear nobody got hurt. I've been watching for the place to open up again. You've got the best coconut cream pie I've ever tasted over there, and I have surely been craving some pie lately."

"Well, Mike. Like I said, we're in a bit of a jam, and if you could see your way to help us out, you can have a piece of pie, any flavor, on the house, every day for the next month."

His eyes lit. Bingo. "What can I do to help?"

"We need a place to stay and your…um…friendly receptionist seemed to think the hotel was full."

"The hotel is full. The rodeo's going on in Great Falls this weekend, and with me working on these rooms, I'm out of space. I'd like to help you out, though." Mike scratched his head and appeared to be thinking quite hard.

The man must really like pie.

He shrugged. "I haven't really started work on room six yet. I probably wasn't gonna get to it for another couple of days. It's kind of a mess in there, and there's no television. But you're welcome to stay in there, I guess. I could probably knock off twenty dollars a night for putting up with the mess."

His words were music to her ears.

She could put up with a mess and no television if it saved her twenty dollars a night. "That sounds great, Mike. Can we get into the room now?"

Mike looked down at Sam and the little dog at his feet.

Rex happily wagged his tail and gave an excited bark at being noticed. "The only problem is we don't allow pets. Especially dogs that bark. This hotel has too thin walls as it is. Customers tend to get real unhappy when their sleep is disturbed."

Shit.

She hadn't thought about the dog. Poor Rex. He was such a sweet mutt, and yet everybody seemed to have it in for him. Reed was giving her hell about getting rid of the dog, and now they might not get a place to stay because of him.

"Listen. You're a reasonable guy. We're staying in a room that's going to be gutted anyway so the dog hair won't hurt anything. And we'll be in the far room so no other guests should hear him."

"And we'll keep him real quiet," Sam said. He was smart and must have recognized the desperation in her voice. "He won't be any trouble."

"Just for tonight," Cherry said. "And then we'll figure out something else tomorrow." Right now she just needed to make it through this night. "And I'll bring you over a whole pie, as soon as the diner is back up and running."

He tilted his head then grinned. "All right. Just for one night. I really like that little dusting of graham crackers you do on the edge of the crust."

"Extra graham cracker dust, you got it." Relief washed over her. "And thanks, Mike. This means a lot."

He waved toward the door. "Go tell my girl to give you the key to room six, and we'll figure out the rest tomorrow. But the dog only stays for one night. Agreed?"

She couldn't look at Sam. She knew he'd be crushed.

"Agreed."

She grabbed Sam's hand and headed out the door before Mike changed his mind.

Big surprise. Mike's girl was still glued to her phone when Cherry entered the office and asked for the key to room six. "I guess you weren't really full after all."

The girl gave her an indifferent look, and Cherry's feeling of triumph deflated like an old balloon.

"That room is pretty bare because of the remodel. I can come over and make the beds for you if you want, but it might be a while." The girl stacked sheets, two thin orange bedspreads, and a handful of travel-sized toiletries on the counter.

"It's okay, I've got it. Besides, you do seem pretty busy." She couldn't help the sarcasm dripping from her voice.

All of her life, her grandparents had instilled in her that treating people with kindness and offering great customer service were the most important part of your business. She made a mental note to start teaching Sam those same lessons.

He was already a pretty great kid and his thoughtfulness of others continually surprised her. Stacy and Greg had done such a wonderful job with him. She saw so much of her kind-hearted cousin in Sam.

She took a deep breath and picked up the stack of towels. There was no time to dwell on that now. She had beds to make, and the thought of a hot shower practically made her knees weak. "Can you grab that key, Sam?"

He smiled at the teenage girl then took the key and led them back across the parking lot. After unlocking the door, he pushed it open, and they got their first look at their accommodations for the night.

The room was bare except for two double beds and a built-in counter/desk affixed to the wall. An ancient lamp sat on the faded and scarred nightstand tucked between the two beds. An aluminum ladder, several new cans of paint, and a canvas tarp were stacked in the corner of the room.

The air smelled faintly of stale cigarettes and mildew. Cherry wrinkled her nose in disgust and opened the window to let in the late summer night air.

Neither Sam nor Rex seemed to mind as they raced into the room to explore.

She dropped the sheets on to the bed closest to the door. "Let's get our stuff out of the car, then we can both get cleaned up."

"Ah, do I have to?" Sam asked. "I just had a bath yesterday."

She grinned. The boy could always make her laugh. "Yes, you have to. There's enough dust in this room to fill a slop bucket, the least we can do is get ourselves clean."

They carried their few things in from the car, Cherry grimacing at her laundry basket luggage.

Mike's daughter crossed the parking lot and handed her a stack of clean towels and a tub full of paper towels and cleaning supplies. "My dad said it might be a little dusty in the room. I can come clean it for you but it might be a while before I get to it."

Yeah, this seemed to be a pattern for her.

Cherry took the tub. "It's all right. I've got it."

Truth be told, she'd rather clean the room herself anyway.

Sam and Rex wrestled while she scrubbed the tub and shower area with an abrasive cleanser. When she was satisfied that the bathroom sparkled as much as the old fixtures could, she ran a tub full of bubbled water for Sam.

Thankfully she'd packed enough of their bathroom supplies to cover them, because the sample bottles of shampoo and lotion they'd been given at the front desk weren't going to last long.

While Sam soaked and splashed in the tub, she dusted and cleaned the rest of the room and made up the beds.

Hearing the water draining from the tub, she hollered toward the bathroom. "You need any help in there?"

"No, I got it." Sam emerged from the bathroom, his pajamas stuck to his still wet body. He'd made a half-hearted attempt to comb his sopping hair, and droplets of water ran down his neck and into the collar of his pajama top.

Cherry laughed. "Geez, kid. Did you even use the towel at all?" She marched him back into the bathroom and toweled off his hair then combed it down again.

The smell of his shampoo filled the damp air of the bathroom and caused her heart to ache with the love she felt for him.

She knelt down and wrapped her arms around his tiny body. She spoke against the side of his wet head, her throat thick with emotion. "I love you so much, Sam. Don't ever doubt that. I always have, and I always will. I love you to the moon and back."

He grinned at her reference to the children's book that she used to read when she visited him at Stacy's. They had played this game since he was a toddler. "I love you to the moon and back. One thousand times."

She tickled his sides, loving the giggles she elicited from the small boy. "I love you to the moon and back, seven hundred and four thousand times."

"Wow, that's a lot." Sam wiggled free of her grasp and

jumped onto the clean-sheeted bed. "But I love you to the moon and back. One thousand gazillion-trillion times." He fell over in mock fatigue, as if quoting the tremendously large number had worn him out.

Rex jumped on the bed and licked at Sam's face.

"Sam, we need to talk about Rex." Her voice was gentle. She knew how much the dog meant to him.

The fun, giggling moment passed, and Sam's expression sobered. His arm wrapped tighter around Rex's neck. "I don't want to talk. He's my dog now, and I'm not giving him away."

After the dog had bit Taylor, Cherry had talked to Zack and Charlie about keeping the dog with one of them, just until all the legal stuff was settled.

Sophie had overheard the conversation and excitedly offered to keep the dog for Sam. She hadn't shared that information with Sam yet, knowing how much it would upset him to lose the dog.

She'd hoped that it wouldn't come to this, but with the pressure of the motel manager and Reed, she felt like she had no choice. Her cousin had texted her twice in the last week or so to check on Sam and asked if she'd taken care of getting rid of the mutt. She hadn't answered either text.

She'd thought about asking Russ to keep him, but figured she'd caused enough trouble for the Johnson family. And Sophie was actually excited about keeping the little dog.

"Sam, I'm so sorry. I know how much you love Rex, but we can't keep him here with us right now. You heard the motel manager say we couldn't keep him, and your Uncle Reed is claiming that it's dangerous for you to be around him."

"Rex isn't dangerous. He loves me." The dog's head rested in Sam's lap.

"I know he does. And I know he's a good dog." She reached out to pet Rex's head, and the dog softly licked her hand. "Sophie has offered to keep him out at their farm, just until we get everything settled. You like Sophie, right?"

Sam nodded.

"You know she would love Rex and take good care of him. And he would be so happy out at her farm. He could run around and chase rabbits, and Zack would be there to help take care of him, too."

"But he'll be sad without me. And I love him." His bottom lip quivered slightly but he didn't cry.

"I know. And I know you'll be sad without him. But you have to think about everyone that's involved and do what's best for Rex. Sometimes you have to love something so much that you're willing to let it go. You have to love him enough to want him to be happy too."

Deep emotions rose to the surface for her. Memories of similar discussions with her cousin and her grandmother filled her head. She remembered being scared and alone and feeling so much like this child across from her who seemed so innocent and young and yet had to make an adult decision.

She laid her hand gently on his arm. "I know it's hard to let go of something that you love so much." Boy, did she *ever* know how hard that was.

She had given up the thing that she loved the most in the world. Given him up in hopes that he would have a better life. That he would be surrounded by love.

And he was.

Actually he was still surrounded by love. The intensity with which she loved this child was like a fierce ache in her chest. Like something bigger than she'd ever felt before.

Letting Rex go live with Sophie for a while would be hard, but it would be worth the sacrifice if it meant she had a better chance of keeping Sam with her.

"Do you understand what I'm telling you?" she asked.

Sam nodded. "Yeah, I get it, but I don't like it. Not even one little bit."

She smiled. "I know. I don't like it even one little bit, either. But at least Rex will be with Sophie, someone we know and trust. And we'll be able to visit him all the time. Every day if you want."

"I'll still get to see him? You promise?"

Cherry leaned down and kissed Sam on the forehead. "Yes, I promise." She patted the bed next to him. "I need to take a shower. You going to be okay?"

He nodded and snuggled closer to Rex.

Cherry grabbed a T-shirt and gym shorts from her laundry basket luggage. She pointed at the door. "I locked the door and set the chain. Don't let anyone in. You understand me?"

The boy nodded solemnly. "I won't."

"All right. It will only take me five minutes." She nodded at the wall across from the bed. "I would tell you to watch TV, but they didn't provide one in this luxury establishment, so you'll just have to imagine a show in your head. Or better yet, make up your own story. You can tell it to me when I get out of the shower."

"Okay." Sam twisted around to rest his head on the pillow, his face wearing a thoughtful expression.

She was pretty sure he was taking her instructions seriously, and she fully expected him to have a story ready by the time she had finished in the shower.

Ten minutes later, she emerged from the bathroom,

wearing the clean T-shirt and shorts, a towel wrapped around her wet hair.

She plopped down on to the bed next to Sam. The shower had done wonders for her, and now she just wanted to pretend today never happened.

"Did you think of a story?"

Sam grinned. "Yep."

"All right, let's hear it." She pulled the towel from her head and blotted at her wet hair. She'd found her hairbrush and cautiously pulled it through the tangled, wet strands while she listened to Sam's story.

"Once upon a time, there was a brave knight named Sir Samuel…Adams."

"Sam Adams?" She wondered if it was a coincidence that the hero of the story was named after Taylor and Russ's favorite beer.

"No, *Sir Samuel* Adams. Don't interrupt," he admonished.

She held up her hands in surrender. "Okay, sorry. Go ahead."

"This knight had a huge green fire-breathing dragon named Rexasaurus. And Sir Samuel and Rexasaurus were best friends, and they had lots of exciting adventures together. But Rexasaurus was very clumsy, and he got in trouble a lot. His tail was too big, and sometimes he would accidentally bash down people's houses with it or knock people over if they got too close to it. And he really loved eating pepperoni pizza, but it made him burp, and every time he burped, fire came out of his mouth, and he would burn something down."

Sam's eyes twinkled with delight and he giggled as he told the story. "And the pizza gave him bad gas, too, so every time he would toot—"

"All right, I don't need to hear about dragon toots." She laughed and tickled his stomach. "Tell me about one of these exciting adventures Sir Samuel and Rexasaurus went on."

"Okay. Okay. I'm getting to that. So even though Sir Samuel and Rexasaurus were best friends, like the best-est friends in the whole wide world, there was an evil king, and he didn't like Rexasaurus. He thought he was danger-ous, and he banished him from the kingdom. Which made Sir Samuel and Rexasaurus very sad. And Rexasaurus cried giant dragon tears. So many tears that it made a lake and then they went swimming in it. And the next day, Sir Samuel decided to run away with his best friend, and he climbed on Rexasaurus's back and the dragon flew away."

Sam took a deep breath then continued his story. "As they were flying over the mountains, they saw a princess hanging off the side of a cliff, and she was ready to fall. They yelled at her to hold on and flew so fast to her. But she'd been there for two weeks already and couldn't hold on any-more, and she dropped off the cliff. She screamed as she fell, but Rexasaurus swooped down, and he caught the princess on his back and saved her life. The princess was the daughter of the evil king, and he was so happy that the dragon had saved his daughter that he said Rexasaurus was no longer banished, and he and Sir Samuel could stay together and be friends forever. The end."

"Hmmm. Well, that was quite a story. I really liked the part about Sir Samuel and the dragon saving the princess."

Sam grinned up at her. She really wanted to say that she didn't like the part where the knight and the dragon ran away, but Sam looked so pleased with his story that she didn't want to dampen his enthusiasm with a negative critique.

Surely this was just a story he made up.

Obviously, she recognized the parallels between Sam and Rex, but hopefully Sam wasn't actually considering running away.

She looked down at the scruffy brown dog and laughed as she tried to imagine him as a huge fire-tooting dragon. She rubbed the little dog's head. "You are a sweet little doggie."

Sam pulled Rex into his arms and lay down. He pulled the coverlet over both him and the dog. "He's my best friend."

She stood and tucked Sam and Rex in. She bent forward and placed a kiss on Sam's forehead. "I know, sugar. I know."

She crawled into the other bed and reached for her cell phone.

The display was black. No missed calls. No text messages from Taylor.

He hadn't even called to touch base or see if they had found a place for the night.

Cherry turned off the light and settled her head on the pillow. She'd been exhausted before but now lay wide awake, staring at the water-stained ceiling of the motel room.

What the hell was she doing? How was she going to provide for Sam?

She had no money and no place for them to live. She had them holed up in a crappy motel that smelled of the detergent she'd had to use to clean the room herself, which barely masked the underlying smell of mildew.

Choking back tears, she calculated what was left on her credit card and wondered how many nights she'd even be able to afford this dump. Even with no television and the do-it-yourself maid service.

And now she was going to make Sam give up the one thing that was making him happiest right now.

Maybe she didn't deserve to have Sam with her. Maybe he would be better off with her cousin and his wife. At least they could give him a nice house and a yard to play in.

She balled her fists in anger and fought to keep from beating them against the bed.

Why?

Why did Stacy have to die?

Why did Taylor have to leave?

Why was life so unfair?

She heard a soft whine and turned her head.

Rex was watching her, compassion in his brown eyes as he lay his head across Sam's peacefully sleeping chest.

Sam looked like an angel when he slept, and a new resolve filled her as she watched his small chest rise and fall.

It didn't matter that they were in a crappy hotel or that she was broke. Nothing else mattered but Sam and keeping them together. She would live in a cardboard box under a bridge if it meant holding on to her son.

Screw Reed and Olivia. Screw her Aunt Bea.

They were not taking her son away from her.

Whether she had Taylor or not, she was not giving in to their threats of taking Sam from her.

She checked her phone again. The screen remained black.

That's okay.

She didn't need Taylor Johnson. Screw him, too.

She'd been on her own before he came back to town. She could be on her own again.

Except this time she wasn't alone.

And she wasn't giving up without a fight.

Chapter Twenty

Taylor felt like he hadn't slept a wink all night. The clock next to his bed read seven a.m.

He'd watched it turn from two to three to four and figured he must have fallen into some type of fitful sleep the last few hours.

His eyes were gritty and raw, and he had the urge to punch something.

Or someone.

He had the insane thought that he hoped an actual crime would be committed today so he would have someone to take his rage out on.

How could she have done this? How could she have lied to him all those years?

How could she have lied for the past several weeks?

He alternately swore at Cherry then missed her like crazy.

She'd only been gone one day, and yet his bed felt all

wrong last night. Empty without her soft body curled up next to his. Too quiet without the sound of her even breathing in his ear.

He missed the feel of her. The sound of her voice. He resisted the urge to press his face against her pillow just to inhale her scent.

His cell phone vibrated on the end table next to his bed, and in the deepest part of his heart, he wished it were her calling. Calling to say it had all been a mistake. That she hadn't lied, hadn't betrayed his trust. Hadn't been pregnant and never told him.

But she did.

She did all of those things.

But without those things, there would be no Sam. No sweet blond-headed boy who loved his dog and someday wanted a pet monkey. Whose laugh could light up even the darkest heart.

His phone continued to buzz, and he reached over to pick it up.

Not Cherry.

It was the office. His half-hearted wish had come true, and a crime had indeed been committed.

"I'll be right there," he told the dispatcher and hung up the phone. He reached for his pants and hurriedly got dressed.

His dad was standing in the kitchen and had just poured him a cup of coffee. "Wow. You look like hell, son."

"I feel like hell." He pointed to the cup. "Can I get that to go? I just got a call."

Russ poured the coffee into a travel mug and handed it to Taylor. "What are you going to do about Cherry and

Sam?"

Taylor raked a hand across his stubbled face and let out a weary sigh. "I don't know, Dad. I don't know what to do. I just feel like I need some time alone. To think and sort out what my next move is."

His dad cocked an eyebrow at him. "Are you considering an actual move? You aren't really thinking of leaving again, are you?"

"I don't know what I'm thinking. I can't seem to wrap my head around this whole thing." Taylor took the cup from his dad and headed for the door. "All I know is that I got a call, and I've got a job to do. That's all I can focus on right now."

He let the screen door close behind him as he headed for his truck.

It would be so easy to get behind the wheel and just drive away. Keep driving until his problems were mere specks in the rearview mirror.

He climbed into the truck and started the engine.

Cherry's heart was literally breaking.

The living breathing organism inside of her body was being ripped apart and torn to shreds as she watched her son hand his dog over to Sophie.

It was mid-afternoon, and she'd put it off as long as she could. She knew she still had a few hours of work to do at the diner and hoped that she and Stan could keep Sam's mind off of missing his companion.

They had been out at the Cooper farm for close to an

hour now. Cherry wanted Sam to see how much fun Rex would have here and to feel comfortable knowing that Sophie would take good care of him.

She swallowed at the emotion rising in her throat. "Come on now, Sam. We've got to get back to the diner. I told you we can come out and visit Rex tomorrow. You'll be apart less than a day."

Sam's voice was small, and she could tell he was trying to be brave. "But he's used to sleeping with me every night. What if he gets scared tonight when he goes to bed?"

Sophie gave Sam an encouraging smile. "Don't worry, Sammy. I'll take really good care of him. He can even sleep on my bed tonight."

"You will?" Sam's eyes were wide with doubt. "You promise?"

"Of course I promise. And if he looks even the slightest bit sad, I'll give him a special treat and tell him it's from you."

Sam nodded solemnly. "Okay, that's a good idea. He'll like that. But don't give too many 'cause then he might get fat." He reached out his hand and patted Rex on the head. "Be a good boy, Rex. Be good for Sophie."

He turned and hurried to the car as Sophie carried the little dog inside.

Cherry slid into the seat next to him and opened her arms.

Sam scrambled across the seat and into her lap, throwing his arms around her neck.

She hugged him tightly against her. "I'm sorry, Sam. I'm so sorry. I wish we could keep him. We'll come out and visit him all the time. And as soon as we get all this custody stuff figured out, and I find us a suitable place to live, we'll come back out and get him. Okay?"

Sam nodded against her shoulder, his small head bobbing up and down. "I already miss him so much, and it makes it hurt down inside my chest."

"I know, baby. I know."

Sam pulled his head back and looked into her eyes. "Did it hurt like this when you had to give me to a better home?"

She blinked back the tears, but a single one escaped and rolled down her cheek. "Yeah, honey. It felt like this, only about a thousand times worse."

Sam reached up and swiped at the tear on her cheek. He offered her a weak smile, and the knife in her heart twisted once more.

He was trying to be brave for her. "At least we still got each other. Right, Mom?"

Her heart stopped, and her breath caught in her throat.

Time seemed frozen. Frozen in that one still moment when her son called her "mom" for the first time.

All she could do was nod and try not to fall apart.

She took a deep breath. "That's right, Sam. We still got each other." She squeezed him tightly then let him go. "You better get your seat belt on. We've still got work to do at the diner."

Cherry started the car, trying to control the shaking of her hand. She turned on the radio, and neither of them spoke as they drove back in to town. They listened to music, and Sam looked out the window as she concentrated on driving.

Everything in her world had gone to shiz-buckets. She'd lost the man she loved, her business was in shambles, and her home had practically burned down.

But her son had called her "mom."

Everything was going to be okay.

Ten minutes later, she walked into the diner and instructed Sam to go find Stan.

She set to work on the books she'd left piled on the counter. The insurance company had about a zillion forms, and if she didn't complete each one exactly right, they could deny the claim.

Stan emerged from the kitchen a few minutes later and plopped down onto the seat next to her. "Hey, dude. How're you holding up?"

She gave him a tired smile. "I'm okay. Or I'm going to be okay."

He flashed her his easy-going grin. "Yeah, you are. I've known you a long time, and you're one tough chick. Whether you think so or not."

She had told him that morning that she and Taylor were really Sam's birth parents. She didn't know how long it would take the rumor-mill to pick up their juicy piece of gossip, but she wanted Stan to hear it from her first.

He'd reacted with his trademark casual ease, giving her a hug and stating, "That's cool."

Stan wore a red-white-and-blue bandana tied around his forehead doo-rag style. He scratched at the knot at the base of his neck. "So how did it go with the dog?"

"It sucked. Like I mean sucked to the ten-thousandth degree. I'm surprised I'm still sitting here because I think I left my broken heart in little tiny pieces in the Cooper's driveway."

"That bad, huh?"

"Yeah, that bad."

"Sorry, dude." He shrugged. "I wish I had something to make it all better. Too bad we're not in Colorado. They've got 'feel-better brownies' and they're legal."

She laughed. Stan could always make her laugh. "You dork. I don't need that kind of 'feel-better' medicine, but maybe a glass of iced tea would help for now."

"One iced tea coming right up." Stan got up from his seat. "Oh yeah, Russ Johnson called and said he wanted you to call him when you got back. He said he tried your cell but you must have been out of range."

Why had Russ called her?

Had something happened to Taylor?

Cell reception was notoriously bad in Montana, especially if you ventured out of town. They'd been at the Cooper farm for over an hour.

What if Taylor had tried to call her? She pulled out her phone and called Russ's cell.

He picked up on the first ring. "Hello, this is Russ."

His voice sounded so much like Taylor, she almost had to hang up. Her words stuck in her throat, and she couldn't seem to speak.

"Hello? Cherry? You there, darlin'?"

"Yes, I'm here." She swallowed and was thankful when Stan set a glass of iced tea on the counter in front of her. "Stan said you called." She took a sip of the blessedly cool tea.

"Yeah, I just wanted to tell you that I was in town this afternoon, and I dropped Sam's bike off behind the diner. I thought he might want to have it to ride around town."

Cherry smiled at the thoughtfulness of the man who had been so close to being her father-in-law. "Thanks, Russ. That was really nice of you."

"It was no trouble. I just threw it in the back of the truck."

She heard him take a sip of a drink and imagined him sitting on the front porch having his afternoon iced tea and cookie break.

It hurt too much to think about the way Sam would always join him, his small legs swinging from the seat of the rocking chair next to Russ's. Sometimes she would hear them talking, other times they would just sit comfortably together, rocking and eating cookies as Rex lay nearby waiting for the inevitable crumbs to fall from Sam's mouth.

"How are you two getting along? Did you find a place to stay?" Russ asked.

"Oh yeah. We're fine. We got a nice room at the motel in town."

Russ gave a half-hearted laugh. "Well then you must have found a different motel than the one we have in this town, because nobody I know would describe those rooms as nice."

"I'm working on my positive outlook."

"I'm sorry—the way things turned out. I was—pulling for you all." His words cut in and out. He must be walking around the house. Stupid Montana cell reception.

"Thanks. Me, too."

Okay, now just say goodbye. Do NOT ask about him. Don't do it. Actually, just hang up.

"So, how is Taylor? I haven't seen him in town today." She regretted the words the minute they slipped from her mouth.

"No, you wouldn't. I'm sorry, Cherry. He's gone—"

The phone beeped in her ear, and the 'call failed' message flashed on the screen.

Her heart stopped. She couldn't breathe. Couldn't move. Gone?

Cherry set down the phone.

"What's wrong, dude?" Stan asked. "Your face just went white as a sheet."

"Taylor's gone. His dad just told me." She clenched her hands into fists to keep them from shaking. "I knew he needed time alone. He told me he just needed to think. But he's gone. He really left."

Her phone buzzed on the counter, and Russ Johnson's name appeared in the display.

Cherry turned off the phone. She didn't want to talk to him again. Didn't want to hear his excuses for Taylor. They'd been down that road before.

The first time that Taylor left.

She shook her head in disbelief. "I'm just stunned. I wanted to believe in him. Believe that he'd changed. That he wanted Sam and me to be part of his life. But he hasn't changed a bit. He did just what I thought he would. When the times got tough, he bolted."

Stan shook his head. "That surprises me. I thought Taylor was a pretty good dude."

"Well, I guess it shouldn't surprise me." But it did.

Her feelings warred back and forth between disbelief that he actually left and the inevitable certainty that she knew he would do this all along.

Stan rested his hand on her shoulder. "Why don't you go home for the rest of the day?"

She checked her watch. There was still time to make a

couple of calls to the insurance company. "No. I've got work to do. No use crying over spilled milk." Or deserting sheriffs. "I'd rather stay busy. Thanks, though." She smiled bravely at Stan.

Using the cordless land line, she dialed the insurance company's number. It was better to leave her cell phone off and shut out the world of Taylor Johnson.

Two hours later, her head throbbing, she hung up the phone. She'd spoken to three different agencies, trying to get the new stove ordered, installed, and covered by insurance.

Pushing through the door of the kitchen, she called out for Sam. Stan stood at the counter, pages of inventory lists in front of him, and a pencil tucked behind his ear.

He gave Cherry a questioning look. "Sam? Why are you looking for Sam?"

"Why wouldn't I be looking for Sam? I'm finally ready to go home. Poor kid must be exhausted. Thanks for keeping him with you this whole time so I could deal with the stupid stove situation."

The color drained from Stan's face.

"What? What's wrong?" Alarm bells sounded in her gut.

"Cherry, I haven't seen Sam all afternoon. I didn't even know you brought him back with you. I thought you left him at the Cooper farm."

"What? No. When we got here, I sent him back to the kitchen to find you, then you came out to talk to me." She opened the pantry door as she spoke, checking to see if he'd fallen asleep on the floor of the cupboard.

"I swear I haven't seen him all afternoon. I just heard you come in earlier so I came out front to get a pop." He crossed the kitchen. "I'll check the bathrooms."

It didn't take but a few minutes to search the diner, but there was no sign of the boy.

Stan ran out the front door, hollering Sam's name.

Cherry checked the back alley in case he went outside to play, but it was empty as well.

Something about the alley being empty niggled at her mind.

She raked her hands against her forehead.

Where could he have gone?

She reached for her phone and turned it back on, the screen taking forever to come to life.

Two missed calls from Russ Johnson.

Russ. That was it.

She hit the button to call him back, and relief washed through her as she heard him pick up the phone. "Russ, it's me. Listen, did you say you dropped Sam's bike off in the alley behind the diner?"

"Listen, Cherry, I tried to call you back. I wanted to tell you about Taylor—"

She cut him off, her voice rising in alarm. "I don't care about Taylor right now. Tell me about the bike."

"Yeah, I dropped it off in the alley by the back door. Why? What's going on?"

"The bike is missing, and so is Sam." Saying the words out loud was like squeezing a vise around her chest. She couldn't catch her breath.

"I'm on my way," was all Russ said before the line went dead.

Panic swelled like a ball encompassing her chest.

Maybe he was just off riding his bike.

The bell rang above the door, and Stan rushed back in.

"He's not out there. Ed at the Coast to Coast said he thought he saw him riding his bike around, but that was over an hour ago. What can I do?"

"I don't know. I don't know what to do. Oh God, please don't let anything have happened to him." She couldn't think straight. "Just keep looking. See if anyone else has seen him. Maybe he's in someone else's store."

"Got it." Stan hurried back out.

Cherry clutched her chest. Where would Sam go? He only knew a few people in this town. Russ and Sophie and…

Sophie.

Why didn't she think of it before?

Maybe because the Cooper farm was two miles out of town, and she didn't want to imagine Sam riding his bike that far and on the highway.

She quickly called Sophie, and her heart sunk when the girl tentatively answered the phone.

"Sophie, what's wrong?"

Her voice held the quiver of tears ready to fall. "I'm really sorry, Cherry. I don't know what happened. He's just gone."

"Who's gone? Sophie, is Sam with you?"

"Sam, no." She sucked in a breath, as she started to cry. "It's Rex. I think he ran away. I thought he would be okay tied up in the yard while I took a shower. I thought he would rather be outside playing. He couldn't have been out there more than fifteen or twenty minutes at the most."

"Sophie, listen to me, it's okay. I don't think Rex ran away."

"You don't?" She took a deep, shuddering breath.

"No. Not unless he learned how to untie himself. Sam is

missing, and so is his bike. I think he might have ridden out there and freed Rex."

"Oh no. Poor Sam. I'll tell my dad and Charlie. What can we do to help?"

Think, dammit. She needed to figure this out.

Pushing down the panic, Cherry took a breath. "Okay, yes, get your dad or Charlie, or whoever and drive into town, to the diner. Watch for any signs of Sam or Rex on the road. Maybe he's still riding down the highway."

"Okay. We'll leave now. And I'll call you if we see him."

The thought of Sam out on the highway terrified her. Trucks whizzed down that road all day. What if someone hit him? Or he ran off the road and was lying in a ditch, hurt or bleeding?

What if someone saw him and, God forbid, took him?

The panic was back as every horrible thought filled my mind. She fought to stop the unthinkable images of what could happen to a young boy alone.

She sank into a chair, unable to think of what to do next.

All she could do was pray. *Please God. Please God. Keep him safe. Keep my son safe.*

A sob escaped her as she heard a siren in the distance. The keening wail drew closer as a squad car came flying down Main Street and skidded to a stop in front of the diner. Through the window, she saw Taylor bolt from the car, his face a mask of pain and fear.

The front door crashed open, and Taylor burst into the diner. "Where's Sam? Where is my son?"

Chapter Twenty-One

Taylor tried to contain the rush of panic as he watched the blood drain from Cherry's face.

He crossed the room in three long, quick strides and knelt in front of her. "What happened, Cherry? Where's Sam?"

Her eyes glazed over, as she shook her head slowly back and forth. "I don't know. I don't know where he is." Her voice choked on a sob, and she fell apart.

He swept her into his arms and pulled her against his chest. "It's okay. We're going to find him. I need you to take a breath and tell me what happened."

She nodded, quick little bobs of her head as he watched her try to catch her breath. "We took Rex out to the Cooper's farm this afternoon so Sam could give the dog to Sophie."

"Give the dog to Sophie? Why? He loves that dog."

"Because Reed claims Rex is dangerous and is threatening to use that against us in the custody fight. And because the manager of the motel said we can't have a dog staying there with us."

"Why didn't you bring the dog to me or my dad? We would have kept him."

A sharp look of pain crossed Cherry's face.

"That doesn't matter. What happened after you left the dog there?"

She told him how they'd come back to the diner and how she'd thought Sam was in the kitchen with Stan. "I just got caught up in these dang calls with the insurance agency. I thought he was with Stan." She buried her face in her hands. "Maybe I'm *not* fit to raise him. Maybe he should live with Reed and Olivia."

His heart broke at the way her shoulders shook with sobs. "Hey, look at me."

She shook her head back and forth, her hair a curtain across her face.

He gripped her shoulders. "Cherry. Look at me."

She tilted her head up, pain and misery evident in her eyes.

"I've seen you with Sam the last several weeks and you *are* a good mother. The best. And even more than that. You are *Sam's* mother. And the only one he has left." He swiped at the tears on her face. "And right now, I need you to get it together and be the strong feisty Cherry that I know who doesn't back down from trouble and who doesn't back down from a fight."

She nodded slowly, and he was encouraged by the look of determination entering her eyes.

"Yeah. Okay. You're right. I'm okay."

He watched her swallow then push back her shoulders as she took a deep breath. "I'm okay."

He passed her the half-full glass of iced tea setting on the counter. He had no idea if the drink was hers, and he didn't care.

Evidently neither did she.

She gulped down a swallow then set the glass back on the counter. It must have helped because her eyes were clearer, and she looked more focused.

"Now tell me what else you know about Sam."

"I know that your dad dropped off his bike in the alley, and now it's gone. I know that Sophie tied Rex up in the yard, and now he's gone, too. I'm assuming that unless Rex has learned how to untie a knot, that Sam rode his bike out to the Coopers' and took the dog. Sophie was going to get her dad to drive them into town and look for him on the road." Her eyes started to go glassy again. "Oh Taylor, what if he gets hit by a car or someone takes him?"

"Get it together, Cherry." His voice was probably more firm than it needed to be, but he needed her to stay strong, and it seemed to help her focus. "We're going to go with the assumption that he's on his way back here."

He only wished he felt as calm as he was acting.

He tilted his head and spoke into the mic clipped to his shoulder. "Dispatch, this is double Charlie fifty-two, I need you to issue a BOLO for a Caucasian male, eight years old, blond hair, possibly on a bicycle. Possibly on highway nine. Probably has a small brown dog with him."

"Dispatch responding to Charlie fifty-two. BOLO issued for Caucasian male, eight years old, blond hair."

Cherry's cell phone buzzed, and she made a frantic grab for it. "It's Sophie. Hello, Sophie. Did you find him?" Her face fell, and he knew the answer. "Okay, keep me posted.

And thank you."

She hung up. "Zack and Sophie drove all the way into town and didn't see him. They're going to keep driving around looking for him."

He nodded. "My dad is out driving around, too. He's the one who called and told me Sam was missing. He's probably rallied half the town by now to be on the lookout." He pulled out his notebook. "Tell me everything that happened between last night and today. Could this be as simple as he went after the dog, and he's on his way back, or do you think he actually ran away?"

Cherry's hand flew to her mouth. "Last night. At the motel. He told me a story about a knight and a dragon. And the evil king banished the dragon. And they ran away."

"Does Sam see me as the evil king?" What a stupid question. Plus he shouldn't be worried about stuff like that right now, but it bothered him. And bugged him that a stupid story could hurt his feelings.

"What? No. The evil king was Reed or Mike, the motel manager, or a combination of both. That part doesn't matter. The part that worries me is that the knight and the dragon ran away together."

He hated to admit how relieved he was not to play the villain in Sam's story.

He focused on his questions. "Think back over last night and today. Who you talked to and what you said. Was there anything that Sam could have overheard or misinterpreted? Anything that would make him want to run away?"

She shook her head. "No. Not that I can think of. Like I said, I was on the phone most of the afternoon with the insurance company and ordering the new stove. In fact, I turned off my phone after I talked to your dad."

"Wait, you talked to my dad. What about?"

"He called to tell me that he dropped off Sam's bike and—" she looked away, unable to meet his eye, "—and that you were gone. That you'd left." Her eyes widened, and she gasped. "I told Stan that you were gone. That you had left town. Left me. Maybe Sam overheard."

Anger flared in his gut. "What the hell are you talking about? I didn't leave."

"Your dad said you were gone. I told him I hadn't seen you in town today, and he said that's because you were gone."

"Well, hell. I *was* gone. I had a domestic violence call out on the edge of the county. I left town today, but I didn't actually *leave* town. I was coming back. Why wouldn't my dad tell you that part?"

Tears filled her eyes. "Because I didn't give him a chance. I hung up after he said you were gone. He tried to call me back, but I'd turned off my phone."

The anger sparked, fueling his already heated temper. "And then you bad-mouthed me to Stan. In front of Sam."

Maybe he *was* the bad guy in Sam's story. Or he would be now.

She held up her hands. "No. I didn't. At least I don't think I did."

"Tell me." His voice sounded more like a growl. "Tell me everything you said."

"I told him that you were gone. And that I was surprised you left. That I thought you just needed some time to be alone. Time to think."

He held up his hand. Something about her words triggered something. A memory. "Hold on." He took a deep breath and slowly counted to ten.

There was something there. Something he was missing. A clue. He just had to calm down enough to grab it. He replayed her words in his head. *Some time to be alone. Some time to think.*

He snapped his fingers. "I've got it. I know where he is. When I took him fishing at my grandparent's cabin, I told him it was a great place to be alone. A place to go when you needed to think. I bet he went up to the cabin to find me."

Cherry bolted from her seat. "Let's go."

He held out an arm. "Wait. Someone needs to stay here, in case he comes back."

The door of the diner burst opened, and Russ hurried in.

Cherry ran to him and threw her arms around his waist.

Taylor had just a moment of slight jealousy that she hadn't reacted that way when he'd come through the door.

But she'd also been pretty close to a state of shock.

He didn't have time for these petty thoughts right now. "I'm glad you're here, Dad. Can you stay at the diner? In case Sam comes back. Or if anyone finds him, they'd be more likely to bring him here."

Russ nodded solemnly. "Of course. I'll do whatever I can to help. I'd hoped that he might be headed for the ranch, but I didn't see him anywhere on the road out to our place. Where are you headed?"

Taylor took Cherry's arm. "We think he might be headed up to Gramp's cabin. It's just a hunch, but we're gonna go check it out."

"I trust your hunches, son." Russ pulled open the front door. "I'll hold down the fort, and I've got half the town on the lookout for him." He grabbed Taylor's shoulder as he passed. "Don't worry. We're gonna find him."

He nodded at his dad, unwilling to trust his voice. Knowing it would betray the depth of emotion he felt for his father and his support.

Instead, he hustled Cherry toward the squad car and raced to slide inside. He started the engine and threw the car into gear. The cabin was close to two miles out of town.

He headed toward the city limits.

The mic on his shoulder squawked. "Double Charlie fifty-two, this is Dispatch. Do you copy?"

"Copy that, Dispatch. This is Double Charlie fifty-two."

"Listen, Sheriff, we might have a lead on that missing kid. A couple of guys were just in the Gas-n-Go west of town and claim they saw a boy riding his bike up Highway 5. Said they thought he had a dog with him."

Bingo. The cabin was off Highway 5.

He pressed the gas pedal closer to the floor. "Roger that, Dispatch. We're going that direction now. We think he might be headed to a fishing cabin up that way. I'll check in when I know more."

"Dispatch standing by."

Cherry's knuckles were white as she clasped her hands together in her lap.

He reached over and took her hand. Like it or not, he still loved her, and they were in this thing together. "We're gonna find him."

Cherry faced forward, her eyes trained on the sides of the road. A single tear rolled down her cheek, and his heart splintered into a thousand pieces.

He squeezed her hand and pressed harder on the accelerator.

"I want to get there, too," Cherry said. "But don't go too fast. I don't want to miss him if he's stuck on the side of the road."

She said "stuck" on the road, but he knew she was worried that it might be worse. Much worse. The bends in this road could conceal a small boy on his bike. If someone came around the corner too fast, and Sam were riding in the road, he could easily get hit or run off the highway.

He shuddered and eased back on the gas, watching the sides of the road for any signs of a boy, a bike, or a dog.

They made it to the cabin turn-off without seeing any signs of him.

Taylor turned and drove down the driveway toward the cabin.

"There!" Cherry pointed. "There's his bike." She had the door open and was getting out of the car before he'd even come to a full stop.

Relief flooded him as he saw the familiar red bike leaning up against the side of the cabin. That little turd. He'd ridden all the way up here by himself.

He slammed the door to the car. Cherry had run around to the front of the cabin, and he heard her calling Sam's name.

But he didn't hear any reply. And he didn't hear her exclamation of joy and relief signaling that she'd found him.

She appeared at the corner of the cabin, alarm etched on her face. "He isn't here. How could he not be here? His bike is here."

Taylor examined the bike. It was definitely Sam's.

"I tried the front door, but the cabin's still locked. And none of the windows are broken," she said. "I don't think he went inside."

He scanned the woods around the cabin.

He'd been in law enforcement for several years and grown up in these woods. Using his tracking skills, he followed the trail of crushed grass and broken branches that led away from Sam's bike. "He went this way."

Cherry stuck closely on his heels as he charted the path of the boy and the dog.

They came to the creek, and he lost their trail. His gaze searched the banks of the river for any signs that they'd crossed the creek.

Taylor prayed that the boy hadn't crossed the water and headed up the hills on the other side of the creek.

Who knew what Sam would encounter in those woods? Growing up in these parts, he'd seen bears, mountain lions, and too many nasty rattlesnakes in those hills.

Dusk was settling in, which made it harder for him to see. And he felt an uneasiness settle in his chest as he thought of Sam being out in these hills alone after dark. He nervously paced the bank of the river, searching.

There. A bare spot in the dirt where a boy might have scrambled up. A grouping of rocks crossed the creek in front of the eroded spot on the bank, and he assumed that's where Sam would have crossed.

"I think he crossed the creek here and scrambled up that bank." He pointed to the rocks in the water.

"Let's go then." She barged ahead, but he took her hand to help her across the slick stones in the creek.

Water from the creek splashed against his boots as he stepped across the rocks. He gave her a boost, and she climbed the side of the bank. Red streaks of dirt covered her legs, and mud stuck to her tennis shoes.

Thank goodness she hadn't been wearing those stupid flip-flops today.

He stood at the top of the bank and looked across the wooded hill. Why would Sam cross the creek?

He tried to think. Had he told Sam that he had roamed these hills when he was a kid? Or had he said that he liked to come up here and walk when he needed to clear his mind?

He searched his memories, trying to recall their conversations the day they'd gone fishing. Remembered telling him he liked to hike here.

He suddenly remembered making a plan to bring Sam hiking later that summer. To bring him up to see the cave.

The cave! That was it.

"Cherry, I think I know where he's headed. I just remembered that I told him how I used to hike around up here as a kid and that I'd bring him up here later to show him the cave."

"The cave? Why would you tell him about the cave?"

He'd brought Cherry to the cave numerous times when they were in high school. Was she thinking of the many times they'd laid on the floor of that cave, curled together in a sleeping bag, kissing and touching in teenaged frenzy?

The angry look on her face told him that she was not fondly reminiscing any times with him right now. "Why the heck would you tell an eight-year-old boy about a cave? That's like winning a golden ticket to the mind of a young boy."

Was she pissed at him? For an innocent conversation he'd had while they were fishing? "How was I supposed to know he'd try to come up here by himself? We were just talking. Are you seriously blaming me for this?"

She sighed. "I don't know."

He stepped closer to her and wrapped an arm around her waist.

She resisted for a moment then let him fold her into his arms. He rested his chin on her head. "Listen, babe, there's plenty of blame to go around. But tossing blame and accusations doesn't help us find Sam. Let's just focus on that right now, okay?"

Her hands gripped the cloth of his shirt tightly, but she nodded against his chest.

He tipped her chin up to look at him. "What do you say we go get our boy?"

"Yeah, okay." She let him go and turned to trudge up the hill.

He followed, searching the trees and the ground for signs that the boy had passed through.

She froze. "Did you hear that? I thought I heard a dog bark."

He stopped, his senses alert for any sounds.

He heard the soft whistling of the night breeze as it blew through the leaves of the trees and he heard the trill of a chickadee. He trained his ear to listen for anything out of the ordinary.

Then he heard the dog bark. Once. A loud, sharp yelp. Then more barking followed by the frantic screams of a child.

Pulling his gun from the holster, he raced up the hill toward the sound.

Chapter Twenty-Two

Cherry raced behind Taylor, her lungs burning from running up the steep hill. They crested the top, and her heart stopped.

Sam was there, tucked in between two rocks. Rex was on the ground in front of him, racing back and forth. And barking at a large black bear.

The dog's constant barking only seemed to upset the bear as it swiped its paw in the air toward Sam.

Rex jumped up, and the bear's giant paw caught him in the side. The dog yelped in pain then lay motionless on the ground.

Sam screamed and tried to run for the dog, but the bear stepped toward him, huffing with aggression.

"Sam, get back," Taylor yelled as he pointed his gun in the air and fired a shot.

The sound of the gunfire ripped through the air.

Mustering up her loudest voice, Cherry screamed at the

bear. "Go on. Get out of here."

Taylor fired again, and the bear lumbered off up the side of the hill.

He ran for Sam, then grabbed the boy and lifted him into his arms.

She was only seconds behind him and threw her arms around them both, burying her face in Sam's small shoulder. Pulling back, she searched his body for signs of injury. "Are you okay? Are you hurt?"

Sam looked over her shoulder, and his face contorted in pain. "Rex! He's bleeding. Taylor help him."

She looked down at the dog lying motionless on the ground, his fur matted with bright red blood.

Oh no.

Taylor set Sam down and bent over the dog. "He's got a pretty bad cut down his side. He's still bleeding." He pulled off his uniform shirt and pressed it against the wound.

"Taylor! Help him!" Sam's voice rose to a frantic level and tears streamed down his face. "Don't let him die. Please."

Taylor looked up at her, a question in his eyes.

There was no decision.

"Go," she said. "Run. Take him down the hill. You can go faster on your own. Take him to Zack. We'll hike down and wait for you at the cabin."

"No way. I can't leave you up here by yourselves."

"The heck you can't. I've grown up in these woods. And I can practically see the cabin from here. We can certainly walk down a hill on our own. And I'm not asking you, I'm telling you." She raised her voice in command. "Take the dog and go."

"Take him, Taylor. You have to save him." Sam was

pushing at his legs.

He picked up the little dog and cradled him against his chest, wrapping the ends of the shirt around his little body.

He gave her a nod. "Take care of Sam. Call my dad to come out and get you. And I'll radio him from the cruiser, too."

"We'll be fine," Cherry told him. "Just go."

He turned and raced down the hill.

Please let him get the dog to Zack on time. Please don't let that little dog die.

She picked up Sam's hand. "Taylor will do everything he can."

Sam nodded. "He's a fast runner. He'll save him, right? Right, Mom?"

She couldn't take the heartbreak in his voice. "I hope so, Sam. I know he will try his hardest."

It was getting dark, and they needed to get back down to the cabin.

"Are you hurt at all, or can you walk down okay?" She bent down on one knee and inspected his clothes. His pant legs were encrusted with dried mud, and he had a long scratch down his arm. She picked a dead leaf out of his hair.

"I'm okay. I'm pretty tough for being eight."

He didn't look tough.

He looked small and vulnerable, and she thanked God that they found him and he was okay. "Listen Sam, you can't *ever* run away like that again. You scared us so bad. We didn't know what happened to you, and we've got the whole town looking for you."

Sam looked confused. "I didn't run away. I wouldn't leave you. I just came here looking for Taylor. He said this is where he goes to think, and he told me he likes to hike up here when he needs to figure stuff out. I knew he would be here. And I wanted to tell him not to leave us."

How could she argue with that? She wanted to tell Taylor not to leave them, too.

"He wasn't at the cabin so I thought he must be hiking. And he told me about the cave, so I was trying to find it."

She told Taylor that dang cave was too much of a temptation. "I appreciate that you wanted to help, but you should have told me, and I would have driven you. Taking your bike and riding out by yourself was dangerous. You could have been hit by a car or...worse."

She didn't know if Stacy had had the "stranger-danger" talk with him yet. She didn't want to scare him right now by putting thoughts of evil kidnappers in his head.

"I'm sorry. I didn't mean for anyone to get upset. I just wanted to help. I already lost my mom and dad. I didn't want to lose Taylor, too."

His chin bent all the way to his chest, and Cherry's insides twisted with all the pain that this poor little boy had had to endure the last month.

She pulled him into a hug. "I know. I don't want to lose him, either."

Sam dropped his head and spoke softly into her shoulder. "If I wouldn't have done this, Rex would still be okay. It's my fault that he got hurt."

She pulled back and took his chin in her hand. "Sam, listen to me. You shouldn't have run off like you did, but Rex getting hurt was not your fault. And it really wasn't the bear's fault, either. He was just doing what comes natural to him. And Rex was trying to protect you."

"But he got hurt because of me."

"No, he just got hurt. It was an accident. And accidents sometimes just happen. We don't always understand when people get hurt or even when they die. Sometimes things just happen."

He scuffed his tennis shoes into a pile of leaves, avoiding her eyes. "You mean like with my parents?"

"Yes, like with your parents."

He tipped his head back, looking her in the eye. His voice trembled with emotion. "Is Rex gonna die?"

"I hope not." She pulled her cell phone from her pocket. No bars. No surprise.

She knew cell reception was terrible out here and hoped it would be better the closer they got to the cabin. "Let's get back down to the cabin. As soon as I can get reception again, we can call Russ to come and get us. And call Taylor to check on Rex. Okay?"

Sam nodded and trudged down the hill in front of her. It was getting dark, but there was still plenty of light to see by. She wasn't as concerned about the bear coming back as she was about poor Rex.

It didn't take them long to reach the creek, and she helped Sam across. They headed for the cabin. Taylor had told her where they hid the key so they could go inside to wait for Russ.

She pulled her cell out again. A few bars showed, and she tried Taylor's number. It went straight to voicemail. If he were still driving, it would probably be too much to take care of the dog and answer the phone.

She tried Russ's cell next.

He picked up right away. "Cherry, did you find him?"

"Yes, we found him at the cabin. He's okay."

She heard him breathe a sigh of relief then relay the message to the others in the diner. "They found him. He's okay."

A cheer went up in the background, and she smiled at the support of the town.

Small towns also had their advantages. The members of the town might know all of your business, but they could also be counted on to be there for you when you needed them.

She turned away from Sam and lowered her voice. "So, Sam did ride out to get Rex before he came to the cabin."

"I figured he did, the little stinker. I'll call Sophie to let her know that the dog's okay, too."

"Well, actually the dog might not be okay. Rex was trying to protect Sam from a bear and got hurt in the process. Taylor is taking him to Zack right now. Sam and I are still at the cabin. Is there any chance you could come out here and pick us up?"

"What? Taylor left you at the cabin by yourselves?"

Cherry lowered her voice. "We told him to. Rex was hurt pretty bad. We knew Taylor could move faster without us and get the dog to Zack. We didn't care about waiting here by ourselves. We just want the dog to be okay."

"Okay, I get it. And of course I'll come get you. I'll leave now and be there in ten minutes."

"Thanks, Russ. We'll wait inside. Can you tell Stan to lock up the diner and go home?"

"Sure. See you in a few minutes."

Cherry hung up the phone and turned back to Sam. "Russ's on his way out to get us. Let's find the key, and we can wait inside the cabin."

The sound of a car coming drew both their attention.

A familiar black Denali was speeding down the driveway.
What the heck is Reed doing here?

How would he have even known about Sam running off? How could word have traveled that fast?

And how could he have known that they would be at the cabin?

The car came to a shuddering stop, and Reed threw the car door open. He wore an angry look on his face as he marched toward her. "What the hell were you thinking? I knew this was too much for you to handle."

He reached Sam and knelt down to bring him into an uncharacteristic embrace. "You okay, buddy?"

A tiny flutter of compassion beat in her heart. Reed could be a total ass-wad, but he really did love Sam.

Olivia had been slower to exit the car, but she joined Reed in hugging Sam.

"I'm okay, Uncle Reed."

"Well, you scared the daylights out of us." His angry tone was back. "Don't you ever run away like that again."

The compassion she'd been feeling for Reed disappeared in a flash. It was one thing for her to scold Sam for running away, it was another for this jerk to be yelling at him.

"I already talked to him, Reed," she said. "He's not going to do it again."

Reed stood and pointed a finger at her chest. "You're damn right he's not going to do it again. Because he's not going to have the chance. I knew it was a mistake to even let you bring him here. You're not even responsible enough to take care of yourself. How could you have let him out of your sight for long enough for him to ride his bike all over this damn county?"

"I thought he was with Stan. It was just a mistake."

"The mistake was in letting you have Sam for the last several weeks. This is the last straw, Cherry. This proves that you're not capable of handling him on your own."

"I'm not on my own," she said, even though she knew she was. "I have Taylor—"

Reed sneered at her. "Don't give me that Taylor bullshit line. I already know the two of you split, and you and Sam are staying at that piece of crap motel on Highway 9. Sam's probably got lice by now."

"I don't have lice," Sam said.

Olivia was peering at his head, her nose wrinkled in disgust.

"Of course you don't," Cherry told him, avoiding the subject of the motel. "Uncle Reed is just making a joke and not a very funny one."

"Can Uncle Reed take us to get Rex now?"

"Rex? That scruffy little dog? I thought I told you to get rid of that mutt."

His accusations were really starting to piss her off. "We did. That's why Sam took off. We left the dog with a friend who lives out on a farm, and Sam took off so he could go out to get the dog back."

"But now he's hurt," Sam explained. "He was trying to protect me from a bear, and he got scratched, and he was bleeding a lot."

A red flush moved up Reed's neck to his face, and he turned to Cherry in fury. "Is he really telling me that he was almost mauled by a bear? That's it. This is over. You've given me more than enough ammunition to gain custody of Sam."

He turned to his wife. "Olivia, put Sam in the car."

Olivia stood frozen in place, as if unsure of her husband's command.

Cherry took a step forward, but Reed blocked her way. "What do you think you're doing? You're not taking Sam anywhere."

Reed clamped a hand roughly on her arm. He spoke through gritted teeth. "Olivia, I said put Sam in the car right now."

Olivia ducked her head, and Cherry almost felt sorry for her, always having to put up with Reed's bullying tactics.

But her few ounces of pity dried up when Olivia grabbed Sam's hand and led him to the SUV.

He looked small and bewildered. "Where are we going? I don't think I want to go with you."

Cherry lowered her voice and narrowed her eyes at her cousin. "Do NOT do this, Reed. I will *not* let you take him from me."

She pushed against her cousin's body. He didn't have Taylor's muscles, but Reed was solid and strong, and his fingers tightened on her arm.

He turned his head to Sam. "Get in the car, Sam. We'll take you to get your dog, then we'll go get ice cream."

Sam reluctantly moved toward the car. "Is Cherry coming with us?"

Olivia ignored his question, as she opened the car door and boosted Sam in.

She pleaded with her cousin. "You're scaring him. And me."

Reed had always been a bully, but she'd never seen him

like this. A chill ran through her at the icy glare he gave her.

"I don't know what my sister was thinking when she named you Sam's guardian. But I am his uncle, his next closest relative, and I will fight you in every court to see that you do not gain custody of this boy."

Her fear crossed into anger.

She was actually Sam's closest blood relative, but she wasn't ready to share that with her cousin yet.

And now wasn't the time for anger. She needed to try to get control of this situation. To diffuse her cousin's temper, not spark it further.

She tried once more for rational, trying to keep the tremor out of her voice and sound as calm as possible. "This is not the way to do this. You're just making it worse on Sam. Why don't we all get together when everyone has settled down? We can talk this through and come up with an arrangement that will make everyone happy."

"What you fail to understand is that I don't give a shit about your happiness. I care about that kid and making sure he doesn't get stuck growing up here in this piss-ant town with you as a single mother. You're a joke, Cherry. You live in a run-down, piece of shit apartment, and you spend your days serving pie to old farmers who leer at your tits then leave you nickel tips. Your mom took off on you, and your dad was a drunk. You have nothing to offer to the kid, and I won't let my only nephew grow up to be the clichéd subject of a country-western song."

Who did he think he was? Emotion choked her throat as she fought to deny that most of what he'd said was true.

Except that she had nothing to offer Sam. She *did* have something to offer him. She had love. Buckets and bushels and baskets of love.

Love to the moon and back.

And she loved that boy with the ferocity of a mother bear.

That fierceness welled inside of her now. Anger and strength filled her.

She would not back down. Not again.

And she would not let Reed bully her.

Not anymore.

She pulled at her arm, trying to yank it free. "Reed, let go of me. Right now." She drew her phone from her pocket. "I'll call the police."

He slapped the phone from her hand, and it bounced into the tall grass. "You can call whoever you want. You're missing the big picture, cousin. You are a nobody who doesn't even have two nickels to rub together. I have wealth and power on my side. I'm a lawyer who owns a nice house and has a wife. No one is going to side with you against me."

His fingers dug tighter into her arm, as he loomed over her.

It didn't matter. Didn't matter if he was six feet tall or ten feet tall. She was fighting for her son. She struggled to free herself from his grasp. "We're not kids anymore, and you don't get to push me around."

He sneered down at her, his face ugly with contempt. "You're wrong. That's exactly what I get to do. And there's nothing you can do about it."

Then he actually pushed her.

Shoved her with enough force that she stumbled back, losing her balance and fell to the ground.

She landed hard on her rump, scraping her hands on the

gravel as she tried to gain purchase.

Her teeth knocked together when she hit the ground, and she tasted the coppery tang of blood as she bit her tongue.

Reed turned and raced for the SUV, climbing in and slamming the door. He threw the car in reverse and backed up, then slammed it into gear and took off, spraying gravel as his tires spun in the soft dirt.

Sam pounded at the window, yelling her name.

She scrambled to her feet, the blood rushing to her head. She chased after the car, her lungs burning as she sprinted toward it.

But it was no use. The car sped down the driveway and turned onto the highway.

And it was gone.

Sam was gone.

Chapter Twenty-Three

Taylor turned into the driveway of the cabin.

His dad had called to say that he was heading to pick up Cherry and Sam, and Taylor had asked him to come to the vet clinic instead. He'd rather have his dad wait around for the dog and let him get back out to his family.

And he knew that Cherry and Sam were his family. It didn't matter that she'd lied.

Well, it did matter.

But he could forgive her. Because that's what you do when you love someone.

You forgive them.

Falling in love was a risky business. You had to put it all out there. Take a chance by offering someone your heart, knowing that they could cherish it or stomp on it.

And Cherry had done both.

She had both treasured his love and torn his heart to shreds.

But the great thing about the heart is its incredible power to heal. He hadn't been sure if he could forgive her. If he could let go of the hurt and betrayal.

Until he got the call that Sam was missing. And then all he wanted, all he needed, was to be with her. When he walked into the diner and saw her sitting in that chair, he knew.

He knew none of the other stuff mattered.

Only her.

She and Sam were his everything. And he didn't care what he had to do to prove that to them. To prove that he was staying.

That he was going to fight for them.

He knew Cherry was scared of him leaving, and he shuddered at his earlier thoughts of how easy it would be to just take off.

But he didn't.

He didn't fill a suitcase or pack a bag. Hell, he hadn't even packed a lunch for the day. Because he knew in his heart that he was staying. That all he wanted was to be a dad to a precious eight-year-old boy and to have a wild redhead curled against his side every night.

What the hell?

Through the windshield, he could see that redhead now, but he couldn't figure out what the heck she was doing. She appeared to be looking for something as she crawled frantically around in the grass in front of the cabin.

Her red hair was a mass of tangles, and her lips were moving as if she were talking to herself. By the look on her face, she wasn't saying anything nice.

Taylor parked the car and stepped out.

"Mother-F-er. Penis-hole. Asshole. Ass-face. Ass-wipe. Scumbag."

Yep. She was swearing all right. A laundry list of hostile titles fell from her mouth.

"Cherry, are you okay there, darlin'?"

She looked up at him, and he swore his heart stopped.

"What the hell happened to you?" He rushed forward and knelt beside her. Salty tear-tracks showed through the dirt on her face, and dried blood crusted the corner of her mouth. Her upper arm was a mess of dark bruises, and her hands and arms were scraped up.

"Taylor, help me find my phone. I have to call the police." Her eyes held that glassy look that told him she was probably in shock.

He spied her phone in the grass and picked it up.

He couldn't have been gone more than twenty minutes. What had happened here while he was gone?

He reached to grab her arm and realized the bruises were shaped like a large hand. Fury filled him at the thought of someone touching her.

He lowered his voice, containing all the anger and fear he felt, and calmly took her hand. "Cherry, I *am* the police. And right now, I need you to take a deep breath, and tell me what's going on. Where's Sam?"

She blinked up at him, and her eyes cleared as if she just realized he was here. She threw herself into his arms. "Reed. That mother-f-ing arrogant asshole Reed Hill. He took Sam. We need to call someone." She thrust back and pushed to her feet. "We need to go get him."

Cherry turned and ran to the cruiser. She threw open the door and jumped in the front seat.

Taylor ran after her, comprehending her frantic words as he leaped into action.

Reed *took* Sam?

That bastard.

Cherry could add that one to her list.

He started the ignition and got the car turned around and headed back to the highway. "Tell me everything, Cherry. Where is he taking him?"

She shook her head. "I don't know. Home, I guess. Yes, I'm sure he's taking him back to Great Falls."

Taylor turned that direction and stepped on the gas. His speedometer inched to ninety as he flew down the highway.

He passed her a half-empty water bottle that had been stuck between the seats. "Here. Drink some of this. I need you to focus. Sam is counting on us."

She nodded and drank some water. She took a deep breath and pushed her bangs out of her eyes. "Okay. Okay. You're right. I'm all right. I lost it there for a few, but I'm back. I would do anything for Sam."

"I know you would. Take another sip."

She took one more drink then screwed the lid back on the bottle. "I'm good now. I'm ready to tear that bastard cousin of mine a new one."

And there it was. He knew "bastard" would eventually make the list. "How much of a lead does he have on us?"

She shook her head. "I don't know. I didn't know what to do. He showed up at the cabin with Olivia, and he was so angry. I can't figure out how he even knew Sam was missing, let alone that we were at the cabin."

He grimaced. "I can. I was talking to my dispatcher on the way back out here, and she told me that she'd overheard one of my deputies in his office on the phone. She said he was talking to a guy named Reed, and that he'd been telling him about Sam and giving him directions to the fishing cabin. I guess she flat out confronted him, and he said Reed was an old classmate of his and that he owed him a favor."

He would deal with the deputy later. He wasn't about to put up with that kind of disloyalty on his force. He reached for Cherry's hand. "I'm sorry. I had no idea I had a spy in my own camp."

She squeezed his hand back. "It's not your fault. Knowing Reed, he probably has something he's holding over the guy."

He sped past a blue pickup. "I don't understand how he took Sam."

"Neither do I. He said some terrible things to me, and he told Olivia to put Sam in the car. I tried to stop him. I swear I did. Sam was screaming, and I tried to fight him. But he shoved me back, and I fell. And then he took off. I ran after the truck. I don't know what I thought I was going to do, grab the bumper and hang on, I guess."

"Why didn't you call me?"

"I tried. Reed knocked the phone from my hands. After they turned out of the driveway, I ran back and was searching for the phone. I couldn't remember exactly where I'd been standing. I don't know how long I was searching before you got there."

Rage flared in him, and he wanted to punch Reed Hill in the throat. "Your cousin is a bully."

"I know. He has been his whole life. And I swear to you, Taylor. This is it. This is the last straw. I'm done backing down to him. Sam is my son, and I will do whatever it takes to fight for him."

There she was. That was the Cherry Hill that he knew. "Correction. Sam is *our* son. And you're not in this fight alone. I'm right beside you."

"I thought you needed time to think. Time to be alone."

"I've had time. And I'm sick of thinking. Too much thinking just gets you in trouble. I love you, and I love Sam."

He shook his head. "I can't believe I'm declaring my love for you while we're flying down the highway at ninety-five miles an hour. It's not very romantic. But maybe that's what love is supposed to be like. Like this highway, where sometimes you're just steadily driving along, and it's easy, and sometimes you're flying down the road at break-neck speed, heart racing, hitting bumps and hoping you don't crash. Maybe being in love is like one big long road trip."

Squeezing her hand, he kept talking, afraid to look at her. Afraid if he paused, he wouldn't get out what he wanted to say.

What he *needed* to say.

He felt like his words were coming out as fast as they were hurtling down the road. But he couldn't stop. "And I don't want to be taking this trip alone. Alone sucks. I want you in this car with me. You and Sam. Playing the music too loud and obnoxiously telling me when I miss a turn. I want a messy car filled with toys and snack foods and laughter. But I'll tell you what I don't want. I don't want to miss this trip. I don't want to miss my chance to be on this road with you."

He stole a glance at her. She had turned in her seat, and her eyes were filled with tears.

And filled with love.

Love for him.

He recognized that look. Had dreamed about seeing

that look in her eyes again.

He cleared his throat, swallowing back the deep emotion that had settled there. "So, are you okay with that?"

"I guess that depends." Her voice was light, teasing.

"Depends on what?"

"If you agree to sometimes let me drive."

He grinned. "Okay, it's a deal. I will sometimes let you drive."

She smiled and squeezed his hand. "And sometimes you'll let me play with the siren."

He laughed and gave her a naughty grin. "Babe, you can play with whatever you want."

She let loose a hearty laugh, and it was music to his ears.

Keeping his eyes on the road, he reached up and cupped his hand around her neck. He ran his thumb along her cheek. "So, we're okay then?"

She tilted her face, and laid a tender kiss against the knuckles of his hand. "Yes, we're okay."

A shiver of sensation ran through him at the feel of her lips on his skin. He hazarded another glance her way.

She smiled at him, and he was sunk.

Yeah, he had it bad. And he was in this thing all the way up to his ears. He grinned back. "You are ridiculously beautiful."

"Not hardly." Putting a hand to her tangled hair, she pulled down the visor of the passenger seat and gasped as she caught a glance at herself in the mirror. "I can't believe you took pictures of me looking like this."

She scrubbed at the dirt on her face and opened the glove box of his car. "Do you have some napkins or something in here? I should at least wash the blood off my face before we get there."

She found a stack of napkins and used the water bottle to wet a couple and wash her face. "Nice shirt by the way."

He looked down at the yellow T-shirt he was wearing. The words, Cooper Veterinary Clinic, were printed on the right breast side. "Zack gave me a shirt to wear when I got to the clinic. I'm sure he'll tack it on to my bill."

She took a deep breath. "I'm almost afraid to ask about Rex. Was Zack able to save him?"

"Yeah, he said the wounds were superficial, and he should be able to just stitch him up. He'd lost a lot of blood, and it's good that we got him there so quickly. I left my dad there to wait with him so I could come back for you and Sam. Now I'm kicking myself for leaving you guys alone."

"Don't do that. You did the right thing. Saving Rex was the most important thing to do at the time. Reed might have taken Sam but he's okay. Reed's not gonna hurt him."

"But he hurt you."

"I'm okay, too. Actually I'm more than okay. I've backed down to my cousin my whole life. He's always used bullying and scare tactics, and they worked. Until today. Today I had something important enough to fight for, and I stood up to him. For the first time in my life, I stood up to him. And I'm okay."

"Have you seen the bruises he left on your arm?"

She held out her arm and winced at the purplish marks. "Yeah, those are pretty bad. But they're just bruises. They'll heal. I bit my tongue, and I've got a sore rump where I fell, but that's it. I still stood up to him. I didn't back down. He did his worst, and I'm okay. In fact, I'm good. I feel like I'm finally free. Free of his hold on me."

"Good for you. I still intend on punching him in the face when we get to his house."

"You'll have to stand in line." She laughed. "But I think we need more of a plan to get Sam back than just a face-punching receiving line."

Cherry was right. He mulled over their options in his head. "You said earlier that we needed to call the police. That we needed to call someone for help."

She shrugged. "Yeah, sorry about that."

"It's okay, but it's got me thinking. Maybe it is time we called in some help. Some real help. But it means people are probably going to find out. Find out that you and I are Sam's birth parents. Are you okay with that?"

He could tell by her pause that she was thinking it over. "Yeah, I am. Sam already knows, and so does your dad. I'm not ashamed that I tried to do what was best for my baby. I was practically a child myself when it happened. I hadn't even turned eighteen yet. And Stacy and Greg were great parents. They loved Sam."

"I know they did. But now they're gone, and it's up to us to make sure that their wishes are carried out and that Sam stays in a home where he's still loved. That he stays with us."

"Agreed. But how do we do that?"

He dug his phone from his pocket. "I've got some ideas. And some calls to make."

Chapter Twenty-Four

Cherry and Taylor pulled up in front of Reed and Olivia's lavish home. They'd made one stop on the way into Great Falls, but it had been an important one.

"You ready to go get our boy?" Taylor asked her.

"You bet your sweet buns I am."

She felt like she was ready to take on the world. She was no longer afraid of standing up to her cousin, and with Taylor in her corner, she felt armed for anything he threw at her.

She nodded. "Yes. Let's do this." She got out of the car and pushed back her shoulders. Taylor came around and took her hand.

He didn't look quite as official as he usually did in the yellow vet clinic's T-shirt. But the holstered gun riding on his hip and the gold badge clipped to his belt gave him plenty of authority.

Olivia answered their knock and let them into the house.

She shook her head at Cherry. "I'm so sorry. I didn't know he was going to do that. I thought we were just going out there to check to see if Sam was all right. Are you okay?"

Cherry gave her cousin's wife a serious look. She felt sorry for Olivia, but she wasn't ready to let her off the hook that easily. "I'm fine, but we're here to get Sam. And we *are* going to take him home with us."

"I know," she answered in a soft voice. She pointed down the hall. "Reed's in the study. I'll go get Sam."

They crossed the room and found Reed in his study sitting at his desk.

He looked up from his computer when they walked in, a startled expression on his face.

They'd probably just caught him looking at porn.

"What are you doing here?" he asked. "I told you we're keeping Sam. I'll contact you when I have a court date."

"There's not going to be a court date," she said. "You think because you're a lawyer, and you have your so-called wealth and power that I'll just bow down to whatever you say. But I won't. Not this time. This time I have the law on my side. We would have been here sooner, but we stopped in at Judge Simmons's house."

Reed's face paled. Everyone in the county knew the head judge John Simmons. And they knew him as one tough but fair judge.

Cherry took satisfaction in seeing Reed's shocked face and stood up taller. "Judge Simmons and Taylor's dad go way back, and he's known Taylor since the day he was born. We told him about our situation, and he explained to us the laws of guardianship in the state of Montana. Stacy and Greg named me the guardian of Sam, period. That *will* hold up in court. You would have to prove that I was grossly negligent in order to even contest their will."

"And you're not going to do that," Taylor said.

Reed's lip curled into a sneer. "I sure as hell *am* going to do that. She *has* been grossly negligent. She wasn't watching the kid and let him run away where he almost got mauled by a bear. I know the law, too. And she doesn't have a leg to stand on. She's completely unfit as a mother. She doesn't have a home or an income to provide for him."

"Yes, she does. She lives with me."

"Don't start that crap again. I already know that she and the boy spent last night at that fleabag motel on the edge of town. So don't try to pull that over on me again." He gestured at the gun on Taylor's hip. "Besides, even if they were living with you, that wouldn't help. I think we've already established that being around you puts them in contact with dangerous elements, like the recently released inmate that showed up armed at your house. The one that you shot."

Taylor's voice deepened. "Oh you mean Leroy Purvis? I stopped by the hospital to check on old Leroy, and he told me that his lawyer, Reed Hill, was the one who set him up by informing him that his ex-wife would be at my home."

Reed's face paled again. "He's lying. I did no such thing."

She pointed a finger at his chest. "No, Reed, you're the one who's lying. What were you thinking? Sending an unstable ex-con to our engagement party? It seems like there might be a few people that would frown on a person in your profession sending one of his own clients, that he knows to be dangerous, to the area where there's a restraining order against him."

"I would never do that. It's his word against mine," Reed

stammered, but his conviction seemed to be waning.

"It doesn't matter anyway, Reed," she said. "We're not going to use that information against you."

"You're not? I mean, why not?"

"Because we don't need to," Taylor said. "We just wanted you to know that we knew in case you got any ideas about coming after us again."

"But I don't think you will," she said.

Reed narrowed his eyes at her. "Why not?"

Cherry took a deep breath. "Because I'm Sam's biological mother. I had him when I was seventeen, and I let Stacy and Greg adopt him. We kept it a secret from the family. The only other person who knew was Grandma."

A stunned look crossed Reed's face, then his eyes cut to Taylor. "I suppose you're that boy's father."

Taylor nodded. "And *that boy's* name is Sam. Cherry and I just filed an acknowledgment of paternity with the state which creates an immediate presumption of paternity under the state law of Montana."

"So, I'd say that about covers all of our bases," she said with satisfaction. "And in case you're wondering, Judge Simmons agrees with us."

Reed sunk into his desk chair and sighed. His look of defeat told her that he'd given up. And that they'd won.

The door to the study opened.

Sam came running in and threw his arms around her waist. "Mom, you're here. I knew you'd come for me."

She hugged Sam tight. He grinned up at her then turned to Taylor. "Is Rex gonna be okay?"

Taylor laughed. "I see how it is. I rank right in there after the dog."

Sam shrugged.

"Rex is going to be fine. I called Zack on the way to town, and he told me that he stitched him all up, and he's going to be okay."

"I knew it. I knew he'd be okay." He turned to Cherry, a pitifully sad look in his eyes. "Does he have to go back to Sophie's house when he gets better?"

Geez, did this kid know how to play her heartstrings or what?

"No, he'll be coming home with us."

"Yay. Yippee." Sam danced around the room then threw his arms around her again. "I get to come home with you, too, though. Right?"

"Yes, of course. You're coming home with Taylor and me tonight." She pointed at her cousin. "Your Uncle Reed has decided that he wants you to have the dog *and* he wants you to stay with Taylor and me. He's not going to try to take you away from us again."

"I never said this was over," Reed said begrudgingly.

"Yes, it is." Olivia had been standing by the door.

She crossed the room and put a hand on her husband's shoulder. "We're through with this. Let them be, Reed. It's what's best for Sam, and it's what Stacy would have wanted. Think about your sister for once. This would make her happy."

Reed lowered his chin to his chest and waved them away. "Fine. Go on then. Go back to Broken Falls and live happily ever after. This whole thing just exhausts me, and I'm done trying to be the good guy in all of this nonsense."

What?

When had he *ever* been the good guy in any of this?

But she kept her mouth shut and looked at Taylor, trying her hardest to keep her eyes from rolling.

They exchanged a silent look of understanding, and she reached for Sam's hand. "Right. Well, we're gonna take off then. We'll show ourselves out." She crossed the room, and Taylor followed.

He stopped at the door of the study and turned back to Reed, a steely glare in his eyes. "And just so we're clear, Mr. Hill—Cherry and Sam are *my* family now. And if you ever threaten or lay a hand on either of them again, I will not hesitate to arrest you. Or worse. Are we clear?"

"Yeah, yeah." Reed used the sulking voice of a child. "I told you I'm done. Just go home."

Home.

He didn't have to ask her twice. They hurried out of the house and to the car. Although Taylor's words made her warm and fuzzy inside, all she wanted to do was get out of this place and go home. Back to the ranch. Back to the life they were meant to have. Back into Taylor's arms. And Taylor's bed.

Yeah, she couldn't wait to get back there.

Chapter Twenty-Five

Cherry looked through the lace veil and up the aisle of the small church.

Taylor stood at the altar, a broad grin on his face. He looked out-of-control handsome in his white tux and dress cowboy boots.

How could this be happening? Could she really be getting everything she ever dreamed of?

After all these years, could she really be about to marry Taylor Johnson?

The last two weeks had been a crazy whirlwind of activity with planning the wedding and the final renovations happening to get the diner ready to reopen.

Cherry and Sam had officially moved in at the ranch, and she'd enrolled Sam in school at Broken Falls elementary.

So many changes were happening, but all of them good.

Knowing she wanted more time with Sam, Cherry promoted Stan to manager, and he was going to move into the apartment above the diner.

Most of her old things had been destroyed in the fire, and they had basically gutted the little apartment and started over, using the insurance money to re-drywall, paint, and lay new carpet.

They'd filled the bed of Taylor's pickup with the smoke-damaged furniture and hauled it to the dump. As she cleared out the apartment, Cherry felt like she was tossing out all the old baggage of her life and getting a clean slate.

A fresh start without all the history weighing them down.

She and Taylor were different people than they'd been in high school. They'd grown and changed, but the underlying current of love that they had for each other remained the same.

Taylor had proven that it didn't matter how bad things got, he was in this thing for the long haul.

And she had learned to trust him, to stand up for herself, and to believe in herself that she could be a great mom for Sam.

She no longer saw herself in the role of the single girl who got left behind in a nothing town.

Instead she saw her life as leading up to this moment.

This moment where she saw herself as a valued member of a community, a business owner, a mom, and a wife that was cherished and adored.

She had friends and a new family, including Taylor's dad, who had always treated her like his own daughter. He'd actually teared up a little when she had asked him to be the one to walk her down the aisle.

Now they stood together at the back of the church, the music leading up to the moment that she would begin her new life, her new journey, as she walked down the aisle and into the arms of the man she loved.

Russ looked down at her and smiled. "You ready?"

"Absolutely." She looped her arm through his and took a deep breath.

This was it.

Sam fidgeted in front of her. He looked adorable in a small white tuxedo. She'd combed his blond hair down, but a small cowlick still stuck up in back.

He was the official ring bearer, and they had given him a satin pillow in the shape of a heart to carry down the aisle. Cherry watched as he took hold of the ribbons of the pillow and swung the pillow in a circle.

"Sam, stop it." She laughed as she tapped him gently on the head. Thank goodness they hadn't put the actual rings on the pillow.

She looked up to see Taylor grinning at Sam.

At their son.

Today would make it all official.

She was marrying the man of her dreams, and she and Sam were both taking Taylor's name.

They would be a real family.

"You ready?" Charlie whispered to her. She looked gorgeous in the soft pink bridesmaid dress. "Don't our men look handsome?"

Taylor had asked Zack to be his best man and Cash to stand up with him as well. They stood at the front of the church, the groomsmen wearing tuxes in light gray with pink accents.

Cherry had scrambled for another bridesmaid to even out the wedding party and realized that besides Charlie, her closest friend was Stan.

He'd grinned and given her a trademark "Totally" when she'd asked him to be a 'brides-man' instead of a bridesmaid.

She didn't ask him to hold flowers. She just wanted him to stand up with her, on her side, as her friend.

Stan wore white linen slacks and a pink button-down shirt, and his grin couldn't have been prouder as he strolled down the aisle leading the procession of him, Charlie, and Sam.

The wedding march began, and she walked down the aisle toward Taylor.

The walk took forever.

All she wanted to do was take off her high heels and race down the aisle. Run into his arms and stay there forever.

But she didn't. She walked slowly forward, savoring each step, each moment, because something the past few months had taught her was that sometimes she needed to slow down and just enjoy the journey.

That things didn't always happen right when you think they will or when you want them to. Sometimes the best things take time and have hard lessons along the way.

But that's what makes them the best.

The anticipation of the moment finally happened, and she stood in front of Taylor.

Russ lifted her veil back, kissed her sweetly on the cheek, and placed her hand into his son's.

Taylor linked his fingers with hers and smiled down at her. "I love you," he whispered.

A huge grin spread across her face. "I love you, too."

She couldn't be happier.

She and Taylor had both kept their hearts hidden away,

their feelings for each other buried, letting the years pass until they could be together again.

But now the secrets of the past had all been revealed, and the future gleamed bright before them.

He squeezed her hand and grinned down at her, a look of love shining brightly in his eyes. "Ready to marry me?"

She peered down at Sam, at the little boy whose eyes looked just like his father's. She glanced out at the people in the church, their community, friends who cared about them.

Sophie sat in the front row and held Rex on her lap. She'd made him a pink bow-tie and bedazzled silver gems onto the edges.

This was her life now. Her big, beautiful, messy life.

And she couldn't wait to start it.

She looked up at Taylor, trying to convey all the love she felt for him in her eyes. "Yes, you bet your hamhocks I'm ready. I can't wait to be your wife."

Taylor laughed and slipped an arm around her waist, pulling her close and turning them toward the front of the church.

"Dearly Beloved…" the minister began.

And with those words, so did their new life.

Acknowledgments

My thanks always goes first to my husband, Todd, the one who supports me and believes in me. The one who listens to freshly written chapters, and to my new plot ideas, and to all the latest in industry news. I love and adore you. Thanks for taking this and all journeys with me.

Thanks to my sons, Tyler and Nick, for your love and support. You guys make it all worth it.

Thanks so much to my amazing editor, Allison Collins for your hard work and dedication to making this book happen. And thanks to the whole crew at Entangled Publishing for giving your valuable time and energy to publish this book.

My thanks goes out to Michelle Major, Lana Williams, Anne Eliot, and Cindi Madsen for your critique help, your honest feedback, and your steadfast friendship.

Special thanks goes out to Candace Havens and Kristin Miller for helping me plot this story in Vegas. And thank you Todd for buying us pizza since we missed lunch to plot.

Kristin- your friendship and plotting help is invaluable.

I am so fortunate to have the friendship and support of amazing writers, and I can't express enough gratitude to the Colorado Indie Author Group and the Colorado Indies.

My biggest thanks goes out to my readers! Thanks for loving my stories and my characters and for asking for more. I can't wait to share my next story with you.

About the Author

Jennie Marts loves to make readers laugh as she weaves stories filled with love, friendship and intrigue. Jennie writes for Entangled Publishing in both the Select line and Lovestruck, the newest line of romantic comedies. She's also the author of the romantic comedy/cozy mystery Page Turners series, which includes: *Another Saturday Night* and *I Ain't Got No Body*, *Easy Like Sunday Mourning*, *Just Another Maniac Monday*, and *Tangled Up in Tuesday*.

She is living her own happily-ever-after in the mountains of Colorado with her husband, two sons, and two dogs whose antics often find a way into her books.

She is addicted to Diet Coke, adores Cheetos, and believes you can't have too many books, shoes or friends.

Jennie loves to hear from readers. Follow her on Facebook at Jennie Marts Books, Twitter at @JennieMarts, or Goodreads.

Be the first to find out when the newest Jennie Marts

novel is releasing and hear all the latest news and updates by signing up for her newsletter at: Jenniemarts.com

If you enjoyed this book, please consider leaving a review!

Discover the **Hearts of Montana** *series...*

TUCKED AWAY

New Yorker Charlie Ryan hits rock bottom until she inherits a Montana farm called Tucked Away. Now her hands are full of wheat, cows, and one very hot veterinarian. Zack Cooper is wary of this sexy city slicker and her hot-pink cowboy boots. He's been burned once, and knows Charlie might get bored and head back for the bright lights of the big city. Their hearts have been tucked away too long...do they dare risk them for a new love?